# THE
# PLANTATION

## Michelle Larmer

**Published** by MPA Publishing
Paperback ISBN: 978-0-6453083-0-3
**Cover Design** by Nimo Pyle
**Edited** by The Editing Pen and
C.A. Larmer, with gratitude.

# DEDICATION

For Peter xx

# PROLOGUE
## PNG Mount Hagen, September 1990

He had been driving for over an hour before the tyre gave out. He hadn't been going fast, due to the state of the road more than anything else. But fast enough. When the rubber burst, the vehicle skidded violently off the road and into the dense undergrowth.

Getting out, he crouched down to inspect the shredded front tyre.

It was then that he sensed someone behind him and began to turn, catching a momentary glimpse of a weapon.

The hard barrel of the gun pushed forcefully into his temple, preventing further movement.

Without a word of warning, the blast sounded. And in that moment his whole life flashed before him—his work, his travels, the beautiful, lonely Sarah and romantic Gumawa—before there was nothing.

Blackness came instantly.

# CHAPTER 1: JESS

The open-plan newsroom was buzzing with activity, furious typing on keyboards, a competing wall of television monitors broadcasting news twenty-four seven and mid-morning exchanges around the Nespresso coffee station near Jessica McCann's cubicle. Yet she could only hear her heart beating louder as she sat reading the internal email that had just pinged into her inbox.

Leading News *is seeking a reporter for the PNG posting. Short-term contract. Immediate start.*

Was this the sign she had been waiting for to propel her mediocre media career? Or, if not something so cosmic, perhaps the life-changing opportunity to make a name for herself before her career ambitions headed south.

For the past six years Jess had worked at *Leading News*, the country's largest media organisation, and had risen to the ranks of senior reporter two years before. She was now becoming restless in her career stagnation. She'd literally jumped for joy when she'd landed the job in the Sydney HQ. The reward for slogging it out for four years in the bush as a rural reporter where she had refined her journalism craft on a forgiving country audience.

But now her passion had waned, and she was in jeopardy of losing it altogether. She wanted to feel that excitement again. Of landing something extraordinary.

As she looked around the office floor at the fifty or more monochrome grey desks that blurred into the distance, she pictured the opportunity ahead. Swapping her drab high-rise office for a tropical adventure. Stepping out from behind her boring office desk and roaming the jungles and idyllic islands of the Pacific. It could also be a chance to indulge her love of nature and hiking, experience some of the great treks in Papua New Guinea: the Kokoda Trail, the summit of Mount Wilhelm, Shaggy Ridge. But most of all, it would be an opportunity to be a foreign correspondent—a lifelong career dream.

Without further thought, Jess pushed back her chair and marched to the News Editor's office.

\*\*\*\*

'Papua New Guinea? Are you serious?' Frances gasped a few hours later, looking at her with horror sketched across her otherwise beautiful face.

Jess and her best friend Frances met most Thursdays after work for drinks, usually at one or two favourite bars. Tonight they were sitting in a dimly lit wine bar off Bridge Street, a regular with the well-heeled finance sector with its gleaming copper walls and marble bar and proximity across the road from the

Bavaria Bank where Frances worked. The quieter of their regular haunts, Jess was glad they were there and could catch up properly without competing with fellow drinkers loudly kicking off the end of the work week, albeit one day early.

'Yes!' She grinned, reaching for her drink.

'But why?' Frances blustered. 'I'd understand if you wanted to travel in South America or work in New York or London, but New Guinea? It's not safe; it's a basket case!' Frances was aghast at Jess's news. 'Crime! Corruption! You name it. Why would you even want to go? And leave this?' She was dumbfounded as she exaggeratedly waved her manicured fingers towards the stunning view outside the window, which was now revealing a glorious sunset illuminating the harbour skyline.

Placing her hand over her dear friend's, Jess said, 'Because it's time for a change, Franny. I want a radical change.'

Her tone must have resonated because Frances then smiled. 'Well, you'll get a radical change all right!' And they both laughed, harmony restored.

'I'm a run-of-the-mill reporter right now, and to date my career could best be described as pedestrian,' Jess lamented over their second cocktail.

'No, you're a senior reporter,' Frances said, leaping to her defence.

'Oh thanks, Franny,' she gushed, leaning in to peck her friend on the cheek. 'I know I cover some of the big stories, like that police raid in Chippendale and the court case with the NRL, but then I also get sent out to report on the Boxing Day sales and so many of the other lightweight stories that roll around each year.' She rolled her eyes. 'And don't forget the big scoop of the century! Last week's "major report" on Elma Dale's milestone one hundred tenth birthday.' Jess's sarcasm was clear. It had been a definite low point in her quest to be seen as a more senior journalist.

Jess had a couple of great feature pieces to her name, but they had been hard fought for, involving protracted pitching to her News boss and then the Features editor, eventually securing the go-ahead at the expense of her role in the newsroom. Hence the fluff piece with dear old Elma to remind her that she hadn't risen above covering such stories.

'A foreign correspondent role, albeit for three short months, is an opportunity for me.' It would be a chance to impress the bigwigs and land bigger stories with the national site.

Little did she know just what she was signing up for.

# CHAPTER 2: JESS

Two weeks later, Jess sat sipping a gin and tonic and staring out at the mass of white cloud floating past her small window on the plane. She was enjoying the liberal dose of Gordon's gin in her pre-lunch cocktail and feeling a tad sophisticated in choosing it. She was excited but also nervous at what lay ahead. The posting would provide a real chance to demonstrate her credentials to the international news desk whilst showcasing her strength in feature writing, the area she most coveted.

Jess loved the freedom and space of writing features, the greater word count and ability to delve deeper, and the absence of immediate time constraints that governed the daily news cycle. But it was more than that; it was the ability to take the reader on a journey through creative storytelling.

Her gut told her she was making the right decision. After all, what was holding her in Sydney? Certainly no boyfriend. Relationships had been her sore spot, which she blamed on work. If only she poured the same energy into dating as she did into her writing.

She envied her sister's tight family unit. Emma had married her childhood sweetheart at twenty-two and was mum to three gorgeous little girls. The youngest of two, Jess had always looked up to Emma and admired her selflessness and also her clarity in knowing what she wanted in life. Emma had been smart enough not to aim for the grand trifecta: career, marriage and children. Perhaps that was where Jess was going wrong, still not prepared to concede a life without all three in blissful balance. She would miss seeing Emma and her nieces over the next three months but would Zoom each week to catch up.

When the plane landed a few short hours later, the heat hit her like a brick wall. She walked tentatively down the metal stairs to the searing tarmac. Humidity at ninety percent, the temperature above thirty-five degrees Celsius and the sun blazing down so harshly it produced a glistening sweat immediately.

Thankfully she was back into air-conditioning minutes later as she entered the airport terminal and walked to the Passport Control counter queue. She didn't mind the wait; the cool temperature was heavenly.

'You a journalist?' the official asked, now flicking through the pages of her passport as if looking for something in particular.

'Yes, I have a work visa!' she said smugly. 'It should be in there. At the front.' She wanted to be helpful, directing the man to turn back to the early pages where the visa had been inserted. But the man ignored her, beadily scanning page after page. She began to feel worried the visa wasn't enough and rummaged in her backpack for any additional paperwork in case it was needed as proof of her employment.

'What are you here for?' he said abruptly.

Stopping midway through her search, she replied politely, 'I'm filling in for three months with *Leading News.*'

The official frowned and left his desk and moved to the next counter to consult with a uniformed colleague who had been processing another passport. The passenger, a man about her age, revealed his annoyance at the interruption, imploring the official to finalise his document first, then seamlessly switched to another language to address them both. They duly ignored him, and he glared over at her. Jess tried to pass on an apologetic smile, but his gaze didn't soften, and he shook his head as he turned back to the counter.

Eventually the consultation between the officials ended, and a minute later both Jess's and her fellow passenger had been cleared to move through. As Jess walked over to the baggage carousel, the unfriendly man put on his Akubra hat and strode towards the exit, carrying a small bag on his shoulder. In addition to his fierce manner, his imposing stature made him stand out. Over six feet tall, he wore low-slung jeans and a billowing white shirt with rolled-up sleeves. Handsome in a Keith Urban sort of way, he looked more suited to Nashville than Port Moresby, she thought. Just a shame he wasn't as nice as he looked. She sighed.

A sea of faces looked up at her as she wheeled her bag through the exit and into the Arrival Hall. Hoping one of them would be the resident cameraman, Ronnie Walker, she feigned confidence in striding through to the waiting crowd.

'Jess McCann?' She met a pair of friendly brown eyes and a warm smile. 'Welcome to Moresby. I'm Ronnie. Let me take this.' He reached for her suitcase.

Tanned and fit, like he had not long before stepped off a windsurfer or catamaran, Ronnie provided a soothing balm to her frayed nerves, not helped by the rude manner of the stranger she'd encountered earlier.

Chatting easily as he led her towards the parked SUV, Ronnie seemed all too familiar with bewildered first-timers arriving into the big unknown. Not only was he a Port Moresby local, but he'd been employed by *Leading News* for the past five years, so he knew the ropes of the country and the media scene.

'Moresby's a great town,' he enthused as he smoothly navigated the chaotic drive into town.

A large truck overladen with timber swerved three lanes in front of them before braking for a skinny dog limping haphazardly across the road. Jess clenched the seat with both hands to brace for the worst.

Ronnie just flicked on his indicator and moved to overtake the offending vehicle, but not before observing her panic-stricken face as he moved back into his lane.

'Yeah, the roads are a bit crazy!' He gave a light laugh. 'But don't worry. I'll get you there in one piece.'

His easy-going attitude was calming, and Jess prised her fingers from the upholstery and relaxed back into her seat.

Competing shouts and loud horns sounded around them as cars, buses and trucks jostled for position along the highway. Up ahead, a rusty, dented ute had broken down on the side of the road, and about a dozen passengers on the back tray leapt to the ground to find alternative transport.

'Yeah, Moresby gets a lot of bad press,' he continued, 'but there's a great lifestyle up here. I wouldn't live anywhere else!'

His strong declaration of affection for the place was infectious, and Jess was assured she'd made the right decision in taking up the posting, despite her first impressions.

Fifteen minutes later they'd veered into a quiet, residential area and up a windy road that Ronnie said was Bastion Hill.

'The company flat isn't too far from the office, but I'll pick you up each morning anyway. And Jenny, the house girl, will sort you out with what you need— you know, food, laundry, that sort of thing.'

Once he'd deposited her at the flat, Jess was alone to roam around her new digs.

The furnished three-bedroom unit was more luxurious than she'd been expecting. Set high on a hill, it overlooked Ela Beach and was stylishly furnished in spotless beige sofas, safari chairs and an eight-person dining table displaying ornately carved legs. The apartment was also immaculately clean, despite the hasty exit of *Leading News'* permanent correspondent, Warwick Hargraves, to cover the USA Election campaign. No doubt the tidiness was all down to Jenny, the smiling and gentle housekeeper she'd met on her arrival.

Moving to the windows overlooking the beach, she was struck by the external bars on each window.

'Why are there bars on these windows?' She was surprised, given they were seven floors up.

Jenny nodded and said, 'Good security,' and began to point out the deadlocks on the front door. Jess had already seen the security guards stationed outside the high-rise when they'd driven in, plus the cameras inside the building and lifts, but window bars were a definite first. *Wasn't it all a bit much? And if not... what had she signed up for?*

After farewelling Jenny for the night, Jess rummaged in the fridge and grabbed a small bottle of Coke. Flopping into a chair on the balcony, she took a gulp and looked out at the far-reaching view across the water. The overhead fan was doing its best to keep her cool, but combined with the icy soft drink, it was no match for the dense, sweat-inducing heat.

Yep, welcome to Port Moresby indeed.

# CHAPTER 3: DOM

Dominic Jonson sat restlessly in the uncomfortable armchair, flicking channels, switching between the US PGA Golf and the late-night news. Neither was taking his mind off things, but it was too early for him to go to bed. He was still wired from the day and seeing his feisty father Clancy again.

He'd nearly missed his tight connection after the flight delay and the mucking around at immigration in Port Moresby with that bloody blond tourist. Anyway, he'd managed to make his Mount Hagen flight, although he now wondered why he'd bothered. His father was being a prick.

His first night back and Clancy was already at him about his "responsibilities". What the hell?

Thank God the old man had retired for the evening. He was getting on, but surely that didn't mean he had to step in, did it? Whilst he had a quiet respect for what his father had achieved in his forty-five years in PNG, he didn't feel the same connection to the place or share his dream. At least not since he had been ten.

It was then that his idyllic life growing up here had changed. Playing with kids from the town and neighbouring plantations—swimming in the river and cycling up and down the roads as they raced each other on their bikes—had come to an abrupt end.

The death of his mother, immediately followed by the exclusive boys boarding school in Brisbane, had created a crevasse between him and this place. The change had been too great. Despite coming back three times a year for school holidays, the plantation never felt like home again. The ever-widening divide between him and his father had a lot to do with it. Clancy was a man singularly focused on the plantation and bugger anything or anyone else. Including his son.

His gentle mother had always been the affectionate one. The glue that cemented their small family together. Without her, they were now two self-centred men with separate lives and very little in common.

It might have been different if he had had a sibling, but he didn't allow his mind to go there. The "what could have been?" if his mother were still alive.

His father was the only family he had, which was why he'd eventually agreed to return home for a long weekend. He'd been flat out at his Sydney law firm but after putting it off for six months, he'd finally nipped it in the bud. Just two nights to go and he'd be out of there.

****

'This will be yours soon enough, Dom. I know you have your life in Sydney, but I need you here,' Clancy announced the following afternoon as they sat on the back veranda, drinking a beer and watching the last of the sunshine fade over the distant mountain range.

'I don't want to be here,' he'd said through gritted teeth but determined not to get into a fight. 'I've told you that this isn't where I want to live. I haven't lived here since I was a kid.' He avoided saying 'Since you banished me to boarding school!'

He had hated his father at that moment in his life, and the resentment still simmered nearly thirty years later. He'd been punished for his mother's death, packed off to boarding school on his own. One minute he was being enveloped in his mother's warmth and the next he was sharing a chilly, dark depressing dorm with a group of twenty boys, feeling as abandoned as he had ever felt in his life. Nothing had since come close to that feeling of utter rejection and sheer loneliness. He hadn't let it.

The painful emotions of that time felt like only yesterday, and he had to let the wave of fury pass as he sat glaring into the eyes of the man who'd once been his idol.

But then something changed.

His father looked away. A first. 'Look them in the eye and show them you mean business,' his father had always instructed when negotiating something you wanted.

*If Dad wants me to step up to run the place, why isn't he using his age-old technique?*

'What's going on?'

'Nothing. I just want you here. It's time.'

'Bullshit. What's going on? I'm heading back on Tuesday morning, so let's get it out on the table. Tell me what's going on?'

His father took a long slug of his beer and sat back for a few minutes before finally responding.

'I've got to go away for a bit. Have an operation.'

'What operation?'

'Heart. Doctor wants me in Brisbane in a month's time,' his father said gruffly.

The news hit Dom like a physical blow. Hard and unexpected. This dominating, egotistical, arrogant man succumbing to sickness? Surely he wouldn't let it get past first base? Seeing his father as suddenly vulnerable was not something he'd ever experienced before. It was disturbing.

'Okay,' he breathed out. 'I'll sort something out. Give me a couple of weeks to get the office in order. Then I'll come back and run things for a bit.' But for how long, Dom wondered, and he suspected his father was thinking the same thing.

# CHAPTER 4: JESS

'Good morning, Jess! Ready for day one?' Ronnie greeted her with a cheeky smile behind his black Ray-Bans as she slipped in beside him in the air-conditioned SUV.

She'd chosen a pale blue sleeveless tunic dress and wedge sandals for this morning's press conference at Parliament House, which she hoped would look the part. Her usually loose blond curls were secured in a high ponytail in a combined effort to look professional whilst keeping the frizz at bay.

As Ronnie steered the vehicle out of town towards the government precinct, they fell into an easy chatter.

She'd now been in the bustling capital for three days, and during that time he'd escorted her to an assortment of media offices, introducing her to colleagues at the government-owned TV and radio networks, as well as various foreign media bureau offices.

He gave her a rundown of what to expect at

this morning's conference, and she noted down various names and background information. *Wow, she was the Leading News' overseas correspondent,* albeit temporarily, but still, she was actually here, doing this. Her nerves jangled with the responsibility she now felt.

Since arriving, she'd learnt that *Leading News* were the big guns in town; their sizable operation was the envy of the other news bureaus. The office included a large studio for television and radio interviews, two state-of-the-art edit suites and a host of equipment from lightweight camera gear to industrial-strength tents and generators for remote locations.

In addition to writing news stories for the International desk, Jess would also be producing video and online content to support the company's multiple platforms—online news site, social media channels and wire service.

Her apprehension was now giving way to a desperate hunger to get started. She felt the stirrings of passion for her craft being restored.

Manoeuvring the SUV through the security watchhouse and into the visitor car park, they loaded themselves up with the camera gear and made their way to the conference room.

The sight of ten or twelve media already assembled sparked Jess's fears again. *Would she be good enough? Would she look like the novice here today?* But as her self-doubts threatened to creep in, she heard her name.

'Jess. Ronnie. Morning,' Larry cheerily called over from the lectern where he was setting up a BBC microphone. He had been one of the reporters she met on her familiarisation, and she gave a wave.

'Morning,' she and Ronnie said to the assembled group, and she smiled at the synchronicity she'd already established with her cameraman. They waved and shook hands with the group as they moved to the camera pool.

'This is quite a turnout,' she whispered to Ronnie, impressed and surprised at the large media contingent.

'Hey, Ronnie, my man! Good to see you again, Jess,' their neighbouring cameraman enthused as they began unloading their equipment and setting up alongside the others. Whilst Jess couldn't remember many of their names, she instantly felt like one of the gang. A sense of solidarity and team spirit abounded between everyone.

'Hi,' she replied before extending her gaze around the room.

It was so different to the competitive environment back in Sydney, and Jess was relieved.

Within ten minutes of their arrival, three executives walked in and took their seats at the front of the room.

A smartly dressed professional stood up to speak. 'Welcome everyone to today's official announcement on the launch of the Kikarlo Iron Ore Mine. I'm Muriel Blick, the head of corporate affairs at Ester Mining Company, and I'd like to welcome our CEO David Burgess and investment partner, Xi Peng, the Chairman of the China-PNG Development Group. But first it is our honour to have Papua New Guinea's Minister for Trade, Sir Joseph Igarro, here to officially launch the project.'

Resources rich, Papua New Guinea was a treasure trove of oil, minerals and other precious commodities, and over the following hour Jess heard details about the new agreement that would mine iron ore in the north of the country for export. The deal would apparently deliver the people of Papua New Guinea with new roads and schools due to the millions of dollars it would bring into the country. How much of the riches would actually get distributed would remain to be seen, and Jess made a note to keep a watch on this.

'I can't believe we've been here for two hours,' exclaimed Jess, glancing at her watch as they walked back to their vehicle.

'Yeah, there's always a pretty good morning tea at these things.' Ronnie smirked.

'I'll say. And everyone was so nice. I was a bit nervous about stepping into all this. Filling Warwick's size thirteen shoes.'

'Nah. Piece of cake, Jess.'

Before Ronnie had even exited the car park, Jess's hands began to itch, and she reached for her notebook and pen. She quickly scribbled the outline of her news story and then began drafting her online content pieces.

Her motivation was back! A bubble of happiness filled her, and she couldn't help but smile like a loon all the way back to the studio.

The next few weeks followed a similar pattern. Ronnie picked her up at nine o'clock each morning en route to a media briefing or an interview they'd prearranged or to the office. Each Monday and Thursday they had mid-morning Zoom meetings with the News and Features editors in Sydney, and for the rest of the week, Jess was left alone to immerse herself in sourcing, interviewing and writing. One story she was particularly interested in was a successful coffee plantation in a remote place called Gumawa, so an unexpected phone call had her yelping with delight.

'What's going on?' Ronnie asked, leaning out of the edit suite as she ended the call.

'We've got the green light to go to the highlands for that coffee story! You know the plantation getting all the international acclaim?'

'For real? Mr Coffee Baron?' Ronnie said.

The coffee baron—as she and Ronnie had quickly termed Clancy Jonson—had been in PNG since the 1970s when a post-university backpacking trip had turned into a permanent lifelong adventure in a remote area halfway between the highland towns of Mount Hagen and Goroka. He was now the owner of a multimillion-dollar operation that rivalled those in Africa, Asia and beyond.

'So, pack your bags, Ronnie! We're going to the highlands on Monday!'

It was an inspiring story, and Jess couldn't wait to meet the man behind it all.

# CHAPTER 5: JESS

'What took you so long?' were the first words Jess heard as she alighted the 4WD. Having travelled for four hours by small plane and truck, Jess assumed the formidable male voice was making light of their travel ordeal but couldn't be sure.

Clancy Jonson wasn't what Jess had expected. He was debonair in both appearance and manner, greeting her in the European fashion of kissing both cheeks and shaking Ronnie's hand. He was both charming and commanding in his presence, instilling a sense of respect at first meeting.

'Leave your bags in the truck. Kila will get them later. I want to get you across the plantation before dark,' he said before striding away, knowing that she and Ronnie would follow. She wondered if this assuredness had been the secret to his success.

Settling quickly into his dual cab truck, they traversed the expansive farm, which was as dense in coffee plants as it was in the overgrowth and jungle on either side.

The plantation was astonishingly beautiful—a stately homestead positioned among a green backdrop of plants, trees and mountains in the distance. But there was also a feeling of remoteness and isolation— the thick rainforest seemed to be a living, breathing presence all around them. A slight shiver passed down Jess's spine, which she shook off as she tuned in to Ronnie and Clancy's chatter in the front, swapping stories of mutual friends and acquaintances in PNG.

'What time's sunrise?' Ronnie asked. 'I'd like to capture the plantation at first light.' Jess could see that like her, Ronnie was enjoying working on this feature, which offered them so many more creative possibilities than the straight news stories they had been covering. She, too, could see the visual opportunities this story promised.

'Six, thereabouts. We get moving at that hour at any rate. The growers and machinery head out before it gets too hot,' answered Clancy as he began explaining which allotments they were working and the process of planting, nurturing and picking the valuable beans before leading them into the enormous iron sheds that housed the cleaning and roasting processes.

The sun was setting as they returned to the homestead, and a feeling of exhaustion now swamped Jess as she plodded through into the house. After being directed up the large timber staircase and into the bedroom she had been allocated, she showered and avoided looking at the tempting four-poster bed. Instead, she quickly dressed and joined Clancy and Ronnie on the large timber deck at the rear of the house.

'There you both are.' The coffee baron moved towards them, smiling at Jess and then looking beyond her, his gaze softening.

Turning around, she noticed a striking older woman who had been walking just a few steps behind.

'Allow me to do some introductions. It's my pleasure to introduce you to Mika Julen, a dear friend,' he said, taking her hand and kissing it. 'And this is Jessica McCann, the Australian journalist I was telling you about, and Ronnie Walker.' Ronnie gave a wave.

'Now let me fetch you both a drink.' And with that he was off.

In her early sixties, Mika looked like an artist. Curly brown hair, stylishly framed glasses and a montage of colours merging in her flowing kaftan. Glamorous with an engaging smile. Mika shook hands politely with Jess and suggested they sit on the safari chairs nearby.

'Is this your first visit to the highlands?' she asked in a strong European accent that had Jess mentally wondering who Mika might be. She had read that Clancy's wife had died many years before and his adult son was working in Australia, but the research hadn't mentioned anything about a new partner. Or was she a sister-in-law given her foreign lilt?

'Yes, it's my first time. It's beautiful up here in the mountains,' Jess replied.

'It's intoxicating for sure. Even after fifteen years, I'm still awestruck by the beauty of these mountains. I live in the property just across the valley.'

'I detect an accent?' Jess enquired, eager to learn more about Mika and what had brought her so far.

'Yes, I am from Germany—Stuttgart, but it has been many years since I have been there. At least forty... maybe longer.' She shrugged, pondering for a moment. 'I have always loved to travel, see new places. Since coming here, I don't want to leave.' She smiled wistfully, her face lighting up as she looked to where Clancy now stood with their drinks.

'Here we are,' he said, handing over chilled glasses of gin and tonic.

'Mika has made an enormous contribution to nurturing the highland arts,' he said, fondly squeezing her shoulder as he continued to expand on her accomplishments in supporting the arts and culture of the region.

He told her that Mika had an in-depth knowledge and appreciation of the region's indigenous arts and had been instrumental in identifying and supporting local artists in getting their works shown and sold globally.

'If you had time, I'd encourage you to visit her gallery in Mount Hagen. A fine collection,' he praised.

'Perhaps on our next visit,' Jess responded, sensing a second story in the making. And also wondering about the mutual admiration between the two. Long-time friends or something more?

# CHAPTER 6: JESS

Jess woke feeling deliciously refreshed after collapsing into bed late. Stretching her body out in the enormous four-poster bed, she kicked her feet with the joy of being here on the exotic coffee plantation.

She let her eyes roam around the white-walled bedroom, which she'd had scant time to appreciate since arriving. The white muslin curtains wafted in the light breeze coming through the flyscreened windows, and the lazy turning of the fan above added a peaceful ambience. An assortment of small paintings hung on the far wall, indigenous artworks in reds, browns and greens. She wondered if Mika had been involved in the selection of them.

It was early, just gone seven, and Ronnie and Clancy would be out driving around the farm. She'd arranged to interview Clancy at nine, and it felt decadent just lying there without needing to rush. She had the whole day to focus on her feature, and it felt fantastic.

Eventually pulling back the sheet, she got to

her feet and went to have a shower. Later, dressing in a pair of white capri pants, sleeveless navy top and flat sandals, she added a dash of BB cream and lip gloss to her face. She tied her hair into a ponytail and went downstairs in search of coffee.

In the morning sunlight, she could now fully appreciate the beauty of the plantation-style house. Timber floorboards throughout, thick brown shutters and glass louvres shaped just right to ensure a constant airflow aided by overhead fans. A shaded section on the back veranda indicated breakfast, and she sat down and admired the stunning view across the mountain ridge as far as Mount Wilhelm, the country's highest mountain and one that Jess hoped to climb during her brief time in the country. Although sadly not this visit.

'Morning, miss,' said a pretty woman around ten years older than Jess, who had come out with a coffee pot in hand.

'Good morning. Oh! I'd love one of those.' She nodded eagerly at the pot and picked up a clean cup from the table. 'I'm Jess,' she said whilst her coffee was poured. 'I hope this is one of Clancy's brews?'

'Yes, very good coffee at Gumawa,' the woman said meekly, putting the pot on the table and smiling warmly before leaving.

No one else was about, and so she helped herself to the fruit platter, a rich bounty of paw colors, bananas and pineapple all neatly sliced and displayed.

As she poured another cup of coffee, she continued staring out at the mountains, wondering what stories they contained. And pondering when she'd get a chance to trek one of them.

'Sleep well Jessica?' Clancy bounded in, startling Jess with the unexpected company. 'Lena looking after you with everything?'

'Yes, thanks,' she murmured as Clancy and Ronnie took up seats on the veranda and Clancy began pouring out coffee.

'I've got a few things to take care of in town, so do you think we could get into the interview now?'

'Of course.' So much for the leisurely start, she thought, as she left to fetch her notebook.

After settling back at the table, she set her iPhone to record whilst Clancy topped up their coffees. Ronnie drifted off with his coffee mug into the garden below.

Jess took the opportunity to sit directly opposite Clancy so that she could really look at him and gain a greater sense of the man behind this business empire.

He was dressed in a pair of beige trousers and a white long-sleeved shirt, which highlighted his glowing tanned face and forearms. His tousled grey hair was slightly longer than conservatively worn, and he had an urbane yet cavalier appearance. Stylish yet rugged. Charismatic yet unnerving.

'So, tell me, Clancy, what brought you to PNG nearly fifty years ago?' Jess began as the interview unfolded for the morning.

\*\*\*\*

Clancy eventually called a halt about an hour later, eager to get on with his errands in town.

Jess was now a lot more informed on Clancy's success. How he'd pioneered a new coffee bean that delivered the increasingly sophisticated beverage market exactly what it was after—a subtle, smoky flavour, sharp taste and delectable aroma.

'It's a unique blend that appeals to the discerning palates of Australian and European coffee drinkers, as well as catering to the mainstream American market, which has huge potential. In the US there's a preference for a slightly sweeter taste, and they'll typically complement their brew with flavours such as vanilla or caramel. But this bean has its own sweetness,' he explained.

As a twenty-four-year-old backpacker travelling through the highlands, Clancy had met widower Harold Spotnik at a social club called the Anzac Club in Gumawa, nestled around sixty kilometres west of Mount Hagen. After visiting his nearby plantation, the very next day, he never left. It was, Clancy said, the moment he had absolute clarity about what he wanted to do with his life and whom he wanted to share it with.

After a whirlwind romance with Harold's nineteen-year-old daughter Sarah, he began working on the farm—initially in the labouring and clearing of paddocks, the planting of fruit trees and coffee plants, and later in the planning and management of the farm. He married Sarah two years later, and within three years, he had become a father and also taken over the reins of the farm. During this time, Harold had died suddenly from a heart attack, forcing Clancy to end his apprenticeship and become manager at the relatively young age of twenty-eight. From that day on, Clancy had set about reworking the mixed farm into a coffee plantation and innovated it to become a multimillion-dollar enterprise.

Jess knew from her research that there was more tragedy in this success story. Sarah had died young, leaving him to raise their son alone.

After attempting in vain to get Clancy to open up about that time in his life, she had to concede defeat. Clancy simply repeated what she already knew that his wife had died prematurely at just thirty-five years of age when their son, Dominic, was just ten.

Clancy's evasiveness wasn't particularly unusual—Jess had encountered this before when people she had interviewed didn't wish to shine a spotlight on some aspect of their lives, instead hoping to steer a writer into a more flattering line of questioning or towards topics more favourable. However, she couldn't shake off the feeling that there was something else going on here. References to Sarah were minimal in the interview, and evidence of her existence was scarce in the homestead. That surprised Jess, considering that this had originally been Sarah's family home where she had lived with her father before Clancy's arrival.

Whilst there were some photos displayed throughout the house, just one of them captured Sarah with Clancy, and it was hung alongside about half a dozen others in the small study/library at the rear of the ground floor. Taken at an agriculture conference in Cairns in 1978, according to the caption, Sarah and Clancy Jonson smiled happily at the camera, holding up large bronze-looking goblets. Clancy was dashing with his engaging smile and mop of dark hair, and Sarah looked glamorous in her beehive hairstyle and dark pantsuit.

The only other images Jess had managed to find were in their ageing *Highlands Annual* magazines. One of them included a black-and-white photo of Sarah, still a teenager at the time, standing shyly with

her father and the farm workers at the end of harvest—
all smeared with dirt and smiling at the camera.

The newspaper reports at the time had
described Sarah's death as sudden but qualified it with
the words *no suspicious circumstances*, which she knew
from years in the media to be a pseudonym for suicide
or accidental death. She'd read the reports online
before flying up here and knew that Sarah had died on
November 12, 1990, at home, and the local doctor had
issued the death certificate for *death from natural causes*.
Slightly odd, thought Jess, given she was just thirty-five
years old at the time—not much older than Jess was
right now. Had she been ill for some time or possibly
taken her life?

As she sat poring over the historical magazines,
Ronnie knocked on the doorframe.

'When do you want to head over to the
roasting shed?' he asked, brandishing his camera.

'What about now?' she answered, keen to
shake herself out of her dangerous line of thinking.
Together they headed over to the iron-clad shelter on
the southern side of the property.

Once inside, Jess felt the tension in the room.

'What the bloody hell are you doing!' Clancy
yelled as he stormed in from the rear of the shelter.

'Turn the power off! Turn if OFF!' Immediately
the large shed went silent.

Clancy pulled on thick gloves, grabbed a small
spade and began urgently scraping coffee beans into a
second large stainless-steel cylinder, barking for the
others to follow suit.

'What's going on?' Jess quietly asked Kila, as he
and another worker she hadn't yet met gloved up and
prepared to assist Clancy.

'Temperature's too hot,' came the murmured reply as he hastily moved over to work with his furious boss.

The team quickly transferred every last bean into the new cylinder, saving the batch from a certain fate.

'Are the beans okay?' she worriedly asked as Clancy began removing his gloves.

Kila and his fellow worker silently monitored the recovered beans as if their life depended on it.

'Yes,' Clancy growled, punching a touchpad on a large computer, which controlled the temperature setting.

'You've got to have eyes in the back of your head.' He shook his head, a frown taking over his face. Yesterday's showmanship had slipped to be replaced by worry and tiredness.

'The device keeps playing up because of the humidity up here. We're only using this roaster because we're doing an urgent order. Bloody stupid thing!' He thumped the machine.

Ronnie and Jess exchanged a look, silently agreeing to abandon today's planned photo session. There would be time enough in the morning when hopefully the mood would be lighter and Clancy's charming demeanour restored.

Some hours later, over dinner on the back veranda, it became apparent what was contributing to Clancy's dark mood. His son, Dom, was reluctantly returning the following week but apparently just for a *short-term* period. It was clear Clancy wanted something more permanent, gritting his teeth at the words.

'I love this place,' he said. 'But it needs young blood to run it. Kila's great and so are the other local men I've got, but with a plantation this size and the sales we're doing…' He sat back in his seat shaking his head.

'What about Dom?' Ronnie bravely asked as Jess eagerly waited for Clancy's response.

'Good question,' he grumbled, before quickly recovering, remembering his company. 'I'm very proud of my son. He's a fine man, but he's got his own ideas on what he wants to do. He'll be up next week for a bit but has told me on many an occasion that this isn't his life, it's mine.' A fatigue seemed to come over Clancy then. He abruptly brought the night to a close, saying he needed an early night and would see them in the morning at the coffee shed for the final photos before they departed.

Not long after, Jess followed Ronnie up the stairs, wondering how father and son had drifted so far apart.

****

Two days later, Jess sat beside Ronnie at the large Mac computer screen, poring over the images he had captured from their highlands trip.

'What a place, hey? What a life?' Ronnie pondered aloud, as he clicked from one image to the next—row after abundant row of coffee plants spreading towards a dense jungle and mountain range to a portrait image of a commanding-looking Clancy proudly surveying the hive of activity all around him.

'Yes, such an interesting man,' she agreed, failing to shake off the feeling that there was something missing in the editorial feature she had just drafted. Whilst she had captured the inspiring story of a young

Australian dreamer creating an empire in the remote highlands, she felt there was a dimension she hadn't included in her piece.

Her mind kept returning to the mysterious wife, Sarah, and why Clancy didn't expand beyond his initial comments about his instant attraction to her. And the son, Dom, and his reluctance to return.

She moved over to her desk and began to consider ways she could add the much-needed personal family angle to the story. Perhaps the son's input into the family success? She could reach out and make contact with Clancy's son. He was, after all, on his way to PNG. She could possibly snare an interview with him during his stopover in Port Moresby where most travellers were forced to stay over before making their connection. Or perhaps she could track him down for a phone chat?

Excited with the prospect of filling in the blanks, she found Dom's details on LinkedIn and typed up an instant message requesting a catch-up.

# CHAPTER 7: DOM

Dom stared at the unanswered message that had been sitting in his email for much of the past week.

When it had come through, he had still been in Sydney, working mad hours at the firm he'd set up with best mate and fellow solicitor, Marcus Cowley. The pair had always divided the work fifty-fifty, and he felt guilty leaving Marcus to run things for one whole month and possibly two.

'Mate, don't worry about it. You've worked more hours in the past two weeks than I have in the past two months, so we'll be more than square on that front.'

Both sets of eyes fell on the copious client folders that Dom had just deposited on Marcus's desk, with comprehensively detailed file notes attached to each.

Dom had worked diligently in the past fortnight, anxious to clear the decks for his return to PNG. He'd averaged fourteen-hour days at the office, getting his matters in order, keen to minimise the disruption caused by his absence. He hadn't spent any time worrying about Clancy's health. After all, what could he do about it? He would be okay, surely?

'Dom? Dom?' repeated Clancy, snapping his fingers and managing to bring him back to the present.

'Sorry,' he mumbled. 'Where are we up to?' Dom paused his tense fingers on the computer mouse, awaiting Clancy's next update. An expansive Excel spreadsheet occupied the screen, outlining the complicated schedule of orders to be filled over the next six weeks.

The scale of the coffee business was impressive and far exceeded Dom's expectation. Customers spanned Australia to the UK, Canada and now the US, with over one hundred clients on the rota—from cafés and restaurants, to retailers, food wholesalers and hotels. An average of seven new enquiries were coming in each month.

For much of the weekend Dom was holed up in the office, learning the ordering system, accounting program, and familiarising himself with the critical dates for invoicing, deliveries and supplier payments.

'Right,' Clancy resumed in his professional voice. 'Pay attention. Now, there are twelve orders to dispatch while I'm away; that'll take us through to the end of October when I'll be back,' Clancy said with certainty.

'Only this order here, the one I've highlighted in blue, is a new client, *Paradiso Santa Monica*. It's our third new one from California in as many months, so word is out, son. Americans are learning the art of fine coffee,' Clancy said with a wry smile.

Dom noted the order down in his own notebook, ensuring he'd be extra mindful.

'So, you know the drill?'

Dom nodded, now all too familiar with the additional inclusions in an introductory shipment to a new client.

'Yeah, I know the drill. The gift set, brochure, extra beans.' Dom repeated the elements needed to wow first-time customers, reading from his notebook as he went.

'Too right. And the letters are in this file, already printed with my signature. So just include as you go. And any additional orders whilst I'm away, just prepare one yourself and sign it as acting manager, okay?'

*Now wouldn't he love that*, Dom thought. *My name on the Gumawa Plantation letterhead.*

Clancy's enthusiasm at having Dom sit in his chair for the weeks ahead was clearly obvious. He'd no doubt be hoping his son's passion for the place flourished, of that he was sure.

'Righto. I think that's enough for today,' announced Clancy. 'I'll go see about dinner.' There was an unmistakable spring in the old man's step as he left the office.

Dom entered the kitchen a short time later, slipping his mobile on the charger.

'Marcus and the contractor are both at a client do, so I've decided to call it a day as well.'

Clancy looked up momentarily before resuming his task of chopping up tomatoes to add to a salad bowl. Beside him, working harmoniously, was Lena, Clancy's long-term cook and housecleaner. She had been a loyal employee to Clancy for the past fifteen years, and Dom observed them quietly functioning in sync.

'I told Marcus to sing out if he needed me—or it might be the other way around?' He laughed. 'After all, here I am in the middle of the jungle without cable TV or a decent bar, so I'll be crawling the walls once we have the orders sorted. My non-existent social life is about to get a whole lot quieter!' He opened the fridge to grab them both SP beers.

Opening the bottles, he sat down at the kitchen bench and pushed Clancy's beer towards him. Taking a mouthful, he said, 'I heard you did an interview with *Leading News*?'

'Yeah, they're doing a story on the farm,' Clancy replied, not looking up from his chopping.

'What sort of story?'

'Oh, you know the type. How the farm became a coffee plantation, the rise and fall, that sort of thing. Every couple of years we get a journalist up here wanting to write about the place, and it's all good publicity, so I naturally agreed.'

He stopped cutting and turned to look at Dom. 'Has it already run?'

Dom shrugged his shoulders and took another swig of his beer.

'Well then, how did you know about the piece?' Clancy looked confused.

'I got a note from the journalist, Jessica McCann.'

'Yeah, that's right, Jess. She was a really nice girl. Well, I should say woman, as she must be in her late twenties, maybe older. I can never tell. She said she'd email the article through before she sends it on to the editor. What did she want with you?'

'That was the same question I had. I've got absolutely no idea. She just said it would be good to catch up. She'd heard I was visiting and thought we could connect in Moresby. Something about getting additional insights and quotes for the story.'

'Well, she's more industrious than most,' replied Clancy. 'You should speak with her. In fact, why not get her up here again? Whilst you're here?'

'No, no, no. I think I've enough to sort out while you are away. Plus I'm not a big fan of the media.'

'Come on, son! Even if you leave it a few weeks, why not arrange it for mid-September? The bulk of the orders will be done. I'll be bored out of my head in Brisbane waiting for the all-clear, and you'll be lonely as hell. It's a good opportunity for the plantation; the story's going online, which means good marketing everywhere.'

Dom took another mouthful, not responding. He had no intention of calling the journalist back. As he watched his father and housekeeper prepare the meal, he had a sudden flash of his mother, of all they had lost. She had been such an avid cook, had never needed any help. Demanding she have the kitchen all to herself. His missed her terribly, even after all these years. He took another good gulp of his drink and walked away.

# CHAPTER 8: SARAH
## Gumawa, 1974

Sarah had always enjoyed her own space. A shy child, and an only child, she was perfectly happy in her own company. Raised by her father, Harold, following the death of her mother in childbirth, Sarah arrived in the world resourceful, no fuss and quietly content.

A veteran of boarding schools—initially in France and later Australia—she had followed her father from Europe to the Pacific and was well rehearsed in looking after herself.

Despite their absences, she had a very loving and close relationship with her father, and when she was on school holidays, she spent her time almost exclusively with him—wherever his latest adventure took him. From the Swiss Alps where she was born to the pastures of France where her father first tried his hand at agriculture—growing olives and sunflowers— to the highlands of PNG where she would later reside after her father's decision to set up a farm when she was twelve.

A small all-girls boarding school had been found in the southern highlands of New South Wales, and she would spend the next six years commuting between Australia and her home, three thousand kilometres away in a different type of highlands altogether.

She loved the untamed beauty of Papua New Guinea and the quiet serenity of the mountains where she and her father lived. The wild jungle was such a contrast to the manicured lawns and foreboding buildings of the French and Australian boarding schools where she had spent so much of her youth.

Upon graduating from school, she had returned home to Gumawa, initially for a gap year but had then simply never left.

Perhaps that was due to that fateful meeting with a dashing Clancy Jonson at the tender age of nineteen.

> *Our two souls therefore, which are one,*
> *Though I must go, endure not yet*
> *A breach, but an expansion,*
> *Like gold to airy thinness beat.*

Sarah read the poem softly to herself, just a slight movement of her lips as she mouthed each line, and the sensation of a soft blush creeped into her cheeks.

How she admired the fluidity of John Donne's words—the way he transported you to the heartache of star-crossed lovers in her favourite. *A Valediction: Forbidding Mourning.*

*If they be two, they are two so*
*As stiff twin compasses are two;*
*Thy soul, the fixed foot, makes no show*
*To move, but doth, if the other do.*

John Donne, John Keats, and Emily Dickinson were among her favourite poets, and she could lose herself in their verse for hours, which was what she was doing when her life took its fateful turn.

'Sarah, come and meet Clancy Jonson,' called out her father, arriving at the entrance to the lounge room she had been reading in. Her favourite room in the house, it was filled with soft light and a fresh breeze drifting through the top louvres, circulated further by the two large fans on the ceiling above.

Jumping up from the window seat she had settled into some hours before, Sarah placed the poetry book on the table and obediently went to welcome their guest.

A friendly set of eyes greeted her as she took in this new acquaintance of her father's—one of many to visit their homestead. Harold embraced company, keen to fill the rooms with fresh, vibrant energy.

The handsome stranger had longish blond hair that curled around his collar and, whilst clean-shaven, had the appearance of being a hiker or bushwalker. He wore khaki walking pants and thick boots, and his long-sleeved navy shirt was rolled up to reveal olive skin and athletic arms. His glowing face was highlighted by sparkling blue eyes and a wide smile.

Shyly greeting him, she volunteered to make tea, almost running to the safety of the kitchen. She felt fluttery and nervous in the presence of this striking man. Filling the kettle and putting it on the gas stove, she pulled out three cups and saucers from the drawer and buried herself in the walk-in pantry, looking for a new box of shortbread biscuits.

'Can I help?' Clancy asked, looking in to find her reaching up to a high shelf.

'That would be great,' she murmured. 'Just that box—the red one.' She pointed in the direction before moving away, out of the pantry. He allowed her to pass before effortlessly reaching up to fetch the tin box of shortbread and handing it to her.

'Harold tells me you're a child of the world? Switzerland. Germany. France. Australia. PNG.' He sounded impressed. 'So, where's home for you these days?'

'Wherever father is,' she replied without even considering there could be an alternative.

'Well, you've got an amazing setup here. It makes my life back home seem very boring.' He gave her a dashing smile.

He asked her about her life, the countries she had been to, and she shared her experiences of growing up in Europe, her travels with her father, and her love of the farm. Now that school was completed, she didn't have aspirations to be anywhere else than where she was right now for at least a year, possibly longer, before starting to think about university or travel.

The conversation put her at ease, and together they began to arrange the morning tea.

\*\*\*\*

Within days, Clancy had arrived with his backpack and moved into one of the upstairs bedrooms. He began to work each day with her father on the farm where they grew vegetables and farmed cows.

It was to be the start of a heady romance between Sarah and Clancy. Sly glances followed by longing looks and Sarah's heart racing in anticipation of what would happen next.

Around two months after moving in, Sarah was dozing in the hammock on the back veranda when she felt a light touch to her lips. Opening her lids, she found herself staring into Clancy's hopeful eyes. She blushed.

'I've been wanting to do that since I first saw you,' he said sheepishly. 'I know I should ask a girl before I kiss her, but you looked too beautiful to resist.'

Sarah touched her lips, which had just been warmed by his. 'I don't know what to say.' The sensation was blissful, and she felt dazed for a moment.

Grinning at the response he'd elicited, he took her hands in his and looked at her face longingly, his gaze intensifying on her lips.

'No need to say a word, Sarah,' he whispered, standing up and releasing her touch. She watched him move away and walk over to the shed.

There were to be many more such romantic moments, and Sarah and Clancy's love affair began with Harold's knowing consent. Sarah couldn't recall a time she'd seen Harold more chuffed.

Whether he'd intended to play matchmaker or not, he'd succeeded.

Clancy became a permanent fixture at Gumawa, heading outdoors each day with Harold to work the farm. Sarah kept busy around the house and immersed herself in writing. She discovered she had her own voice and released pent-up feelings of love, passion and desire into her poetry. She was good at it too, with several poems getting published in the *Australian Women's Weekly*, the *London Ladies Gazette* and their local community paper.

Their wedding two years later was a small affair. Harold and Sarah had flown to meet Clancy's family in Brisbane—the first meeting between the two families. Despite being outnumbered by the Jonsons, Harold and Sarah were embraced heartily and warmly by Clancy's family and relatives.

They honeymooned in the Gold Coast before returning to the farm where their life took on a quiet harmony.

Mornings would see Sarah coordinating the chores with Tara, their beloved house girl, and then meet up with Clancy and Harold for lunch. Sarah spent her afternoons working in the thriving garden or sitting at her antique writing desk and crafting her volume of poems.

Three years later, Sarah gave birth to Dominic Eldrik Jonson, the beautiful son they had both hoped for. Sarah's life felt complete.

# CHAPTER 9: DOM

As Dom went to log off for the night, a message pinged on his email. It was another one from the journalist he'd been ignoring.

Switching off the computer, he picked up his phone and turned it over in his hands, undecided what to do. Eventually he switched it to silent, threw it on the desk and walked out.

By the time he'd made it to the kitchen, the landline was ringing, and Clancy reached for it.

'Hello, Gumawa Plantation,' Clancy said smoothly before his face softened, and he quickly glanced at Dom.

'Good to hear from you again, Jess!' He raised his eyebrows at his son, and a broad smile erupted.

'He's actually right here. Why don't I put you on speaker?'

Before Dom could exit the room, a female voice filled the air.

'Thanks, Clancy. Hello, Dom? It's Jess… from *Leading News*. Hopefully you've received my messages?

It's about the story we're doing on Clancy and the coffee plantation.'

'Yes, I've been telling Dom that we need to get you back to the farm to finish your story.' Clancy's mischievous tone was not difficult to miss.

'Really? That's great.' She gulped. 'That's actually why I'm calling. I was hoping to interview Dom for the piece?'

'Dom's been incredibly busy since arriving,' Clancy said diplomatically. 'I'm sure we can settle a time for a few weeks for you to visit. What do you say, Dom? As you're now staying on for a month? Shall we all agree to two weeks from today?'

Jess would never know that at that precise time, Dom was silently mouthing 'No!' at Clancy, but his father wouldn't be deterred.

'Jess, how are you placed to return?' Clancy asked, pausing to listen before enthusiastically continuing. 'Great! Let us know your flight's details, and we'll arrange a pickup at the airport. Dom will have a room ready.'

Dom threw up his hands and went to find a beer. Neither Clancy nor Jess seemed to require his input nor his agreement to proceed with the interview. To interrupt now would have seemed churlish, so he reached into the fridge for a beer whilst Clancy finished the call. A call that was ostensibly for him. But no one seemed to have worried about that either. Gulping down half the beer in one go, he stomped back to the office.

Dom had always had an intense distrust of the media, and he couldn't understand what he could add to the story about the farm. Perhaps it was the lawyer in him. *Say nothing. Put nothing in writing that may incriminate you.* In his experience, the media had a tendency to take words out of context and manipulate the truth to suit the readers and their circulations.

Yet he knew his dad wasn't born yesterday and was both canny and astute.

Switching the computer on again, he sat down to do his own due diligence and find out a bit about this Jessica McCann and the types of stories she wrote.

It didn't take long for the search to reveal her media history from rural press reporter to senior reporter at *Leading News.* Most recently he noted some video pieces posted from Parliament House in Port Moresby on the changes to foreign aid and an editorial feature on the Conflict Islands as the next "tourism mecca for the Pacific".

She wrote reasonably well, he conceded, and seemed to capture the details without voicing a personal opinion. That earnt her a tick.

Oh well, he was going to have to go through this PR exercise for Clancy, he guessed. When Clancy made up his mind, it was near impossible to shift him.

# CHAPTER 10: JESS

Jess arrived at the property on Sunday afternoon. She'd travelled alone as she wouldn't need Ronnie this time; they already had enough pictures to fill the feature. It was just the copy she wanted enhanced.

When she got out of the 4WD, the farm seemed to be deserted. But after following Kila to the front door, it swung open to reveal there was someone home.

A younger version of Clancy stood before her.

Gone was the grey, replaced by light brown tousled hair that looked like it hadn't long been in the shower.

A three-day growth only added to the man's ruggedly handsome appearance, but unlike Clancy, this man's eyes were cool and wary. She felt like she had seen that expression before.

'Dom? Hi, I'm Jess McCann. Thanks for agreeing to meet,' she said, plucking up her professional confidence.

'Hi. And I didn't really get a say.' His smartarse response was softened by a well-timed smile. 'Clancy likes to get his own way.'

She found herself smiling cautiously back at him. 'Well, I'm grateful for that.'

He took her bag from Kila and led the way into the house, which now felt so familiar after her visit just three weeks before. There was something familiar about him too. Had she seen him somewhere? Or was it just his similarity to his father?

'Your home is so lovely,' she prattled to fill the silence.

'Thanks, but it's not my home. I live in Sydney. This is Clancy's place,' he replied, further contributing to her unease.

It struck Jess then that Dom's connection to Gumawa wasn't quite right. Didn't he grow up here? People generally had a soft spot, an attachment for where they spent their childhood, but this didn't appear to be the case with Dom.

'Do you get back very often?' she enquired.

'Not much these days. I'm temporarily running things whilst Clancy's in Brisbane,' he said, not offering more detail than that. 'Come through, and I'll get you a cold drink.' He left her bag at the foot of the stairs.

'Oh, he's not here? Is everything okay with Clancy?'

'Yeah, fine. What can I get you?' he asked, opening the kitchen fridge. 'A juice, soft drink or perhaps something stronger?'

'I can see an SP; that would be great!' she said, keen to relax the mood a little.

'Yeah, a beer does sound good,' he said, pulling out two SP bottles and pouring them into tall glasses.

'I'm getting quite fond of these.' She took her

glass. 'I've been in Port Moresby for two months now, and before that I didn't realise PNG made such great lager,' she gushed, internally rolling her eyes at her nervous chatter. If only she could relax back into her professional persona.

'Let's go out to the back veranda,' Dom suggested, 'and you can tell me what brought you to PNG.'

As they walked outdoors, Jess explained, 'I'm relieving for a colleague, Warwick Hargraves, who's in Washington covering the US elections. I'm only filling in for three months but really loving it,' she said with an enthusiasm she hadn't realised she had for the place. The feeling anchored her. 'I live in Sydney, but the opportunity came up to fill in for Warwick, and I jumped at it!'

They both sat enjoying their beers before Dom then switched the conversation to the reason for her visit.

'So, tell me about the story and what you are hoping I can add. If anything?' he asked, assuming the role of interviewer—or perhaps interrogator, Jess thought unkindly.

She looked up from her beer and addressed Dom in a playful manner. 'You're the heir apparent, as it were.'

'Hey, Clancy's not going anywhere. This is his show,' he snapped back.

'I'm sorry.' She backtracked. 'I didn't mean it quite that way.' He was incredibly defensive, and she'd clearly hit a sore point. 'What I meant to say is that you're Clancy's son. You were here when the farm really transitioned into Gumawa Coffee, and I thought it would be good to get some more of the personal story behind it all. You know? Family life, growing up with the dynamic Clancy Jonson?' She was desperately hoping to make Dom lighten up.

'Yeah, well, I went to boarding school pretty early on, so I'm not sure I can add anything relevant. But sure, let's knock it over.'

'What, now?'

'Yeah, why not? Unless you're too tired from the trip? I thought it was pretty urgent?' he recounted.

'Okay,' she said. 'Let me just grab my gear.' *Like father, like son, she thought...*

# CHAPTER 11: DOM

Dom recognised her instantly as the young woman at the passport desk at Port Moresby Airport a few weeks back. The same curly blond hair and button nose, which was now supporting a large pair of dark sunglasses. Much of her face was hidden by the designer shades, but he knew she was the same woman. However, he wasn't going to alert her to their earlier exchange, as he hadn't been his most charming that day. And for some reason he wasn't being his most charming now either.

As Dom began recounting his childhood in the interview, he felt something release inside him.

'Yeah, I guess you could describe it as an idyllic place to grow up. So much freedom to roam around, ride our bikes, take the canoe out on the river, things like that.'

It had been the perfect playground for a kid. The largest backyard you could ever wish for, with adventures and games and space. So much space. He remembered the weekend gatherings of all the neighbouring families at Green River or Princess Falls, or even at the Anzac Club, splashing about in the pool as the adults sat back with their cocktails and conversation. He loved the water and must have easily spent half of every day submerged in it.

'How did your family dynamic play out?' Jess asked, moving the interview along.

'Well, you've met Clancy.' He raised his eyebrow knowingly. 'He was always hands-on with the business, and it was really just getting going back then, so he was consumed by it. My mother was always around, either working in the garden or cocooned inside with a book. She loved reading but also writing her own verse and sometimes short stories. I wonder where they are now?' he pondered, only now contemplating the fate of his mother's poems and stories.

'Tell me more about your mother,' Jess encouraged after a brief pause.

Dom immediately recalled the warm smile on his mother's face when he would rush in after playing outside all day.

Ready with an ice-cold water or a chilled Fanta on special occasions. Tearing open a Band-Aid and ever so gently affixing it to his latest scrape. Always wanting to hear about his adventures. A constant, gentle presence in his childhood.

'Mum was beautiful. A true caring soul. She died too, too young.' He looked away, shaking off the sadness that still flared when he thought of his mother. Lying helpless, lifeless on the floor.

'Do you mind telling me what happened?'

'She had a fall. On those stairs.' He looked over at the wide timber staircase leading to the upstairs bedrooms. 'It was just a tragic accident.' He shook his head, biting his lip as he focused on maintaining his equilibrium in front of this nosy journalist, but it required an enormous effort, even after all this time.

'That must have been really hard for you, especially at such a young age. You were—what—about ten?' she probed carefully.

'Yeah… but it happened and life moves on.' He shrugged his shoulders, shaking off the memory. 'I then went to boarding school in Brisbane, later on to Sydney for university, and so as I said, if you want to know about the growth of Clancy's business, I can't really help you there. I've lived most my life in Australia.'

He was being deliberately evasive and short, but he didn't want to get into private family stuff with a journalist. This was supposed to be an article about Clancy and the Gumawa Coffee Plantation, and that wasn't anything to do with him.

The interview wound up after another twenty minutes with the writer asking hopeful questions about Clancy as *a role model for his son, a leader in the community* and as *someone who must make Dom so very proud?*

I'm not sure, perhaps, and sure were his curt replies.

Retreating to the office shortly afterwards, Dom logged on to a Zoom meeting with his office in Sydney before sorting out a logistical hiccup with one of the coffee deliveries. It was over an hour later that he emerged and found Jess sitting in the back garden, quietly studying the expansive mountain range. It was nearly dusk and possibly the most beautiful time of the day with a spectacular sea of pastels flooding the sky. He grabbed two beers and wandered down to join her.

'It's so pretty here at sunset,' she said, accepting one of the beers.

'It is. A great way to switch off,' he said, signalling a cheers with his beer and taking a swallow.

'I'd love to climb Mount Wilhelm while I'm in the country,' she said wistfully. 'She's magnificent, isn't she? So majestic.'

'She's majestic all right. All 4,500 metres of her!' He laughed. 'I've trekked up there a few times. It's a hard climb, but the views are worth it. Green as far as you can see.'

They sat companionably and chatted about the trek before moving the conversation to their careers.

He enjoyed her self-deprecating tales of being a naive country newspaper reporter, straight out of university, and the embarrassing mistakes she'd made before graduating to the big league in Sydney with *Leading News*.

'And sometimes I'm even elevated from a run-of-the-mill reporter to the lofty heights of Features writer, depending on staffing levels that month.' She laughed, although he detected a note of frustration in her tone.

'The good news when you run your own show is that you have more control about the work you take on. Theoretically at least,' he said, sharing a sympathetic smile.

Jess asked lots of questions about his career in law and the firm he'd founded, revealing she too had done some due diligence of her own.

'Yeah, like you, the first five or six years were tough. I was at Collier & Jones, and like all young graduates, you were handed briefs at the eleventh hour and had to work your butt off to get them ready in time. You needed the billable hours, and so you'd just put your head down and work through the night if you had to. The workload was unrelenting but good practice,' he explained. The manic pace had prompted him to look at alternatives to working in a large-scale law firm, and eventually he'd set up his two-man practice with university pal Marcus Cowley.

'I love the pace, and of course working with a mate is a bonus. We opted to specialise in corporate and tax law, and the cut-and-dry thrust seems to work for both of us. Although you would think we were a couple of architects or creatives in the space we bought in The Rocks, it definitely doesn't conform to your image of a typical law firm,' he said, glad they'd created a workspace that didn't feel restrictive or claustrophobic like Collier's.

He left out that a key factor for the change had been the demise of his marriage to a fellow lawyer at the firm. His brief but intense relationship with Lauren had spectacularly failed after they got married. Within four years, they'd gone from newlyweds to divorcees, and whilst he sailed into smoother waters in a boutique legal firm, she went on to become one of the city's toughest litigation lawyers.

Looking at his watch, he noticed it was getting on and suggested they go and get ready for dinner, mentioning his seven-o'clock booking at the Anzac Club.

Within the hour, they were being seated in the restaurant at the club with drinks and he felt himself relax. He'd observed Jess's friendliness to the motley crew at the club as she answered their enquiring questions as they'd made their way to the table. Ostensibly stopping the pair to ask about Clancy, the conversation invariably moved to Jess, and she'd been gracious under scrutiny.

Some hours later, they returned to the homestead, bade each other a good night, and went to their rooms. However, it took a long time for Dom to fall asleep, his mind a whirlpool of fuzzy memories of his mother and especially of that tragic night so many years ago.

# CHAPTER 12: SARAH
## Gumawa, 1974

Sarah had never intended to sleep with him. Being unfaithful was something she had never contemplated nor ever considered in her fourteen-year marriage to Clancy. It had just happened. Such a cliché, but so true. She would never discount that things *just happened* for the rest of her days, after all it had *just happened* to her. Simple as that.

'Sarah, come and meet Ryan.' Elena had beckoned her over to the bar as Sarah moved through the Anzac Club that breezy, carefree afternoon. She was sans Clancy, who was absent again, and her cousin Elena had been staying with her this past month. Clancy had spent a lot of his time lately either in Port Moresby gathering government support for his expansion's plans or in Australia at meetings. She knew this was a critical period in his export vision but felt neglected in his quest.

'Hello.' Sarah extended her hand to Elena's new friend.

'Your cousin here is filling me in on the highlands. It's my first trip up here.' His easy smile and warm eyes lured her in to stay and have a drink. At least ten years younger, he projected youthful exuberance, and she couldn't help but be reminded of her husband when she had first met him, before he had become consumed by the farm and business.

The enigmatic Ryan explained that he was travelling through the country, photographing everything along the way for a feature he was doing for *National Geographic* magazine.

'I'm a bit of a nomad, but I wouldn't have it any other way,' he said, the happiness of his life choice clear.

Intrigued by his work, Sarah spent much of the evening talking to him about his travels not only in PNG but around the world as a photojournalist. Whilst he had started writing and photographing for the *Australian Geographic* magazine initially, he had switched to the global title and was now a citizen of the world.

'I envy your travel experiences,' she said wistfully, wondering if she might have let something slip through her fingers by being such a dutiful daughter, and now wife. Whilst she loved living on the plantation and raising her young son, she couldn't help feeling that she hadn't really lived—especially after hearing of Ryan's adventures through South America, photographing rare bird species in the Amazon and his recent safari in the plains of Kenya.

'Ryan, you should score an invitation to Gumawa Plantation—that would be worth including in your piece,' suggested Elena, noticing the rapport between them as they bade their farewells hours later.

'Of course!' Sarah agreed. 'You must come.

Wednesday?'

'I'd love that.' His reply was instant. 'I've got to be in Mount Hagen on Thursday, so I'll need to keep moving, but one more day here would be magic.'

And magic it was.

Ryan arrived at lunchtime; his timing was perfect. It had given her something to look forward to after the early-morning departure of her beloved Elena, who was commencing her long haul back to Zurich.

Sarah had kept herself busy since Elena's leaving, carefully laying out the table with linen napkins and fresh flowers from the garden—the crimson bougainvillea setting off the table beautifully. With Clancy still away and Dom spending the day with Robbo, at his best friend's house, she had the place to herself. Again.

She wasn't sure why her nerves were rattling away inside, but later it would all make sense.

'Welcome.' She greeted Ryan with a kiss to both cheeks, happy to see her new friend again so soon.

'Wow, this place is beautiful,' he said, walking through the homestead and following her onto the veranda.

They ate a lunch of cold smoked salmon, iceberg salad and chilled wine and talked about travel, their favourite places—Sarah sharing her global growing-up experiences—and life in general.

After a late-afternoon stroll around the gardens, they returned to the house and sat comfortably over coffee and liqueurs in the cool of the late afternoon. As the sun set, there was no mention of Ryan leaving, as if they both had a tacit understanding of what the night would entail.

Taking her glass and putting it on the low coffee table, Ryan looked at her knowingly, and she led him upstairs.

The lovemaking had been slow, tender, and yet also fierce and urgent. Their souls met in a fury as if they had known they would. For hours they loved each other, savouring each inch of the other, before falling into a blissful sleep as the rain began to fall outside.

It seemed just hours later—but had to be much longer as the sun was rising outside—when Ryan gently stroked her face, causing her to awake.

'I've got to hit the road.'

And she knew he did. Surprisingly, as significant as it had been, she knew this was just a brief, delightful interlude for both of them—each absolved from their real lives for just one afternoon.

Sarah found herself smiling throughout the days to follow at the delicious encounter with Ryan. She resolved to place the memory to the back of her mind, to pull out when she wanted to give herself a lift, but for now she must concentrate on what was most important—her life here with Dom and Clancy. They were her life.

# CHAPTER 13: JESS

After settling back into her desk at the office in Port Moresby a few days after her trip to Gumawa, Jess eventually finished the feature and filed it. But she couldn't shake the niggle that her story wasn't somehow complete.

The sudden death of Sarah Jonson seemed a loose end, yet she had hit roadblocks in her attempts to learn more about it from both Clancy and Dom. A tragic fall in the home... those things happened, and whilst Jess still didn't quite believe it had been as simple as that, she didn't have any reason to doubt it. After all, she wasn't hired as a detective but rather to write an inspiring feature article, as per her brief, and that was precisely what she had produced—eventually.

To celebrate finally submitting the protracted feature article, she joined Ronnie and a few of their press colleagues for late-afternoon drinks at the Yacht Club. It was a spectacular time of day with the intensity of the sun fading and the sea breeze gently wafting across the expansive timber deck as patrons relaxed over beverages and shared chit-chat about their day. As the yachts bobbed and their crews settled into comfortable deck chairs, she wondered where else she would rather be at that precise moment.

'Jess? Earth to Jess?' She looked up from her reverie as Ronnie began to poke her arm.

'Jess! Great to have you back,' he said. She smiled lazily back at him and then noticed a couple standing beside him, watching her politely.

'Jess McCann, let me introduce you to these guys. John Mercedes and Grace Pickering, who are almost as new as you in town.' He laughed.

Ronnie went on to explain that Grace had arrived in Port Moresby about six months ago to work with ARC Surveys. With a smirk, he added, 'The bigwigs in town.'

'Hi,' she said, delighted to meet some new faces after spending so much time either at the office or the comfortable but isolated work apartment.

The beautiful-looking couple had a glow about them. John was nearly six feet tall and pure male with his broad shoulders, rich, dark curly hair and broad grin. Grace was pretty and fair yet had the look of a super fit woman—an athlete perhaps? Her short hair was Scandinavian white blond, and she wore no discernible make-up. Her denim skirt showed off taut, tanned and striking legs.

'How long are you in town for?' Grace asked with interest, now seated beside her. Jess explained about her short-term contract, which was now galloping through its final month.

'We'll have to get you out on one of the next field trips,' Grace suggested, expanding on a large-scale gas project they were working on at present. It was going to pump gas all the way from a remote part of the country to Australia and beyond. A 3,000-kilometre-long pipeline overland and below the sea.

'I'd love to,' Jess enthused, looking at Ronnie for his buy-in. 'It could make a great story, both as a straight news piece on the project but maybe something bigger for Features?'

Ronnie agreed, and so the four of them began discussing the logistics and timeframe for a site visit, the spokespeople they'd need to interview, and what type of access they'd have to information for a news story. As more drinks were ordered, the conversation moved on to more general topics, including what had brought John and Grace to PNG.

It was only then that Jess realised that they weren't a couple in the romantic sense but rather work colleagues.

'I'm all about work these days,' Grace said, explaining that a bitter heartbreak in Melbourne had prompted her to take the PNG job. 'I needed a change of scene, and you can't get more different than this!' Her light laugh didn't quite disguise the hurt, and Jess reached out and squeezed her hand.

'Change is good. Let's toast to that,' Jess said, lifting her drink to Grace's glass.

John's eyes drifted over to them, and he winked at Grace before resuming listening to Ronnie. Jess could see the big-brother role he played in Grace's life. She guessed Grace had many such big brothers in the field she had chosen to work in. How many female surveyors were there? And fewer still, she imagined, in Papua New Guinea. Another human-interest story emerged in her mind's eye.

# CHAPTER 14: GRACE

Grace hummed happily the next morning at work. It was such a fun night last night, and great to meet another expat, and one who she just clicked with. If only Jess was here for longer, she thought, she would be cool to hang out with.

Grace would get the Kooto Gas site visit organised for Jess as soon as she could. But first, she had to finish checking the series of maps she was studying, which were for a different project altogether. She was reviewing imagery captured by the drone they had used to provide high-tech visuals of the typography below the dense jungle of the PNG Highlands.

A new highway was being built adjacent to the run-down roadway that linked Goroka to Mount Hagen, and Grace was inspecting the best route for one of the steeper sections of the 170-kilometre roadway.

Drones had really shaped the direction of surveying and ensured that what had taken countless weeks could now be achieved in days, with the high-tech equipment providing near-accurate mapping of distance, heights and terrain.

A shading on one of the maps prompted her to zero in and enlarge the image, curious what had caught her eye.

Was that a rubbish pile she was looking at? Or possibly the remnants of some type of shed? Or was it a vehicle? She magnified the area further before pausing the image and calling out to John.

John took control of the mouse, moving it over the imagery for another ten minutes.

'Yes, you're right. It's a vehicle. It's probably run out of fuel. Don't worry about it, these images would be from last week, at least, and I'll bet it's now back on the road and probably halfway to Moresby.'

'Oh, okay,' she said, closing the file without giving it further thought.

Grace was keen to begin organising the media trip with Jess, so reached for the QAP client file to make the arrangements.

Little did she realise what she had stumbled on.

# CHAPTER 15: JESS

Within a week, Jess was strapped in tightly beside Ronnie in a helicopter preparing for lift-off. Grace sat upfront beside the pilot, Cedric, who had been preoccupied with switches and nobs since they'd buckled up.

'Apologies for the early start folks,' Cedric said through her headphones, his soft Irish lilt bizarrely comforting despite being out of place so far from her home. His sing-song voice had Jess instantly forgiving him for the agony of getting up at five to make the trip.

'The weather around these parts is notoriously unreliable. Mist, fog and wind can roll in without warning. Especially when the day be getting on. So, we'll get up there early, have a couple of hours on the ground and be back by early afternoon. Sound all right, Grace?'

'Perfect, thanks, Cedric.'

'Rightio. So, we'll be off,' he announced, switching on the rotors, and in no time they were effortlessly lifting away.

The flight took them northwest of Port Moresby across a never-ending expanse of jungle. Every now and again there was a clearing, and Cedric and sometimes Grace pointed out landmarks below, including small village settlements or rivers.

Two and half hours later they landed in the remote community of Kooto—which looked to have more gas employees than local residents.

On one side was the village, around a dozen thatched huts and two larger open traditional-style pavilions. And opposite was a scattering of at least twenty shiny demountable buildings, no doubt belonging to the QAP Gas project.

Alighting, Jess stretched and gulped in the moist, fresh mountain air. As her eyes roamed the site, she noted the contrasting blend of traditional villages and the ultra-modern mining camp. A small group of children had gathered to watch the helicopter land and were now observing them curiously. A group of women sitting nearby shyly smiled, and Jess waved hello.

Grace strode over to the village on her own, greeting the women in fluid Pigeon English and fluffing the hair of the younger children, who giggled with glee.

A middle-aged man wearing a faded grey T-shirt and navy shorts came out to greet them, and Grace shook his hand before calling Jess and Ronnie over to meet the tribal leader. After a few more minutes of conversing in Pigeon, Grace led them towards the mine site.

The QAP Gas head office was located in the largest demountable. Its modern, fabricated structure was at odds with the thatched village homes nearby.

'Welcome back, Grace,' said a bearded man dressed in khaki pants and a white polo shirt emblazoned with the QAP Gas logo. He stood up as they entered the air-conditioned office.

'Great to see you again, Andre. As promised, I've brought the *Leading News* team,' she said before introducing them to the site manager and fetching cold soft drinks.

Half an hour later, Ronnie had set up the camera and tripod on a small rise overlooking the site, and Jess began to interview Andre about the project. He elaborated on the level of technological sophistication being used by the crews as they mapped out the route for the new pipeline—of which just one-fifth would traverse the overwhelming geography of the country, and over 2,000 kilometres would stretch along the ocean floor.

'The drones we use can efficiently map out the terrain, shaving hundreds of hours off what was manual labour in the old days, and by "old days", I'm talking as few as five, ten years ago.' He chuckled.

'They're fitted with camera gear that picks up everything—gradient, mass, typography—even ancient burial sites.'

Jess was intrigued to know if they had ever detected any such thing. 'Not here, but in Indonesia we did. It wasn't a traditional burial site but sadly ended up becoming one for an American couple. They were reported missing in the area years before. I can't recall how long. But apparently a landslide had just swallowed them up. Anyway, the drone located them buried below metres of soil sometime later.'

'I can't believe they vanished just like that,' Jess said, shocked.

'Oh, there'd be others,' Andre said confidently. 'Dense jungle, thick forest, gorges, crevasses… Yeah, nature has bountiful places to conceal just about anything.'

It was an eerie thought, and Jess was grateful to return to the mining story.

Handing out hard hats, fluoro vests and heavy boots, Grace walked them over the site, explaining the project as they went. Ronnie captured footage of the large-scale drilling operation, and Jess occasionally stopped Grace for some on-camera comments.

Exactly two hours later, they were back on the chopper.

The mental overload and early start were now taking their toll on Jess, but she wanted to get the guts of her story written whilst it was fresh. Reluctantly extracting her laptop from her bag, she began typing as the helicopter lifted away.

This would be her last feature story before returning home to Sydney, and whilst she couldn't wait to see her family and friends, she also felt a tinge of loss at leaving this adventure behind.

She reached for her iPhone and scanned the photos she had taken over the past three months. There were hundreds, and she clicked through eventually reaching her final shot. It was one that she'd taken less than an hour ago of the group of them at the mining site. Her eyes roamed the faces of Cedric, Andre, and Grace and a dozen or so uniformed pipeline employees. She'd insisted the tribal leader join in, and his toothless smile was dazzling. Her now good pal Ronnie grinned in the photo, and so did she. She looked different and not just because of her clothes and pulled-back hair. But her face, her eyes, her posture. She almost didn't recognise the smiling, confident woman looking back at her.

# CHAPTER 16: SARAH
## Gumawa, 12 November 1990

Sarah paced nervously. She loved her husband; she really did. But she also loved this child growing inside her… The problem was, it wasn't Clancy's. A careless, carefree dalliance—so exciting and liberating—was now the cause of so much inner turmoil.

Her lover had long departed, a magnetic attraction that had caught her off guard. So intense she'd been powerless to resist. Clancy had been away—again—and she had thrown caution to the wind, perhaps for the first and only time in her life.

The conception was instant. She had felt it almost immediately. The seed of joy filling her with so much elation and hope. For three months she had concealed her pregnancy from everyone, including her husband, but time was now against her. Her dalliance would be exposed as her body revealed the wonder within.

For at least a year now she and Clancy hadn't made love. It was as if he was never there. Late nights, much too early starts, and increasingly frequent business trips that took him away just that bit longer each time.

She moved her hands to her abdomen to feel the small miracle inside and trembled with excitement... but also exhilaration, and was that fear? She would need to speak with Clancy.

Some hours later, as they were preparing for bed, Sarah sat down at the mattress edge and swallowed the lump that had been in her throat all evening.

'Clancy, I have to tell you something. It's important.' Her voice trembled.

Her tone must have conveyed the significance of what she had to say because Clancy stopped immediately, abandoning his walk towards the wardrobe to undress. He turned around to face her, expectantly. A frown on his face.

'I'm having a baby,' she breathed out the words. Clancy took a moment to register what she'd said. His face froze before a flash of joy turned into a look of confusion. He had no doubt mentally registered the impossibility of this baby being his.

'What? How?' he spluttered, puzzled, not quite understanding what she was telling him.

'I'm three months pregnant.'

His shoulders visibly slumped at the words, and he let out an enormous sigh.

'I'm so sorry, Clancy. Not for having this baby but that I was unfaithful.'

Nodding mechanically, Clancy whispered, 'Who?'

'No one, or at least no one you know, no one important.'

'Who? Tell me!' he persisted, louder now, clenching his fists.

'Clancy, please…'

'I demand to know! Who is he? When?' he yelled at her.

Steadying her nerves and in an attempt to defuse the escalating mood, she decided to just get it over with. Clancy wouldn't let up until he had all the facts, she knew that.

'You were in Port Moresby, again, for coffee business, the export summit I think?' She didn't mean to sound critical, but in a way she was. For months now she had been left to her own devices.

'He was just someone passing through, photographing a story on the highlands for a magazine. It was one night, that's all,' she whispered, hoping to allay his upset.

'Where?'

'Clancy, why? Why does it matter?' she pleaded.

His fierce stare had her continuing.

'Okay! Elena and I were at the club. It was my cousin's last night, and I was already feeling down about her leaving… you both going away.' She noticed his face turn red with anger at the implied criticism.

'I'm not blaming you, Clancy. I'm not! But I was lonely. I'm here so much of the time without you, and yes, I was flattered… maybe? No, that sounds too superficial. It wasn't like that… We chatted about his travels, and I wanted to capture some part of myself. Some part I was missing out on…' She trembled. Tears were falling, but Clancy's body remained rigid. Unmoved.

'Right. Well, you'll have to get rid of it,' he

shouted, looking at her with disgust. 'No wife of mine bears the child of any other man,' he added proprietorially.

'I can't,' she cried, moving from the bed towards him. 'Clancy, please… We have wanted another child for so long, please, let's talk about this.'

Clancy just shook his head, refusing to look at her but not walking away either.

'Please support me on this. Support *us*. I only want to have another child. It wasn't to hurt you,' she begged, noting the quiet desperation that was entering her voice.

'No!' Clancy said, becoming increasingly agitated and moving past her to the door. Opening it, he stormed out.

Sarah rushed after him begging, 'Clancy, wait.' Reaching out to grab his arm, he violently pushed her away.

# CHAPTER 17: DOM
## Gumawa, 12 November 1990

Dom had snuck outside to lie on the front lawn and stare up at the full moon, imagining what it would be like to be a space man up there. Walking about in those strange spacesuits, floating so far from Earth. Maybe he'd be an astronaut when he grew up. Or would he? He must have dozed off at some point and woke with a start.

Sitting up suddenly, he felt alert. Some type of loud noise had woken him. Shouting, a crash? Something was wrong. Very wrong. The enormous moon now looked foreboding, and he quickly got to his feet and walked back inside.

But when he opened the front door, his heart stopped.

His mother lay at the foot of the stairs, her limbs askew and her face staring blankly at him.

At first he couldn't move. It was as if time stood still and he could only stare, trying to work out what her motionless eyes were conveying. And then he screamed, 'Mum! Mum!' and ran towards her.

As he crouched down, trying to shake her, his father came crashing down the stairs.

'My God! Sarah?' he screamed, kneeling to pull her up into a sitting position.

'Come on, Sarah! Love? Please!' The panic in his voice was frightening, and Dom moved backwards away from the distressful scene.

'Sarah, Sarah darling, are you okay? Sarah, talk to me!' His father's panic had now become futile pleas reverberating in the silence of the hall.

'I'm so sorry, Sarah, please, please…' he repeated over and over as he knelt over her lifeless form. Dom was still cowering a few steps behind him, and it was only as his sobs intensified that his father paused to look over to him. But he didn't reach out to his son; instead, his eyes darted around the room as if looking for something. Someone.

'Dom, call Mika and find Willy and Giro. Now!' he shouted.

Obediently, Dom went to the telephone to call their neighbour before sprinting out of the house in search of Dad's workmen.

Returning breathless, he then watched the three men slowly lift his mother and take her upstairs with care. Mika's steady arms were soon wrapped tightly around him, and the tears fell.

'Let's go into the kitchen. I'll make some sweet tea,' Mika said, ushering him away from the staircase where he hadn't moved.

It might have been minutes but was more likely an hour before he saw his father again. This time conferring quietly with the town's only doctor at the front door. His father looked pale and old. His body sagged with defeat.

The two men immediately stopped talking when they saw him.

'Dom, it's important that you get some rest, hey?' Dr Willis spoke softly, nodding at him. 'I've given Clancy something to help you both sleep tonight. I'll check on you tomorrow… well, later today now,' he said, looking at his watch. He then nodded at Clancy and headed out to his car in the pitch-dark morning.

An eerie silence filled the house as Dom watched his father, still standing at the front door. Dom knew he was waiting for something, but he wasn't sure what. Perhaps reassurance that everything would be okay in the morning.

Eventually Clancy spoke, his voice sounding hoarse and low. 'Sorry, son. Mum had a fall.' He gulped, swallowing before continuing, 'It was too hard on her small body. She's passed.'

Clancy's shoulders shook as he struggled to get the words out. Tears streamed from Dom's eyes, but he didn't move, instead beseeching his father for more. But only silence filled the space.

'But… What happened?' Dom's voice was so quiet he was surprised his father had heard him.

There was a flicker of something in Clancy's eyes before he shook it off and looked up, past Dom.

'Mika, good. Would you take Dom upstairs and get him into bed?' His father now had full command of himself again, and the moment was lost.

Handing something to Mika, he said, 'Dissolve this into some water for Dom. Son, make sure you drink this before you go to sleep. Okay?' Clancy squeezed his shoulder in a small sign of comfort as he handed over the sedative before hastily retreating out the door and into the silky darkness.

Dom lay awake, wondering where his father was. He also tried to recall what it was that he'd heard earlier when he'd been lying on the grass outside, watching the stars. What was the sound that had startled him out of his slumber? Was it the sound of his poor mother falling down the stairs? Or did it sound more like voices? Yelling? Eventually the drug oozed him into a deep sleep.

# CHAPTER 18: JESS

Jess felt like an observer, sitting on the top deck of the bus as it crawled into the city, inching painfully forward in the morning peak-hour traffic crossing the Harbour Bridge. Sydney commuters competing in cars, trains and a never-ending chain of buses to reach the skyscrapers ahead. It felt surreal to think that this time last week she was sitting beside Ronnie in the work SUV, navigating around potholes and overcrowded buses on their morning commute, laughing at some anecdote or workshopping today's story. She missed Ronnie and his endless tales of people and crazy adventures. She missed the craziness and also the simplicity of Port Moresby.

Jess looked around at her fellow commuters—some with grim, stony faces staring out of the large windows and others impatiently tapping and swiping their smartphones, eager to make inroads to their workday. *Would any of you have any idea of what another version of your life could look like?* She felt smug in her memories.

Jess was so thankful that she'd put her hand up for the foreign correspondent role. Not only for the amazing experience she had had in her short time away but because she was now returning to work as Features editor. Being the head of the Features department was something she had coveted for some time, and the recent staff changes would give her both a taste and a much-desired opportunity to showcase her talent.

'We love what you did over there,' the News editor Paul had said when telephoning her to announce the promotion late last week on her return to Sydney. 'You have a natural ability to really transport the reader into the story, and we'd like to see you take this further. We're offering you the role from Monday. Let's see what you can do with it.'

Jess was brimming with story ideas to take to her first editorial meeting at nine thirty and excited to catch up with her friends and colleagues again.

Getting off the bus at Wynyard, she walked the short distance to the office, queuing to buy an almond latte on the way.

'Where've you been?' Fred the barista enquired with interest, as he adeptly ground coffee beans, refilled the machine, grabbed cups and pressed buttons seamlessly as he worked to satisfy his waiting customers.

'I've been learning about all this,' she said, waving at the espresso machine. 'I've been in Papua New Guinea for the past three months.'

'PNG, hey? Now, they grow good coffee. My cousin's brother-in-law used to live up there. Pretty dangerous, hey?' he said, managing to maintain their conversation amongst the frantic pace of producing coffees for time-poor city workers who were alternating their glances between him and their phones.

'No, not if you know the drill.' Jess smiled. 'Anyway, I'll fill you in next time,' she said, indicating the busy crowd around them. Taking her latte, she headed in the direction of the office.

After offloading her laptop and oversized handbag on the desk, she took her coffee and notepad into the meeting room, savouring the aroma emanating from her cup and also the precious few minutes before the conference began.

'Jess McCann, welcome back!' boomed Paul as he strode into the room, followed by a stream of others, some of whom she knew and a couple she didn't.

Eventually ten of them were gathered around the morning conference table, which was staged in the larger of the two meeting rooms on the newsroom floor. Surrounded by glass, it felt a bit like being in a goldfish bowl. Jess had never been sure who was watching whom but guessed it was designed so that Paul could continue monitoring the action on the main newsroom floor whilst attending these meetings.

The news editor was accompanied by his assistant, Joyce, and there were seven other editors present, each overseeing the various rounds from State and Federal Politics to Business, Entertainment, News, Courts, Health, the Environment and Local Government.

'Jess will be attending the morning meetings from now on,' explained Paul. 'We've promoted her to the Features role.' After a round of congratulations from her colleagues, the morning conference began in earnest.

When it came to Jess's turn to put forward her

story ideas, she began with gusto, running through four different features she had developed—from an inspiring entrepreneur who had set up a new tech company that only employed school dropouts, to an exclusive with the gorgeous Sasha Downs, who was a rising star on the global stage and outdoing Nicole Kidman and Margot Robbie in the popularity stakes.

It was decided that Jess would kick off with the Sasha Downs piece before the other media got their hands on her.

After lining up the interview for the following day with Sasha's agent—who just happened to be a good friend of Frances (hence the 'in')—Jess sat back with glee. She knew it wouldn't always be this easy to secure sought-after celebrities, but for now she was happy to be off and running.

After work, Jess met up with Frances at a new bar that her girlfriend had discovered in Jess's absence.

Also in Jess's absence had materialised a very handsome work colleague.

But introductions were delayed as the pair embraced, jumping up and down, squealing.

'You're back! Finally!' Frances squeezed her tighter. 'I really missed you!'

'Me too,' replied Jess, giving her girlfriend a tight hug.

'Now, let me introduce you to Edward Acland. He's also at Bavaria Bank with me,' said Frances.

Jess liked the look of the gorgeous Nordic-looking man standing before her. Piercing green eyes accentuated a stunning face with high cheekbones and dark cropped hair. His suit was straight out of a Calvin Klein campaign, and she was relieved she had put some effort into her own attire for her first day back.

'Great to meet you,' he said warmly, kissing her on both cheeks. 'Frances told me all about your New Guinea trip.'

'Hi,' she squeaked as they took seats on high stools around a small circular table. Frances had just rushed over to another table to chat with apparent colleagues, leaving Jess and Edward to their own introductions and conversation.

She learnt that he had only recently joined the boutique investment bank in Sydney but had worked with the company in Singapore, Hong Kong and originally in Munich—his home city. Since arriving in Sydney in July, he had rented an apartment at Bondi, was a keen surfer and spent many weekends heading up and down the coast to see the beaches that made this part of the world famous.

'I'm here for a two-year contract and keen to explore everything all at once,' he said, taking a sip of his beer. By the time Frances had returned, they were enthusiastically debating the merits of the south coast versus the north coast and which road trip offered the better coffee.

'You Australians and your coffee.' He laughed. 'Before I arrived, I didn't know you were such caffeine addicts!'

'I know. I nearly died without my regular almond lattes when I was in Port Moresby for three months, and this morning's was sublime.' She exaggerated a sigh, feeling more confident and cheekier. 'Let's just say that whilst they may have good coffee beans, they haven't yet discovered the joys of mixing them with almond milk.'

'I don't know about "joys", Jess. I can never understand how you can drink that stuff. It ruins a great coffee. Give me a short black any day,' scorned Frances.

The conversation soon moved to her stint up north, and she entertained Frances and Edward with the people she had met and the logistical challenges of reporting in such a remote country. Power blackouts, unreliable telecommunications and difficult terrain just to name a few. Telling the stories made her feel nostalgic.

'My favourite was this intriguing family dynasty,' she began, playing it up. 'This handsome, swashbuckling Australian backpacker makes good, marries a Swiss beauty, they have a son, and he develops a globally successful coffee business. But I can't help feeling there's something I missed in my feature.' She pouted.

'What do you mean?' enquired Frances. 'I remember that one. I loved that story!'

'Thanks. It's just something I can't quite put my finger on. Something about the sudden death of his wife. No one wanted to talk about it.'

'But that's obvious. It would be deeply distressing,' Frances said.

'Or she may have met with foul play?' suggested Jess, widening her eyes at them both.

'Jessica, you are a suspicious one,' Edward said, jumping in, and she liked the way her full name sounded on his lips.

'Yes, I think I'm drawing conclusions from very little. After all, it was nearly thirty years ago.'

'Thirty years! God, Jess, move on,' Frances reprimanded impatiently. 'That's a lifetime ago. Even just thinking of ten, fifteen years seems an age! Remember when we couldn't get enough of *Talking*

*Heads,* Long Island ice teas and chunky shoulder pads? Edward, you really should have seen Jess's hair back then.' Frances steered the conversation to their days of trying to be sophisticated eighteen-year-olds straight out of school and keen to experience everything on offer.

The memories were embarrassing and hilarious, and in no time Jess's suspicions were left far behind.

# CHAPTER 19: JESS

It was late Friday afternoon, and Jess sat rereading her article on Sasha Downs. She adjusted a word, only to return seconds later to the same paragraph and click Undo. The copy was fine, and she knew it. The only thing her story needed was to be saved and sent up the ladder to her editor.

Before taking the final step, her office phone rang. Recognising the Bavaria Bank landline number, she smiled and sat back in her chair to enjoy the distraction.

'Hi, Frances.' She sighed.

'Hello, Jessica? It's actually Edward calling,' he stumbled. 'Frances's colleague from the other night? I hope you don't mind that I looked up your work number?' His awkwardness was endearing.

'Of course not,' she replied with a small flutter in her stomach. 'How are you?'

'Good.' He let out a relieved breath. 'I wanted to see if you had plans next weekend. I've been invited to a function at the German Australian Pacific

Association next Saturday night, and I was hoping you could join me as my plus one. You'd be doing me a huge favour. I don't really want to go. I'd much rather hit the coast, but I committed myself to attend.'

'Wow, you really know how to pitch a tempting offer.' She let out a loud laugh, and he joined in.

As she put down the phone a few minutes later, she thought, *A date! Wow, maybe it's not so bad being back in Sydney? And maybe my luck is changing!*

Jess decided to end the day on a high note, pressing Send on her Sasha Downs feature and closing down her computer for the weekend. As she picked up her handbag, she noticed her forlorn-looking swim bag under the desk and made a decision to go via the pool on her way home. She hadn't swum since she'd gone up to PNG, and it had been way too long.

She loved swimming for both the exercise and the quiet meditation. Her favourite place to swim laps was outdoors, and the North Sydney Olympic Pool was a hub of activity when she arrived just after six. Squads dominated the fast lanes, and post-work types like her were sharing the remaining lanes, each keen to knock over a kilometre or more before heading into the weekend.

Beautifully situated beneath the arc of the Sydney Harbour Bridge, it was a haven for stressed-out office workers keen to stretch out their limbs and enjoy the silent contemplation of following the black line up and down the pool. The peak-hour traffic crossing the Bridge above dissolved into a faint hum as a hundred or so swimmers powered up and down the fifty-metre pool below.

After a quick change, she tightly tucked her blond curls into her swimming cap and fitted her goggles before going to wrestle space in a lane. Thirty minutes later, she had done her laps and was under the shower rinsing off, her shoulders and legs tingling with fatigue.

On her short walk home from the bus, she stopped to pick up a Laksa and a bottle of white wine. Just one week back and she was already settling into her city life.

On Saturday morning, Jess went up the street to buy the weekend newspapers. She still preferred the ritual of poring over newsprint and supplements on a long, lingering weekend to the online alternative. She ordered a large coffee and an assortment of pastries at her favourite café, a French-inspired patisserie that she knew her sister loved. The sweet treats were for Emma and her nieces, whom she'd be visiting next. Spending Saturday afternoon with Emma was another weekend ritual, and she was looking forward to seeing them today.

'Jess!' they cried out excitedly a few hours later as she alighted from her car. Their little bodies jumped up and down as Emma protectively shielded them from the road.

'Hello, girls,' she said, scooping both Angelina and Clementine into her arms. Whilst there was just over a year's age difference between the two girls, they could have passed as twins. The blond-haired, blue-eyed smiling five- and six-year-olds were squealing in delight.

Emma gave her a warm hug, leading her into the kitchen where a contented baby looked up from a bouncer on the floor.

Scooping up her newest niece, Annabelle, Jess

gave her loud, squelchy kisses on her stomach, making her giggle. The sound was as sweet as the pastries Jess had just carried in.

'They've really missed you, Aunty Jess,' said Emma, adding, 'I've really missed you too.'

'Back at you sis!' They settled down at the benchtop with cups of tea and a danish each. At a small table in the living room sat Angelina and Clementine happily munching into their flaky croissants with glasses of milk.

Jess loved having her sister so close, providing a much-needed dose of family life to balance her singledom. She spent many a morning, afternoon or weekend at Emma's home, playing with her nieces and helping out where she could. Taking them to the park and stealing a few cuddles and sloppy kisses when curled up reading their favourite story books at night were among her favourite things. Emma's husband, Steve, worked long hours at the Parramatta branch of Westpac Bank, and whilst a doting dad and husband, he was out of the house more often than not, attending meetings and overseeing his young team. He was also a bit of a golf addict, but Emma was adept at juggling the girls alone.

Jess admired her sister's devotion to motherhood, and despite the exhaustion, Emma still had time to be interested in her life too.

'So, tell me about Edward?' asked Emma, who had heard about the handsome stranger earlier that week.

'Well, he's pretty cute.' Jess sighed and began filling her sister in on their upcoming date.

'A cocktail party! I'm envious,' swooned Emma. 'I can't recall the last time Steve and I got dressed up for anything.'

'Me either!'

After discussing what she should wear and agreeing that a blow-dry was a must, the sisters moved back to their favourite topic, the latest antics of the girls. This time it was naughty Angelina who'd taken Annabelle's bottle, and peacekeeper Clementine had done her best to resolve things without Mummy knowing.

'Adorable,' Jess said, pouring more tea as they talked on into the afternoon.

# CHAPTER 20: DOM

Dom groaned as he hung up the phone. Clancy was a stubborn bugger. His father had confirmed that he'd be returning to Gumawa on Sunday, two weeks ahead of schedule. And against medical advice.

'I'm fine,' he quipped when challenged by his son on the earlier return date. 'I can't stay here any longer. I want to be home. This is bloody suffocating me.'

Clancy's return signalled the end of Dom's caretaking stint at the farm. In spite of himself, he'd enjoyed working on the property. He had travelled back to Australia twice over the past six weeks to attend to affairs at his Sydney office, and to check on Clancy's recovery, and had now settled into the routine of the place.

The isolation suited him too. Sure, there were the regular Friday-night drinks at the Anzac Club and a few dinners with neighbours—all keen to keep an eye on him—but what he had most enjoyed was the quiet solitude of the farm. It had been unexpected.

Thankfully, his law firm had sailed on smoothly without requiring too much of his physical presence, although he spent every second or third day on conference calls with his team or at least Marcus, who he missed working alongside.

During his time at Gumawa, he had come to know Mika better. He'd met her a few times over the years, but through their weekly catch-ups at the club, they'd begun to move beyond the small talk, and he had got a better sense of his father's friend.

Before this visit, he'd never really understood what kept her, a single woman, in PNG. Her husband had left many years before, and whilst she had many friends in the district, it still puzzled him.

'But it is so beautiful here.' She shrugged off his question. 'I have my art and my friends. I love to hike each morning and then paint until dusk. I have Clancy—he is very good to me. I am very loyal to him,' she said, glowing with genuine affection for his father.

Dom knew that there was a strong friendship between the pair and had never read more into it than that. A mutual fondness existed, and he almost envied their closeness.

Perhaps sensing his quiet reflection, Mika continued. 'Your father is a very kind and generous man, Dom,' she soothed. 'I know that he is so proud of you in your career and now for being here to take care of things.'

'Well, why doesn't he ever say it?' Dom was annoyed and knew that he sounded like the little boy he once was and not the man of nearly forty years of age that he had become.

'He's a man,' she said simply. 'Pfft. You men never share emotion, feeling, intimacies.' She waved her long fingers in the air to reinforce the point. 'Like you, Clancy never wants to show his true feelings. But I can see. I have always been able to see, sometimes more clearly than Clancy, how he is feeling. What he needs…,' she said somewhat cryptically.

'He's vulnerable, and so are you.' She sat back and gazed at him over her scotch and soda.

'You don't really know me, Mika,' he responded, keen to shake off the psychoanalysis.

'But of course I do. You are Clancy's son!' she said, as if that explained everything. 'Your mother passed away when you were just a boy. You marry young, hoping to fill the void, but it doesn't. You still feel empty and blame your father for this, but it was never his fault,' she continued, getting into her stride. 'You will not find happiness until you move on from the past. It is time to forgive your father for not being two parents to you when your mother died. He too was grieving, Dom,' she added more gently.

Dom downed the remainder of his beer and rose to his feet.

'Mika, always a pleasure to catch up—even with the weekly dose of therapy,' he said, kissing her on both cheeks.

'I care for both of you and just want you to move on. Life is for living,' she said.

The words sounded like an instruction not to be ignored.

When he arrived home, he avoided checking his phone or emails, silently heading straight to bed. But his tiredness didn't prevent the tossing and turning that kept him awake for the next hour or more before finally succumbing to sleep.

Clancy's return created a buzz with the

workers, especially Kila, who had the team all lined up ready to greet the boss when he alighted from the truck. Dom had gone in to pick up Clancy that morning and had driven him back to the farm with caution.

'I'm not a bloody invalid,' he'd barked. 'Put some gun into it! We'll never get there at this rate.'

Shaking his head, Dom stayed his course, and they chatted about the positive prognosis and treatment plan for the months ahead.

'My immune system is the only issue now,' Clancy said. 'But being this far away from people, I told the Doc that I wouldn't be catching the winter flu in a hurry!' He chuckled.

The cardiologist had given Clancy a strict health regime to follow that included plenty of rest, not driving for three months, and no heavy lifting or operating machinery. They had also encouraged him to ease slowly back into his daily routine. He would need to present himself again in three months for a follow-up scan and full blood work, but the cardiologist was confident that he would make a full recovery.

'Sounds like Christmas in Sydney then,' Dom said, calculating the timing for his father's follow-up appointment.

'Fine with me,' agreed Clancy, catching Dom by surprise. It would signal a first in their relationship. Dom had always been the one to travel up to PNG to spend time with his father. This would be a turning point for them, a concession in their relationship. At least he hoped it would.

After a few days together, Dom departed the property with Kila driving him to the airport, where they shook hands and reached an unspoken agreement that he would now watch over things and, in particular, Clancy.

# CHAPTER 21: JESS

The head massage was divine. Jess was reclined at the wash basin at her regular hair salon in Mosman. The soothing hands of the young apprentice, Jilly, worked their magic, deliciously kneading her scalp. After this she would be getting a blow-dry, preferably something a little chic for tonight's cocktail party with Edward.

He'd been in touch earlier that week to firm up their plans, insisting on picking her up. The six-o'clock soirée was being held at the Woollahra premises of the German Pacific Group, or was it the German Asia Pacific Partnership? Jess couldn't quite remember the full name of the organisation but got the general gist. Edward had said it would be a group of professionals—German and other nationalities—all apparently focused on expanding and supporting German business links in Australia.

'More likely they'll be focused on the social aspects and the chance to enjoy a steady supply of German beer,' he'd remarked.

Despite Edward's misgivings, Jess was looking

forward to this evening. Dressing up, going out to a glamorous cocktail party and going on a date were things she hadn't done for a long time. Especially with such a handsome man. Yet despite those piercing green eyes and sculptured face, he also had a fun and cheeky side, which she'd liked instantly. He had been easy company the first night they had met with Frances in the city bar. Not trying to be a show-off or hog the conversation but rather just easing into their company. He had also been a true gentleman in making the plans for tonight, confirming by phone and insisting that he escort her to the function—despite living on opposite sides of the city.

Whilst she wasn't sure where tonight would lead, if anywhere, she knew that there was an attraction—at least for her.

As Jess let herself back into her apartment two hours later, wearing styled curls and clutching a second almond latte and toasted bagel to sustain her for the next few hours, she smiled at the possibilities that the evening might bring.

Kicking off her shoes, she settled onto her sofa with her afternoon sustenance and began to read the magazine insert of the weekend paper before eventually rising to get ready.

Jess felt radiant when she buzzed Edward in promptly at five thirty p.m. She knew her strappy cocktail dress was just the right colour (bolt blue) and shape (clingy, bias cut) to accentuate her best features—her blue eyes, blond curls and slim frame. Or so her sister had insisted in the confidence-building Facetime call she'd just had with her. Emma had repeated how stunning Jess looked, and the flattery had woven its way into her psyche.

Thankfully Edward agreed. 'Jessica, you're a knockout,' he said, leaning in to kiss her softly on both cheeks.

A quick cab ride later, they were walking into a 1930s-style ballroom that oozed elegance and formality. Jess could see that the organisation took its charter very seriously. This was no regular social group but a networking event for grown-ups.

Edward found her hand and drew her over to a small group of men, introducing her to the chairman of the German Australian Pacific Alliance. *She knew it was something like that!*

Enjoying the warm, electric feel of his hand in hers, she felt comfortable and confident and began to settle into the conversation, learning more about the imprint the organisation had on the Sydney business community and the partnerships it had made possible for aspiring businesspeople both here and in Germany.

When Edward disclosed that Jess was a journalist, the chairman beamed and immediately swept her around the room to meet other board members, all the while earnestly discussing the potential of a 'fascinating editorial on the bilateral partnership between the countries.'

Eventually Edward arrived to rescue her, apologising for outing her media status.

'It's fine.' She laughed. 'It's not the first time that's happened, and it was flattering.'

He steered them towards the supper buffet to taste some of the German delights before murmuring that perhaps they could now respectably head off for a nightcap. So, a short time later, he called an Uber and they discreetly departed for a small bar in Double Bay.

Nursing a delicious Baileys on ice, Jess sat back

in the comfortable lounge, watching Edward slowly weave his way back to their table. He had worn a slim-cut grey suit and open-neck white shirt that highlighted his striking eyes and glowing skin, no doubt darkened from his love of surfing and the ocean.

He was undoubtedly good-looking. She knew it wasn't just her opinion, as he created a wave of glances from the other females (and a few men as well) as he moved towards her. She felt a little giddy that it was she who he was with, at least for that evening.

Whilst they had enjoyed conversing at the cocktail party, they hadn't had a chance to really talk until now. Over their cocktails, they exchanged their stories—families, career trajectories, past life experiences.

'My parents died when I had just finished the HSC—my final school year exams,' Jess said to clarify the relevance of this period in her life, knowing Edward wasn't Australian educated. 'I was eighteen, and my sister, Emma, was twenty.' Jess found herself sharing the story of her parents' tragic car accident, the innocent fatalities of a semitrailer truck that lost control on the highway between Sydney and Melbourne. Two other people had died in the carnage, including the truck driver—who was believed to have fallen asleep at the wheel.

It was a tragedy that had cemented the two sisters in their grief and also in their determination to live the lives that their parents had wanted for them. Emma had finished her nursing degree and immediately married Steve, her high school sweetheart, and created a family to share her love with. Jess had focused on her career, reticent to lose her heart again and experience the shattering pain.

'I too have nieces,' Edward said. 'And nephews—six in total—two to each of my three sisters.' He shared photos, pulling out his iPhone and clicking through various images with affection.

Jess liked the way Edward spoke about his sisters and their young protégé, revealing a doting uncle and a protective, proud and caring older brother.

Last drinks were announced by the waiter, prompting Jess and Edward to gather their things and head home. Living in opposite directions, Edward hailed a cab for Jess, kissing her lightly on the lips before bidding her good night. She watched him wave as she headed home from a wonderful evening.

'Well, how did it go?' Her sister's excited voice awoke her the next morning.

'Emma? My God, what time is it?'

'That good, hey?' Emma laughed. 'Sorry to call you so early! I know it's not even eight o'clock, but I am up at sparrows with the kids and have been wanting to call you for the past two hours.'

Sitting up and peering at the light streaming through her shutters, Jess began to recount her evening before.

'He's really lovely. And before you ask, yes, I did get kissed good night, and we talked about catching up next week, okay? Pleased?' joked Jess, so familiar with her older sister's consummate worry about her single status.

'Yee ha!' squealed Emma. 'I'm glad! You deserve a really nice guy, and I'm thrilled the night was such a success.'

The pair talked some more before Jess ended the call to shower and meet Frances for brunch. She too was bursting to know how the evening had gone.

Over the following two months, Jess enjoyed spending more and more time with Edward. Whilst the romance was still relatively new, she felt a growing attraction towards him, looking forward to their regular nights out and late brunches after staying over at one or the other's place.

She enjoyed the casual, no-strings nature of their relationship and the room it left her to catch up with other things in her life—Emma, her girlfriends, her evening swims and of course her feature writing.

'I want us to go away together for a weekend,' Edward announced one evening as they sat at an Italian brasserie in the uber cool stretch of Bondi Beach, where he lived.

Caught by surprise, Jess gulped the mouthful of wine she was savouring before Edward continued.

'I know you're a fan of the north coast, but I want to introduce you to the splendours of the south. I've made a booking at a favourite coastal spot for the first weekend of December, and I'd love you to join me,' he said with earnestness.

'I'd love to,' Jess found herself instantly replying, thrilled to be invited on a weekend away with Edward.

A broad smile lit his handsome face as he lent over the table, meeting her halfway before planting a delicious kiss on her mouth.

They grinned at each other before returning their attention to the menu.

# CHAPTER 22: DOM

Dom had barely looked up from his desk since returning nearly four weeks ago. He had been buried in an unrelenting cycle of client conferences and drafting legal documents. Piles of cream manilla folders tied up in pink ribbons sat on the desk opposite, ready for client conferences tomorrow and the days to follow. He'd moved mountains in the past month.

But he wasn't complaining. He still felt guilty for leaving Marcus and the team for the best part of two months to help Clancy out at the farm, and this was making up time. At least according to him. Marcus kept telling him to slow down. 'Where's the fire?' he'd say as Dom flicked open another client file at the end of the day, eager to make inroads before a new day dawned.

But the late nights were taking their toll, and he now scrabbled in his desk drawer for a few paracetamols and gulped them down with water. Shrugging his shoulders and turning his neck, he attempted to ease the stiffness in his body and massaged his temples to soothe the emerging headache.

As he looked out at the darkness outside, he caught a glimpse of the lights across the harbour and was reminded of the complete darkness of home. Well, not his home. Gumawa, to be precise. Although he had to admit, if only to himself, that he had become strangely accustomed to life at the farm during his protracted stay. He especially missed the sounds of birdlife and the jungle coming to life at sunrise and the spectacular mountain view in the morning as he took his coffee on the veranda.

Clancy would be returning for his scans in two weeks, and Dom was looking forward to seeing him. Their fraught father/son relationship had thawed dramatically since Clancy's diagnosis.

Perhaps realising that time was precious, Dom had been in regular contact since returning to Sydney. His time at the farm had given him a greater sense of the man his father was. Mika, Kila, Clancy's mates at the club had all bent his ear about the support his father had given them. He had been reminded of the pioneering work he'd done in farming, his fearlessness, loyalty and leadership in the small community.

It would be a legacy, thought Dom, wondering what he had to show for his thirty-nine years.

Divorce and his legal partnership. Not much in the scheme of things.

Since his marriage breakdown a decade ago, he had become a workaholic, of that he knew. Initially it was to keep up with the manic workload at the global law firm and make partner. But when he had slipped off that trajectory and set up practice with Marcus, he had no reason to keep up the furious pace. But he had anyway.

Over the years, he had seen Marcus and other friends marry and start families and fill their lives with family vacations and junior soccer games. He'd never envied it before, but now he was beginning to contemplate a different life for himself.

Maybe it was time to start dating again? Since Lauren, he hadn't met anyone special. And he wondered if Mika's analysis of him had any merit. Was he trying to fill a void left by his mother? And if so, *why*?

Tomorrow would be the twenty-eighth anniversary of his mother's death, and it was making him feel reflective and melancholy. He clicked on the Google Chrome icon on his computer and typed in his mother's name, hoping to learn something more about her. Hoping to feel connected to her in some way.

When nothing appeared in her maiden name, Sarah Spotnik, he typed in Jonson. Bingo.

### SWISS PLANTATION WIFE DIES IN PNG

Sarah Jonson, thirty-five-year-old wife of Gumawa Coffee Plantation owner, Clancy Jonson, died suddenly last week at the family home in the remote settlement of Gumawa. Her accidental death has been ruled as not suspicious by Mount Hagen police. Clancy and Sarah Jonson have one son, Dominic, ten.

## OUTPOURING OF GRIEF AT
## YOUNG MOTHER'S FUNERAL

Residents from the remote township of Gumawa and surrounding settlements gathered to farewell a much-loved neighbour this week, as thirty-five-year-old Sarah Jonson of Gumawa Coffee Plantation was buried at the Mount Hagen Cemetery.

More than one hundred people attended the church service, followed by a burial with her immediate family—husband, Clancy Jonson and ten-year-old son, Dominic.

Sarah moved to Papua New Guinea as a child with her late father, Harold Spotnik, in the 1960s and continued to reside in the area, marrying Clancy Jonson in 1976.

It was surreal to read the stories online, and Dom was transported back to that fatal day when his mother died, wondering what had happened to make her fall so fatally down the stairs? Surely it was just an accident… or was it something less innocent? And why was he now wondering that? After all these years?

Despite the late hour, he pulled the business card out of his wallet where it had rested for the past three months and dialled.

# CHAPTER 23: JESS

'Hello?' Jess answered cautiously, unsure and wary at the unknown number flashing on her screen at eight thirty at night.

'Is that Jess McCann?' a man asked, his voice revealing a professional clip.

'Yes?'

'It's Dom. Dom Jonson,' he stated before apologising for the lateness of his phone call and mumbling something about finding her business card.

'Yes, of course I remember you,' she said and listened to Dom's request to meet up.

Intrigued—and relieved it wasn't a pesky telemarketing call—Jess agreed, and a time was set for the following afternoon.

As she sank back into the sofa, she felt even more curious about the call. It was surprising to hear from Dom after all this time—it must have been at least three months since they had met. And more puzzling to Jess was that he wanted to speak to her in a professional capacity. After all, he hadn't been overly enthusiastic with her profession when she'd met him for the interview at Clancy's farm. His distrust of the media had been all too apparent.

The next afternoon, she arrived promptly at the designated café and walked over to Dom. His head was down as he quickly typed into his phone, and it gave her a chance to observe him unaware. She couldn't help but notice his altered appearance. He looked thinner, and his face was drawn. The healthy and vibrant glow he'd possessed when they first met at Gumawa was long gone, replaced by a hollow and grey complexion.

'Dom?' she said quietly after reaching his table.

'Oh, Jess. Hi,' he replied, quickly dispensing with his phone and standing up to greet her. He looked like he was about to stick out his hand to shake hers but seemed to quickly pull it back. Instead, they nodded at each other, and she sat down opposite.

'You had me intrigued,' she said with what she hoped was an easy smile.

After they ordered coffees, she sat back and listened as Dom explained the purpose of their catch-up.

'I want to know more about the circumstances of my mother's death,' he said, studying Jess for a moment. 'You asked me about it when we met, and I know I was evasive, but the truth is I don't really know myself what happened. But I now want to.'

'Why? Why now? What's changed?' she asked.

'Today's her anniversary… the anniversary of her death, I mean. The twelfth of November. I don't know why, but I just can't seem to let it rest without knowing one way or the other what happened.'

'I'm sorry,' she murmured. 'If you have questions, perhaps you should speak with Clancy.' But he shook his head, staring at her.

'Do you think Clancy…,' she began before he cut her off.

'No! That's not what I'm saying. Look, Clancy refuses to talk about any of it. I can't be at peace, wondering if she fell by accident or, God forbid, she meant to or something I can't even get my head around let alone articulate.'

Was he talking about murder? Feeling a little giddy, Jess calmed her nerves before replying, 'Okay. But I don't understand why you're talking to me? How do you think I can help?'

He pulled out copies of the news articles he had read online and laid them out on the table.

'I found these, but that is all I could see online. Do you have access to the newspapers of the time? I want to know if there was any more information in any other media reports, either in the PNG or Australian Press. Being a journalist, I thought you may know at least how to get a hold of the historic news articles— you know, dating back to when it happened?'

Jess considered his request, noting the desperation and tiredness in his eyes. She knew that she could quite easily check the archival database when she was back at the office and felt compelled to at least do that much for him. But she wasn't confident it would reveal much.

'What about other more formal sources of enquiry? Have you also thought of any other avenues to investigate?' she asked.

When Dom looked at her blankly, she expanded. 'Your local doctor in Mount Hagen? The coroner's report? You know, the medical side? They would have had to sign off on a death certificate on the cause of death.'

'I doubt I'll get any answers from the doctor and I wouldn't know how to find him after all these years, but the death certificate might hold a clue,' he said hopefully before adding, 'Unless it just states exactly what these reports say?'

'I won't be able to get the coroner's report without applying for it, and I don't want to raise suspicions by doing just that.' He looked at her intensely, and his voice found a note of hope. 'But you could, couldn't you? You're media! You investigate stories all the time?'

During her time at *Leading News*, Jess had built up a wealth of contacts in the legal system and knew he was right, but she was also miffed that his initial dislike of her profession was something he now wanted to exploit.

'And why would I invest my time to do this?' she asked flatly.

'Fair question.' He had the grace to look a little meek, possibly remembering he hadn't been the easiest interviewee all those months ago. 'I guess I just hoped you would help me. You were curious about my mother when we spoke at Gumawa. I just want to know what happened. And I thought you did too. I'd be happy to compensate you for any costs and your time?'

Testing the waters, Jess said, 'And if there is a story behind it all, and I want to run it? As an exclusive?'

'No,' he snapped before momentarily closing his eyes and releasing a deep sigh. 'I don't want this to be shared in the media. It's deeply personal.'

'But if a crime was committed and it wasn't addressed?' she argued before he cut her off. Neither of them mentioned *who* the crime may have been committed by, neither wishing to acknowledge the awful truth that could lie at the heart of Sarah's death.

'If, and it's a big *if*, someone had a hand in my mother's death, then I'm prepared to consider exposing them for what they did, but I'm not consenting to anything before we know the facts.'

The news hound in her wrestled with her compassionate nature, and she eventually agreed to see what her research would find.

The next morning Jess arrived at work early, eager to get started on Dom's request before settling into her regular work. Jess felt vindicated that Dom suspected there was more to Sarah's sudden passing than was fully explained and thankful that he had approached her with his request to learn more. Not only did she feel a journalistic interest in the story but also a connection to the Jonson family—Clancy and to a lesser degree, Dom.

She first dug up the archives and scanned back to the date of Sarah's death—12 November 1990.

Her online search brought up three articles; the first two confirmed what she already knew and were the same stories that Dom had shown her the day before. The third was a classified's listing for her memorial service.

She then began to log on to the international database to access the archives of the PNG press and was disappointed to see the same stories—the exact same stories. Clearly the writer was filing for both media organisations.

She then grabbed her battered contact book, one that she rarely used these days, and flicked through the pages to *C*, finding her contact at the National Coroner's Office and began punching in the numbers.

'Hey, Jess! Long time no speak,' answered Roger Essex from his desk on the other side of the city.

'Hi, Rog. So good to speak to you. Since I'm not doing the rounds anymore, I don't get the fun of chatting to you guys. I miss you and those daily dawn phone calls.' She laughed, breaking the ice before asking, 'But I do have a little request I'm hoping you might be able to help with?'

After listening to her request, Roger advised that as PNG was a protectorate of Australia up until 1975, they would have copies of coroner reports up to that date, but afterwards, these would all be filed with the PNG courts. Whilst he couldn't help her directly, he passed on a contact for her to try.

Jess telephoned Roger's contact at the court office in Port Moresby but was only able to leave a message, and she asked that they return her call.

Feeling frustrated and impatient to know more, Jess reluctantly put the investigation aside and began turning her focus to this morning's editorial meeting, which was fast approaching.

Many hours later, as Jess was finalising an article for the weekend edition, she received a call back from Brett Delaney at the PNG coroner's office. Excitedly, Jess began to explain her request for a copy of the coroner's report into the death of Sarah Jonson.

Anticipating questions as to why she was seeking such a historic document, Jess was ready to explain that it was all part of her routine research into a potential story on pioneering women in PNG, a fictitious storyline Jess had created moments before.

But she didn't get the chance to explain, as Brett Delaney instantly put her on hold. Returning to the call a few minutes later, he said, 'I'm sorry to say but there is no report on this person in our files.'

She could hear his tapping as he went. 'I'm on our computer system, which holds all of our records, and we don't have her details in the system.'

'How come?'

'I would assume it was either a death of natural causes or she died in nonsuspicious circumstances. Autopsies aren't conducted unless there is a specific request in those occasions.'

After suggesting that Jess speak with the office of Births, Deaths and Marriages, and passing on the details, Jess agreed that she would. Due to the lateness of the day, she doubted the office would have anyone there, but she tried the number anyway. As anticipated, an answering system clicked in, and so after leaving a message, she went home via the North Sydney swimming pool where she thrashed through twenty laps to release her frustration at her lack of progress.

The next evening, Jess met Dom at Leo's wine bar in the CBD, close to his office. He looked slightly better than he had just two days before. Perhaps the decision to share his quest with Jess and begin the journey to find answers had taken some of the weight off his shoulders.

He stood up to greet her as she arrived at the small table, pulling out a chair and signalling to the waiter that they were ready to place their drink orders.

Once the drinks were settled on the table, she began expanding on her research and what she had found.

'I've tried Birth, Deaths and Marriages three times and will give it a final try again tomorrow, but I really think your local doctor at the time is the one who will have your answers,' she insisted more strongly now. 'I know he was a family friend and most probably long retired, but you should start with him.'

Grudgingly Dom nodded, and Jess found herself offering to help him trace the doctor's whereabouts.

They then moved off the topic of Dom's mother and began regular conversation, and it transported Jess back to her short stay at Gumawa with Dom. He mentioned Clancy's imminent arrival the following weekend for medical appointments, just routine he'd emphasised, and Clancy's plans to stay over Christmas.

'Please give him my regards,' said Jess.

'Well, you can pass them on yourself,' he replied. 'That's if you don't have any plans on Sunday? I'd like to include you in a small pre-Christmas drinks thing I'm having with some friends. A sort of welcome to Sydney for Clancy, because believe me it's been a long time. How does four o'clock sound?'

Jess could think of nothing nicer than reuniting with the rogue, Clancy… and confirmed she'd be there.

She also wondered if seeing him again might provide a clue in their search for the truth.

# CHAPTER 24: JESS

The expanse of Seven Mile Beach was breathtaking.

'It's great, isn't it?' Edward beamed at her.

It was Friday afternoon. They had left Sydney two hours earlier, and Jess was mesmerised by the spectacular scenery. Work felt like a lifetime ago, and her whole body melted into the luxurious leather seat of Edward's BMW.

'That view is magnificent. Delicious enough to eat!' She sighed. 'I may just need to concede that the South Coast is pretty impressive.'

'Can I get that in writing?' he said, teasing her before turning off the highway and into a narrow road that led them down to Culburra—a small beachside town that boasted a crescent beach and a lone shop that sold fish and chips, groceries and liquor, all from the same counter.

Before long they were pulling up outside a beach bungalow at the north end of the beach with unparalleled views out to the Tasman Sea.

'I love this place,' Edward said. 'I've become

such a frequent visitor; the owner and I now book privately—off Airbnb.'

'It's gorgeous,' she agreed, following him up to the steps and around the L-shaped timber deck.

It really was superb. The white sand almost touched the banister of the deck, and waves gently lapped the shore mere metres away.

Within twenty minutes, they had unloaded the car and were walking the beach. Swimmers had been hastily pulled on, and Jess had thrown on a kaftan and her wide brim sunhat to keep away the glare.

Edward was impressive in the surf, tackling the bigger waves with confidence and ease.

'Are you sure you're German? You're a natural out here,' she commented with glee before they dived under another wave rolling towards them.

That evening, Edward barbequed fresh snapper that he'd bought at the local fish co-op on their drive south and again impressed her with his flair at the grill. The white flesh was succulent and cooked perfectly in foil packages with lemon and herbs.

He was adept at anything he turned his hand to, she thought fondly, watching him now open a second bottle of chilled Riesling and increase the volume on the jazz wafting from his portable Sonos.

'Madam?' he asked, raising an eyebrow suggestively before topping up her wineglass.

She was feeling deliciously tipsy from the wine, the meal, and indeed the whole evening. The sound of the waves meeting the shoreline were now a balm to her ear and added a relaxed holiday feel.

'I can see why you're a regular here,' she murmured, reaching out to wind her fingers in his. He brought her hand to his lips and kissed each finger before lowering her hand to the table. Eventually he gathered her up and steered them kissing and giggling to the bedroom, laughingly navigating their way through the white mosquito net that would enclose them for the night ahead.

The next morning, she woke dozily to soft kisses from Edward and the sound of crashing waves.

'Is it a big surf? Or does it just seem louder to my poor head?' She pouted playfully, and Edward rolled on top of her for a lingering kiss.

'Does that feel better?' he whispered, teasing her.

'A little.' She smiled into his adoring green eyes.

'Good! Because the sea is calling us, so up you get, lazy pants.' He rolled off her, pulling away the sheet.

'But it's the weekend?' she moaned.

'Yes, and we need to make the most of it! Especially if we still must leave by lunchtime.'

'Yes, we do,' she said, reluctantly getting up.

Plunging into the surf, followed by a fried breakfast and a bottomless cup of coffee were Jess's saviours, making her feel loads better by the time they began to pack up their things. They were leaving earlier than Edward wanted, but she had made a promise to be at Clancy's for drinks, and she didn't want to renege.

The three-hour drive back to Sydney saw the pair return as a different couple to the one who had set out. Their relationship had moved to a more intimate, sensual level, and she felt tingly with the lovemaking and quality time they had enjoyed.

# CHAPTER 25: DOM

She looked radiant when she entered the back garden, her blond hair highlighted by the sun and her captivating smile greeting everyone around her.

Dom realised that he had never noticed Jess like this before. He had always viewed her through a professional lens in her role of persistent journalist, eager for a story. Not this stunning thirty-year-old woman clearly enjoying a life outside of work, judging by her appearance here today. Her white pants showed off her trim figure, and the red halter neck top accentuated her tanned arms and shoulders. She looked fresh with her loose blond curls and carefree smile. He was so glad she had come.

'Clancy!' she exclaimed when his father went over to greet her. Dom wished he had been closer to that side of the garden and the recipient of her warm embrace instead of turning over the steaks on the grill.

He watched the pair chatting like long-lost friends, before eventually seconding Marcus to take over the barbeque so that he could greet his new guest.

'Hi, Jess. I'm glad you made it.' He leant in to kiss her on the cheek.

'I wouldn't have missed catching up with Clancy on his much-anticipated return to Sydney! I'm glad to see your dad looking so well!' she said with sincerity, having learnt the particulars of Clancy's heart operation earlier from Dom.

The afternoon drinks party was in full swing as Dom introduced Jess to his friends, one by one, enjoying the thrill of having her at his home. He was heartened to see the gentle but jovial attention she relished on his father, choosing a seat beside him as they sat down to eat.

Whilst a small group, it was a lively gathering with his closest buddies Marcus, Jason, and Scott and their wives and assorted children. Dom didn't spend nearly enough time with these guys but vowed that would change. The afternoon turned into evening, and in no time, children were being gathered and farewells made as Dom saw his friends out. Walking back inside, Dom was relieved to see Jess had stayed behind, and he joined her as they carried in the final glasses from the outside table.

'He'll get used to this, you know.' Clancy chuckled from the comfort of his armchair.

Shaking her head at him, she walked over to give him a kiss goodbye.

'Let me walk you to your car,' Dom said, picking up Jess's handbag and leading her outside.

'I've located Dr Willis,' he began quickly, excited to finally update her on his research. 'He's now retired and living in a gated community at Batemans Bay, and I've arranged to go down and visit him next Saturday.'

'That's great!'

'Yeah, I didn't want to say anything in front of Clancy.' He shrugged. 'I'd love you to come if you can? I'm sure you could get him to open up a bit more than I could, you know, use those journalistic skills,' he added playfully. He was relieved when Jess agreed, and they discussed travel arrangements before he kissed her on her cheek and watched her drive away.

'It was good to see Jess again,' his father said with a knowing smile as Dom entered the house.

'Yeah, I thought you'd like to see a familiar face today. I'm glad she came.'

'As long it was just for my sake, hey?' Clancy chuckled mischievously, and Dom gave him a wry smile.

# CHAPTER 26: JESS

They drove into the metropolis of Batemans Bay, one of the largest towns on the South Coast, and activated the GPS to take them to the address. Just ten minutes from the town centre they arrived.

As Dom pulled his Jeep up outside the imposing security gates, Jess offered to get out and buzz, keen to stretch her legs after the four-hour road trip.

'Yes?' came a faint male voice from the metallic intercom at the gate.

'Hello. Is that Dr Willis? It's Dom Jonson and Jess McCann—we arranged to meet this morning.'

'Yes, yes, come through. Park in front of number one,' he instructed as the gate began to open.

They were approached by a grey-haired man. Thin and frail, he was aged in his late eighties or possibly older and wore beige trousers and a long-sleeved pale blue shirt, as if he was ready to open his surgery despite being long retired.

After polite handshakes and introductions, the

trio made their way into his neat villa.

'Would you like coffee, tea?' he enquired, shuffling into the pink kitchen—circa 1970s—yet not detracting from the spectacular views afforded through the kitchen and living room windows. The coastline was sublime. The villa was built at the end of a headland, giving it nearly panoramic views of the coast and out to sea. Jess had the sense of being at the bow of a ship with only ocean to see in all directions.

'Bev and I wanted somewhere peaceful to retire after thirty years up in the highlands. Although it's just me these days,' he said with a tinge of regret, unloading a large rattan tray containing the tea things.

They settled on the patio, enjoying the strong brew and making small talk for a few minutes.

'Dr Willis, as I mentioned on the phone—' Dom began.

'It's Gerald these days; there's no need to call me Doctor anymore.'

'Of course. Okay, Gerald, I wanted to speak to you about my mother. As you know, I was very young when she died. I was hoping to get things a bit clearer in my head now, because for some reason it feels very important that I do,' Dom said earnestly. 'I distinctly remember you coming over to the house when she fell that night, but I don't remember much more. I'd like you to explain things—medical things—about how she died.'

Surprisingly, Gerald didn't seem fazed by Dom's request, as if this type of question wasn't unexpected. Although thirty years on? Jess was surprised the doctor didn't seem more puzzled.

He sat back in his chair and studied Dom before slowly speaking. 'Sarah was a fine young woman, Dominic. She loved you very much, and it was a tragedy to see her die so young. In her prime.' He paused before continuing. 'I remember the night very well. Very well indeed. Sadly, there wasn't anything I could do when I arrived. Her heart had stopped beating, and it wasn't possible to revive her. To bring her back.'

'Did Mum have a heart problem?' Dom asked hopefully.

'Her heart was compromised—yes—she had a congenital heart disease. Whilst it wasn't life threatening, it was still a lifelong concern for her, as it made her weak, especially in her condition at the time. Add to that a fall, and sadly it was too much.'

'But how?'

'Dominic, your mother fell down the stairs—you remember the steep staircase at the house?'

'Why would she fall down a set of stairs though? I don't understand.'

'It's difficult to be sure, although my recollection is that she had tripped, and unfortunately, the fall was fatal.'

'Are you saying she simply tripped? It was that straightforward?'

'I wasn't there, Dominic, but these things happen, quite frequently I'd have you know. Clancy would be better to explain the accident, if that is what you would like to know about. He was devastated to witness the fall, and I had to sedate him afterwards to calm him down.'

Jess hadn't said anything at that point, but at Dom's silence, she felt it was timely to probe on his behalf. 'Would an autopsy be standard in that situation, Gerald?'

'I didn't see the reason to put Clancy through any more grief. In those days, an autopsy would have meant flying Sarah's body to Port Moresby and waiting weeks for an answer that I felt would be the same one I've just given you. An unfortunate accident.'

'But what about the police? Shouldn't they have looked at the scene, made an assessment if there were grounds for an autopsy?'

'I don't think you understand what things were like up there, thirty years ago. Things were very difficult; we lived in a remote community. No one wanted to harm Sarah. She was a young wife and mother, and very popular. It was clear to me what had happened, and yes of course the police were notified, and we were all confident that the assessment of the situation was correct.'

Jess could see that Dom looked bereft. This ageing doctor had explained the situation quite simply. A devastating fall. Were she and Dom trying to find something that just wasn't there?

But then Jess recalled something the doctor had said earlier and seized on it.

'You mentioned earlier something about Sarah's "condition at the time"? You said it added to the weakness already caused by her weak heart?'

'Sarah was pregnant when she fell. About three months along, I believe. This would have added some additional demand on her heart. It could also have caused some dizziness.'

Jess couldn't contain her stunned look and noticed Dom start back to life at the revelation.

'Mum had a baby?' He had trouble comprehending what the doctor had said.

'Your mother was in the early stage of

pregnancy, Dominic. Unfortunately, the trauma from the fall was too great.'

'I didn't know Mum was pregnant,' he said quietly, 'No one ever said…'

'I'm sorry, Dominic,' Gerald said kindly. 'I wasn't aware she was pregnant until I attended on that dreadful evening. It was an awful shock. To lose two lives.'

A wave of sadness seemed to engulf the room and dull any further conversation for a few minutes.

Nudging Dom, who still seemed dazed after what he'd learnt, Jess nodded and looked to the door.

'Gerald, thank you for sharing all this with us. You've been more than forthcoming, and we appreciate your sensitivity. I think we should head off now, don't you, Dom?' She looked over as he began to nod.

'We can always give you a ring if Dom has further questions?'

'Of course,' Gerald said, standing up as Jess mobilised them towards the door where they said their goodbyes before getting into the car.

Emphasising that he was fine to drive, Dom steered the car out of the villa complex and towards Sydney.

But less than an hour into the journey, he said he needed a stiff drink and to take stock of everything, suggesting they head into the small town of Berry.

After settling into a corner of the Berry Royal Hotel, the pair nursed their drinks—a white wine for Jess and a light beer for Dom.

But it wasn't long before Dom headed to something stronger, and knowing they wouldn't make it home that night, Jess booked two rooms upstairs.

'I just don't get it,' he continued. 'If it's suicide, call it that. But this *accidental death* bullshit just doesn't make sense.'

Jess let him continue to dissect the conversation they had with Sarah's doctor and listened to his anguish unfold.

'Why didn't Clancy ever talk about the baby? No one ever said anything… not ever.'

'Did your mother keep a journal? Or did she have a close friend or someone she may have confided in?' Jess asked. 'That could help paint a picture of your mother and perhaps help you understand her frame of mind.'

'Mum didn't kill herself,' he said strongly. 'She wouldn't. She was carrying a baby for God's sake! She was always so filled with joy.' His face drifted to a faraway memory. 'I recall seeing her so happy in the month or two before she died. Now I know why. But I also don't believe she would just fall. She knew the layout of the house better than anyone. She had been living there since she was a girl. How could she misjudge the stairs?'

'Like Dr Willis said, she might have been light-headed, or fainted, which happens with pregnancy. Or maybe she really did just slip? Accidents happen, Dom.' Jess attempted to soothe him.

'No. I mean yes, of course they do. But Mum was thirty-five, not ninety-seven! I mean, how do you accidentally slip down a flight of stairs?'

'She had a weak heart, so perhaps she collapsed,' attempted Jess once more.

'Well, I didn't know about that either. And I can't recall ever seeing any sign of it.'

Neither of them wanted to speculate about

Clancy's involvement—if any—in Sarah's death.

The conversation continued to go around in circles for another hour before Jess suggested that they order some burgers at the bar. They needed something to help soak up some of the alcohol they'd been consuming steadily for the past two hours.

Over dinner, Dom relaxed and eventually the conversation moved away from the tragedy of Sarah's death.

He shared again with Jess the story of his career ambition and the joy of starting his own legal practice. He also opened up about his short marriage and, despite the brevity of the union, his still fond feelings for Lauren.

'We started dating at Uni. Both got graduate roles in the same law firm and were married by twenty-four.' Noticing Jess's surprise, he added, 'Way too young, I know! It was all over in the four years. But despite it all, I'll always love Lauren,' he said with a weak smile.

'What happened?'

He shrugged, contemplating his answer. 'I guess people change. And in your twenties, the change can be significant… at least it was for us. Lauren was highly ambitious. God, we both were. Lauren was so focused on the next rung up the ladder and lived for successes, winning cases, finding loopholes, anything to prove her acute legal mind. And she was—is— incredibly capable,' he said with admiration. 'Whereas I just wanted to focus on corporate law during the day and then tune out after hours. But not Lauren. She was always permanently on. If it wasn't working late at the office, she'd want to be out networking, expanding her legal contacts, speaking at industry events. It was a side of law that just didn't interest me.'

'I was probably a little bit like Lauren, overly ambitious when I was younger—but most women are as that is our pivotal time to make a mark in our profession,' Jess sympathised. 'Sadly, I didn't have a Dom Jonson in my life to sweep me off my feet,' she said, surprising herself with how flirtatious that sounded.

Seeing Dom's slow smile emerge, she was grateful to have moved him out of his melancholy state but worried she'd given the wrong impression. 'Um… I didn't mean it quite that way,' she said quickly, blushing.

'That's a shame,' he said, now looking meaningfully into her eyes, his face bright and questioning.

Remembering that she was no longer the single twenty-year-old of her youth and instead happily dating Edward, she managed to collect herself.

'Well, thankfully I got over that phase and finally have a boyfriend.' She chortled, trying again to get the conversation on a lighter tone.

'Tell me about him,' Dom enquired quietly.

It was awkward discussing her somewhat new relationship, but she felt that it would be more difficult not to go along with the personal theme of their conversation.

'His name is Edward, and he works in finance. I actually met him through my girlfriend who works with him. He's German and out here on a work contract. It's early days, but he's a really lovely guy. Anyway, I should head up and give him a call and perhaps say good night,' she said, jumping up. 'We have an early drive back in the morning.'

'Jess,' he said, finding her hand and squeezing it.

Their eyes locked for a moment, and Jess was uncomfortable with the rising tension between them. Conflicted by her emotions, or perhaps overwhelmed by the day, she held her breath as he continued.

'Jess. Thank you for today. For listening. I just wanted to say thanks.' He smiled crookedly before releasing her hand, and she quietly nodded before heading to the reception to get her key.

Despite what she'd said to Dom, she didn't feel like speaking with Edward right then. There was something not quite right about introducing him into the day and night she had experienced. As there were no messages from him, she resolved to talk to him in the morning.

# CHAPTER 27: DOM

Dom awoke the next morning with a determination he hadn't had for some time.

He would accept Dr Willis's diagnosis—if that was the right word for it—of the circumstances surrounding his mother's death and put it to rest, once and for all.

For the past twenty-eight years, he had wondered what had happened that fateful night and whether he, or his father, had somehow played a part in his mother's fall. Or if she had, in fact, deliberately hurt herself, although that wasn't a thought he'd contemplated often. Enough was enough. It was time to accept that his mother, his beautiful, gracious, vibrant mother had died from a tragic accident. Whether it was her heart or being pregnant, it didn't matter.

He needed to move forward in his life and cease dwelling on doubt, suspicion, guilt.

He also had to release the thoughts of what could have been... a younger brother or sister.

As he got up, he could see the sun shining brightly from his window, and he listened to the sounds and noise outside, a town coming to life. After showering and dressing in yesterday's jeans and crumpled chambray shirt, he headed downstairs and out on to the street.

Berry was a pretty town, and since the Hume Highway bypass had gone in the year before, it was now free of noisy, heavy vehicles cramming the narrow, two-lane main road. He walked briskly, feeling the fresh air in his lungs and soon completed the length of the main street and was heading out of town towards green fields. Turning himself around, he walked back towards the hotel and soon found a café open. Keen to dull the self-inflicted excess of the night before, he went in to order and sat at a small table in the courtyard.

He felt a small shift within him. Life would go on, and it would be better. Some of the weight he had been lugging around for so long was lifting. He had finally had the courage to probe into what really happened to his mum, and he could now rest easy that he had done that. Despite not learning what had caused her fall, he was reassured that she didn't take her own life. She wouldn't, especially not with a baby growing inside. Not ever.

Around half an hour later his phone pinged with a message from Jess, and he directed her to the café.

'Morning.' Her bright voice caused him to look up from the newspaper he was absorbed in.

After ordering a round of coffees and sourdough toast, she returned to the table. A constant parade of people were now strolling past the window, venturing out, as the village came to life.

'It's so lovely here, isn't it?' she said.

'Like a picture-postcard town, that's for sure,' he agreed, and they chatted amiably over breakfast.

The conversation flowed as they walked back to the hotel and drove north to Sydney. Nothing serious, but insightful all the same as they discussed books, movies, restaurants, cities; each making recommendations to the other and recounting experiences. Laughter too filled the vehicle as they exchanged funny stories, and it brought much-needed levity to the past twenty-four hours.

'Thanks again for driving south with me,' Dom said as he dropped Jess outside her home.

'My pleasure. Speak soon!' She gave him one of her dazzling smiles before waving him off.

As Dom headed home, he silently admitted to himself how attracted he was to Jess. How easy she was to talk to and how envious he was of the man who had swept her off her feet. He would never come between a couple no matter how much he might fancy Jess. After all, he was no catch—with a failed marriage behind him. Yeah, Jess was better off without him.

His thoughts turned to Lauren and what had gone wrong between them.

They had been "the perfect match", according to all their friends and family, and they had been happy for a time. Both enjoying the intellectual challenge of law but also adrenaline junkies at heart. Heliskiing, abseiling, canyoning, sky jumping… they'd done it all. Their friendship circle had been expansive—pals from university, colleagues from work and legal circles, sporting club buddies and random people that Lauren had a knack of befriending. She had kept their social life busy with dinners, brunches, coastal walks… and it made Dom realise that last weekend's drinks at his place had been the first social event he'd organised in a very long time.

He had loved Lauren's fearless attitude to life. Her get-up-and-go. Her ability to make friends with anyone and everyone. So, what had happened?

Marriage? They'd married young at twenty-four in a fancy affair with a traditional church service at Saint Marks and a sit-down dinner for one hundred and fifty people at the Ritz Carlton in Double Bay. And then just four short years later they were signing divorce papers.

The next morning, after failing to quash his thoughts about Lauren, he dialled her mobile. Despite their marriage failing years before, they very occasionally had contact through legal circles, and it had always been amicable.

'Hello. Lauren Smythe,' a crisp, professional voice answered.

'Lauren. Hi, it's Dom,' he began.

'Dom! It's nice to hear from you,' she said with a friendliness he'd remembered. 'How are things?'

Dom began to explain about Clancy's illness and his recent stint in PNG. 'What about you? How's life?'

'Oh, you know, busy as ever.' She laughed.

Sensing a cue to get to the point, Dom jumped in. 'Too busy to meet an old friend? I'd love to catch up properly. I don't suppose we could grab a beer after work one night?

\*\*\*\*

When Lauren arrived, she looked the same as he had remembered her. A pretty face and slim figure wrapped in a charcoal corporate suit and towering heels. Her straight brown hair, the longest Dom could recall ever seeing it, hung neatly down her back.

'You look great,' he said, leaning over to kiss her cheek. She did. She looked more beautiful now than she did when they had met twenty years ago.

'Thank you. You look really well too,' she said before taking the seat he had pulled out for her.

They were at a centre table in a buzzing wine bar off York Street, just down from their respective workplaces. It was just seven p.m. and the after-work patrons were all busying themselves with drink orders and recanting the trials and tribulations of the day. The Christmas holidays would be starting in a few days, and he could feel the manic build-up as everyone moved at double time to tick off work, shopping and last-minute social engagements before the two-week break.

But unlike most of the people around him, he didn't share the same panic as he had decided to work through most of the Christmas and New Year break. He'd been out of the office enough already this year without taking the two-week holiday that many workers did. Sure, he'd take the obligatory public holidays, especially with Clancy staying with him, and that would do him just fine.

'Cool bar.' Dom nodded in approval at Lauren's choice. He hadn't been to it before and admired the sleek art deco furnishings and high ceilings. It was sassy and high energy and would be just perfect for their catch-up.

He didn't know what he expected to get out of the evening, but he felt there was unfinished business.

Returning with their drinks, she immediately enquired about Clancy, and they segued onto holiday plans and then work. Chatting with Lauren had always been vibrant and fast paced, and Dom was enjoying her energetic company after too long. It felt only natural to steer the conversation to what was most niggling him.

'What happened with us, Lauren? I've done a bit of soul searching these past few months, trying to get some resolution about family—my mother's death, my relationship with Clancy—and it got me wondering about us.'

Lauren chewed her lip and took a moment or two before answering. 'I don't know. We got together so young, I guess.' She looked at him with a hint of sadness in her eyes.

'Yes, but we were so compatible, so suited?'

'Until we wanted different things.' She tilted her head to look at him. 'I wanted to reach partner by thirty. You wanted to take your foot off the accelerator and travel, start a family, slow down. I just wasn't ready for that, not then,' she said sympathetically.

Dom could only hear the final two words, as if they'd been left there hanging deliberately.

'*Not then*, or not ever?' Dom asked.

'I wasn't ready then. I'm not saying that I wouldn't have been ready down the track, but we weren't even twenty-five, and I felt we had the rest of our lives to do all that.'

'I would have given you more time,' Dom began defensively, quashing his recollections of impatience to have his way back then. His immaturity to always be right. His envy (or was it jealousy?) of Lauren's commitment and passion for law.

Smiling sadly at him, Lauren said, 'I think we had that conversation more times than I care to remember. But you had a plan for the whole next chapter, and I just wasn't ready. I was still writing the first chapter.'

'When would you have been ready?' he asked, knowing he had missed this window but keen to learn by just how much.

'I just needed more time,' she said, avoiding answering.

Changing the subject, Dom asked, 'Is there anyone special in your life now?' Although he wasn't sure he'd like the answer.

'No. I guess that's the price you pay for making partner,' she said with a gentle laugh, attempting to lighten the tone.

They sat with fresh drinks for another hour, catching up on the past and found humour in their tales of disastrous dating stories.

'My friends put up my profile on eHarmony,' Lauren began. 'It was such an awkward experience, meeting complete strangers and feeling like you were both interviewing for a part in a play.'

Whilst Dom hadn't entered the world of online dating, he had experienced his share of blind dates and knew all too well the discomfort of getting to know a stranger that your mutual friends were so sure you'd hit it off with. No past to share, no mutual experiences to reminisce about, no slow discovery to get to know each other.

They moved on from the bar after an hour, calling into the nearby Italian trattoria for spaghetti and red wine.

It was after ten when they left the restaurant

and jumped in a cab and headed over the Harbour Bridge.

No words were exchanged, but they both knew that there was only one drop-off and it would be Dom's terrace.

Opening the front door and switching on a lamp, Dom took Lauren through and into the living room and selected a favourite playlist on Spotify as he went to fetch the cognac glasses. Handing her a snifter, they sat on the lounge and listened to the soothing tones of Ella Fitzgerald through the sound system.

As the song finished, Dom took her glass from her hand and placed it on the glass coffee table.

He gently touched her beautiful face, once so familiar to him, and kissed her softly. It was like time suspended as he drank in the touch, smell, and comfort of her that rose to the surface.

After a momentary hesitation, Lauren kissed him back. Gently at first and then more urgently.

Their kissing became passionate and desperate, each trying to extract something from the other. A second chance? A memory of happier times?

He moved her down on the lounge and undid the buttons on her white blouse, revealing a sexy pink-and-white-lace bra.

'I want you, Lauren,' he said, his hungry eyes boring into hers.

He began peeling off her blouse, pulling down her skirt and releasing the heels that she had still been wearing and began kissing every inch of her.

The lovemaking had been powerful, fervent and intoxicating. Dom and Lauren rediscovering each other's bodies throughout the late hours before falling asleep, curled up with each other in his bed.

The next morning, Dom awoke alone to the sound of the shower and remembered the perfect night they'd had.

He threw on a robe and went downstairs to heat up the coffee machine and then pulled out a tub of yoghurt and a carton of fresh berries.

Fifteen minutes later, Lauren joined him at the kitchen island bench, accepting a plate and fork and helping herself to the fruit platter.

There was no awkwardness between them. It was as if they had turned back the clock to happier times.

Over a deliciously rich coffee out on the deck, they talked about the night before.

'Bodies don't forget,' said Lauren.

'No, that's for sure. I think they call that muscle memory.' He reached for her fingers.

'Lauren, I don't know what last night was, but it was pretty special. I'd like to see more of you. Try to figure out if there is another chance for us?'

'I'd like that too,' she said, and he moved her fingers to his lips to kiss.

# CHAPTER 28: JESS

Jess grumbled as she got out of bed. Alone. And nursing a hangover from too many glasses of prosecco with Emma yesterday. Actually, now that she thought about it, Emma had been seriously knocking back the bubbly. Sure, it was Christmas Day, but still, it was unusual to see her sister indulge like that. Something she hadn't seen since before Emma had children. For a change it was Steve taking charge of the children, leaving the sisters time to indulge in their sun lounge after lunch.

Still sitting on her bed, Jess looked at her phone to see a message from Edward. It was just a few words with the most magnificent image of a snow-covered mountain and a group of skiers bunched together for the photo.

*Corduroy conditions! First on the mountain! xx*

Sending back a love heart emoji, she clambered into the shower, letting the warm water soothe her aching head and contemplating how she would spend the next fortnight. There would be no Edward to hang out with. He was spending the vacation skiing in Japan and would stay on for work meetings.

Yesterday, she had found herself offering to hang out with Emma all week and entertain her nieces. Steve was working through the holidays, so it would be just the girls.

Over the days that followed, Jess and Emma instigated fun days out with the children, visiting the Zoo and watching the amazing bird show, venturing on a ferry from Circular Quay to Manly where they ate fish and chips on the beach after their swim, and watching the latest *Frozen* franchise from Disney at the cinema.

'I think these are actually my favourite days,' Jess said, sinking back into the outdoor sun lounge after refilling their mugs with tea. 'Just listen to their squeals of laughter!'

Her nieces were playing in the back garden, dashing in and out of the sprinkler system, and their laughter was infectious.

'Simple pleasures, hey?' Emma let out a sigh. 'So, what's the plan tomorrow?'

Jess explained that she was meeting up with Frances for lunch.

'She's back from Paris, and we're having lunch at Chipple.'

'Wow, very posh!' Emma was impressed.

'Why don't you join us? Make it a ladies' lunch?'

'No, I can't. The girls…'

'Can't Steve spend tomorrow with them? Give you a break?'

'No!' There was a tinge of abruptness in Emma's short reply, but Jess decided to ignore it and plough on.

'But it's Saturday. You've been looking after them all week.'

'It's fine, really,' Emma said in an effort to end the discussion.

Although she seemed anything but fine about it. Jess could see that she'd hit a raw nerve. Her sister was clearly annoyed, and she had a feeling that like her, her partner's absence had a big role to play in it.

# CHAPTER 29: GRACE

Grace had managed a few days off between Christmas and New Year and was now back at the ARC Surveys office and busily reviewing the latest maps for the highlands highway project. It had been a few months since she had worked on the project, and hopefully these latest scans would be the final batch before they commenced work on the new roadway.

That's weird, she thought, as her finger paused the mouse. The mystery vehicle she had spotted three months ago was still in exactly the same place as before. It hadn't moved an inch.

Was it abandoned? Was there something more sinister going on? The location was miles from anywhere, and it had Grace intrigued. She went racing to John's office.

Something just didn't feel right.

Overnight they arranged to visit the location and search the area by foot, flying into Mount Hagen to pick up a four-wheel drive. John had advised the local police of their intentions, and two of their team came along.

The location was just a couple of kilometres south of the original highway, almost halfway along the route that stretched between Mount Hagen and Goroka. Renowned for its difficult terrain, the area was made more treacherous by the steep crevasses hidden by vines and dark shadows, and they had to trek a long stretch of it on foot. One wrong move and you could disappear into a hole and never be discovered.

Before long, the young officer at the head of the pack shouted, and Grace could soon see what had caused the excitement. They assembled in front of what appeared to be a wreckage, and as they moved closer, she could see it was an older style four-wheel drive. Eventually peering in, she took a gasp as she saw what appeared to be a human skull.

The team immediately leapt into action.

John and Grace took photographs and measurements of the site and marked the exact location on their survey map, using the equipment they had lugged in with them. The two police officers took their own photographs of the wreckage, careful not to disturb any of what could be vital evidence in the future in discovering what had happened.

Hours later they returned to the township of Mount Hagen, the officers going directly to the police station as Grace and John booked into a local motel for the night. As the sun had faded, it was agreed to convene in the morning at the police headquarters.

John had arranged to visit a friend in town that evening and extended an invitation to Grace to join them, but she gratefully declined, not feeling up to socialising.

As she showered in the small en suite, she felt intensely saddened by the undiscovered body that had lain there in the bush. How long had it been there? Had anyone reported it missing? What happened for that person to be so far off the highway?

She had observed the degrading luggage in the back seat and hoped it would hold some clue as to whom they had discovered.

Ordering room service—a club sandwich and cup of peppermint tea—she curled up in her robe and flicked on the television to keep her company as she ate.

The following morning, Grace and John arrived at the police station to make their statements before their flight home. Detective David Sana showed them into a conference room and offered them coffee.

'We have a forensic team arriving this morning from Port Moresby, and we will then all head back to the site,' he said, explaining that they did not wish to disturb the scene before the scientist had viewed it in situ.

After that, the evidence—including the skull and some bones—would be carefully transferred to Port Moresby for the forensics pathology department to analyse.

'It looks like the vehicle has been there for some time,' he said, explaining that his hunch was around twenty to twenty-five years when the original highway swung around south very near to the location of the scene. 'In the mid-1990s—'93 or '94 I think—it was about then that the highway was improved and altered to the north.'

Grace explained that they were currently working on a survey project on the new highway and would look into the highway's history. She had only been focused on the current route and how a specific stretch would be modified for road safety, but that had now changed.

The pair then provided their statements to the detective, and as they went to leave for the airport, they were asked if they would delay their departure to return to the scene as the forensic investigator was now at the site and had some questions for them.

Grace followed John out to the vehicle, unpacking her overnight bag to retrieve the heavy-duty clothing she had worn the day before. She would change on the road.

Arriving at the scene a short time later, they were sitting down and putting on their boots when the forensic investigator greeted them.

'I'd say a decade at least,' was Dr Gemma Ward's reply when Grace asked how long the vehicle had been there.

'But that roadway wouldn't have been used in decades. It was superseded by the highway we have now, which I believe was finished in 1990,' she said, trying to recollect. Her focus had been on the present and the future, but that had now changed.

'That sounds right.' The forensic investigator nodded. 'There's significant decomposition of the body—which could have been accelerated due to the humidity, insects and bird life, but the surrounding terrain reflects many years of growth. I'll know more when we put his frame back together in the lab,' she said, indicating more skeletal remnants.

'What I was hoping you could assist with is mapping the terrain a couple of kilometres either side so that we can understand the route they may have come from. It may hold some clues.'

They agreed and explained that they had detailed overviews from the drone imagery, but a manual survey could be done. They had a theodolite 3D scanner, battery pack, rod and leveller and began their work.

It was unbearably steamy, but Grace felt invigorated to play some small part in helping out.

By four that afternoon they were finished and began packing up their gear. So too were the large assembly of police officers who had walked the perimeter for any clues. Dr Ward had returned to the station some hours earlier with evidence bags—the body such as it was and the luggage inside the vehicle—a backpack and two small black hard cases. Nothing was opened, as it was agreed that it would be first taken to the lab to preserve the contents.

Grace found herself back in the same hotel room—the one she thought she had farewelled at seven that morning.

But tonight she wanted company, not a club sandwich and an early night.

\*\*\*\*

'I hear the local Chinese is the place to eat,' was John's upbeat greeting half an hour later as Grace alighted the lift, feeling refreshed from a soothing shower. 'After you,' he said, as she walked through the sliding glass entrance doors to the steaming heat outside. A taxi was waiting for them, and John stepped forward to open her door.

The Chinese restaurant had the typical adornments—garish red lanterns and lion statues, large round tables and thankfully dim lighting—which suited Grace that evening. There were a couple of larger groups gathered at the far end of the restaurant, and thankfully they had been seated in a quiet, private corner.

The grim discovery had upset Grace more than she had expected, and she was grateful to have John for company.

'I'd say the vehicle accidentally ran off the old highway, and because the jungle was so dense, it was never discovered,' he said, pouring them each generous glasses of chilled white wine. 'It's a good thing you have such eagle eyes.'

'But surely someone would have noticed? What about the family of this poor person?' she asked, confused that someone could lie undiscovered for so long.

'Yes, that's a good question. You'd think someone would raise the alarm if you didn't turn up to work or hadn't made it home.'

'Imagine just disappearing like that,' Grace said perplexed. 'I wonder who would raise the alarm if I just didn't front up tomorrow.'

Since her broken engagement more than a year before, Grace had somewhat isolated herself from family and friends by jumping on a plane and taking the survey job in PNG. These past few days had highlighted this more than ever. When she had made the decision a year earlier, she had been compelled to run away from the pitying looks of everyone she knew. She had felt like such a failure and a complete fool at not realising her fiancé's betrayal. It was such a cliché to discover a partner cheating with your bridesmaid, but that was what happened. Sure, she hadn't got around to actually asking Claire to be her bridesmaid—because she hadn't actually got around to setting a date in the six months since Jeff had proposed—but Claire was among her closest friends and would have been in the line-up. And Jeff was supposed to be faithful! They were engaged, for God's sake!

John gently nudged her out of her thoughts, reaching out to lightly touch her forearm resting on the table, her fingers tightly gripping the stem of her wine glass.

'Hey, I lost you there for a moment,' he said with concern in his voice before continuing. 'I was saying, a manhunt would be mounted immediately for you, so don't you worry about not being missed,' he said with a reassuring smile.

John was aware of her scumbag fiancé, and whilst she hadn't spelt it out in so many words, Grace could see that he was smart enough to get the gist of what had happened.

He had been a big brother to her since joining the firm where he'd landed a few years earlier. He always seemed so happy-go-lucky and at ease, firmly in the present. Not looking back like she did, and she admired his ability to live that way.

'When are you next taking a holiday?' John asked, changing tack.

'We just had that Christmas break, so that's it for a while…,' Grace replied resignedly. 'Although now I really feel like I need a dose of normal city life to snap me out of things. I'm tired of feeling and looking like an ugly tomboy,' she said, sticking out a rugged boot she was wearing. They both laughed.

'I don't think anyone would describe you as an *ugly tomboy*, more like the prettiest surveyor in PNG,' he said kindly. Given she was possibly the only female surveyor in the country, she laughed at his good-natured compliment.

The next morning, they waited outside Detective Sana's office, and Grace reviewed again the maps and 3D scans on her laptop. There were images of the original highway, and a green marker depicted the current highway, a modified route that had gone in in 1991. There was quite a distinctive change in the route, which made the theory surrounding the vehicle plausible. You could see how a vehicle could have veered off the original road and ended up in dense foliage and remained hidden for so many years.

'We are awaiting DNA testing of the remains,' began Detective Sana when they were later seated in his office with coffee. 'But the contents of the luggage in the vehicle have been looked through, and we believe the victim was a Mr Ryan Reynolds, as this name appears engraved into some of the equipment found in the vehicle. It looks to be professional camera equipment, which is quite well preserved—possibly because of the casing it was in—steel frame, heavy duty, vacuum sealed. Our team is looking at each item closely and hoping to possibly find some unexposed photos that may give us an insight into his travels in the region.'

'My God! It feels surreal to now have a name, an identity.' Grace felt panicked and covered her mouth with her hands at the shock of it all.

John reached out and took one of Grace's hands in his, and she slowly dropped her other hand, settling down.

'I'm sorry. I appreciate this is distressing, Miss Grace,' said the detective. 'But please think of this as you helping us to bring this person—who we believe to be Mr Reynolds—home to his family. That is what we want to do.'

'Yes of course,' she said, collecting herself and gently shaking off John's hand. She felt silly for being so sensitive and emotional about the incident.

Attempting to regain her professional composure, Grace pulled out the laptop in her small backpack and placed it on the desk. It fired up quickly, and she then proceeded to walk the two men through the maps showing the chronological history of the highway, from the original to the current roadway, and the future plans.

'Yes, it's looking more and more likely that this accident was before the current road was built, and so we're looking at some time prior to 1992 when the new highway went in,' said the detective.

They then began to review the 3D imagery of the site, which they'd prepared yesterday.

Apart from the name on the camera gear, little else had been found to identify the man. The police had sent most of his belongings onto Forensics in Moresby to go through, and that would include the photography equipment.

Agreeing that there wasn't much more that Grace and John could do to assist the investigation for now, they left for the airport to catch the afternoon flight back to Port Moresby.

# CHAPTER 30: JESS

'Munich!' Jess couldn't believe that Edward was inviting her to go to Germany with him. He had been back from Japan for less than a week and must have really missed her.

'Yes, Munich.' He raised his eyebrows up and down in that cute way he often did when he was making fun of her.

'But isn't this trip to Munich a family thing?' she said cautiously, delighted yet still puzzled by the invitation.

'Yes. And I very much want you to meet them. My Oma won't forgive me if I don't attend her eightieth birthday, and my sisters won't be satisfied with my description of you. I want you to join me, very much, so we can make a real trip out of it. And we can have a holiday and spend some decent time together—just you and me. What do you say?'

Jess considered his invitation, trying to think of any reason she couldn't go. Edward had insisted on covering all costs: flights, hotels, ski tickets.

'I'm so tempted, and I do have a lot of holidays owing,' she said slowly, starting to picture this invitation of Edward's becoming a reality.

Edward nodded at her, once again raising his eyebrows in expectation as if to say 'So?'

'Okay… I'm in!' she said suddenly, surprising herself with her fast decision-making.

'Yes!' said Edward, punching the air before kissing her and wrapping her in a tight embrace.

The trip was just two weeks away, but Jess knew that she would have little trouble getting the time off. After all, she hadn't made a dent in her annual leave entitlements since starting at *Leading News* six years ago. Six weeks paid leave each year had been accumulating rapidly, with the one or two weeks of leave she took most years hardly making inroads into her tally.

'So much to do!' she exclaimed, squirming out of his hold to grab a pen and paper.

Edward laughed as she began to draw up a list of work and personal tasks to take care of before they departed for their European adventure.

Jess was bubbling over with happiness as she called Emma that night.

'Sounds serious,' Emma said, teasing her. 'Meeting the family. Attending Grandma's birthday party. The girls and I will miss you, but I'm really thrilled for you.'

'I'll be back in no time. You won't even notice I'm gone,' Jess had said, failing to hear the quiet sadness in her sister's voice.

# CHAPTER 31: GRACE

Grace had been anxiously waiting to learn more about the mysterious Ryan Reynolds—the poor abandoned stranger who continued to haunt her. How does a person simply disappear unnoticed?

She knew the detective hadn't forgotten about her, as they had exchanged emails since their meeting last month, and she had also left him a couple of phone messages just the week before.

He eventually called her on Monday morning, just as she was settling back into the office after a much-needed few days break in Cairns—just a short one-hour flight away from Port Moresby. It had been a spontaneous trip, arranged by thoughtful John, who said she needed cheering up after the strain of the grim discovery and a reward for managing heavier than normal workloads.

'I've organised a return flight—on the company—as a belated thank-you for all the work you do and for going above and beyond,' he'd said before pushing her out the door to pack for her impromptu weekend away. The plane would be leaving in a matter of hours.

Thrilled, she had raced home and quickly thrown clothes into a backpack before being taken to the airport by one of the drivers at the office.

The two days in Cairns had flown by in a whirlwind for Grace. She had used the treasured weekend to walk around the buzzing harbourfront, indulge in clothes shopping and visit the cinema—the first time she had seen a film in over a year. She also visited the hotel beauty salon for a haircut and blow-dry and splurged on a pampering facial.

Now feeling revived and a tad more feminine, she stood in the office at eight a.m. on Monday and waited for the kettle to boil before making her morning pot of green tea. Just as she filled the teapot with steaming water, she heard her desk phone ring.

Quickly grabbing the teapot and a cup, she rushed over to lift her handset, relieved to hear Detective Sana's voice. Excitedly she sat down and pulled out a pen and notebook and listened.

'I just thought you'd like to know that the man has been officially identified. His name is indeed Ryan Reynolds, a young Australian who came to PNG in 1990. He is registered as arriving into Port Moresby on 12 August 1990 on a three-month work visa.

'His employer at the time was a US-based magazine, and the police had eventually tracked down someone who had been working at the publication nearly three decades before and confirmed that he was a photojournalist. Because this man was a contributor who provided articles on spec, no alarm was raised when he didn't make contact. The publication had assumed that Mr Reynolds had moved on to freelance with another publication and eventually commissioned other stories to fill his absence.'

'That's harsh,' remarked Grace, although she understood it was a different era. Communication would have been a lot harder between Australia and the highlands of PNG. Email and mobile phones were in their infancy, and getting a signal would be impossible.

'We also had some trouble locating immediate family and eventually spoke with a relative who said that they had lost contact with Mr Ryan sometime ago. His parents are now deceased, and the relative said he was apparently a big traveller and they had assumed he was okay and just not keeping in touch. It seems he may have been a bit of a roamer and free spirit, as no one felt it was out of character for him not to keep in touch. Everyone we've spoken to just thought he was somewhere else, happy and healthy.'

*To think you could so easily just disappear from this world*, thought Grace with sadness.

'However,' the detective began, building up to a climax, 'the results of the autopsy and analysis of the site have confirmed that this is now a homicide investigation.'

Grace suddenly gulped the mouthful of hot tea she was drinking. She had assumed that this poor person had simply swerved off the highway and met his death instantly. But to hear there were sinister circumstances was startling.

'You're thinking it was a murder?'

'Yes, there's no doubt. There's a bullet wound in the spinal cord.'

*My God*, she thought.

'How can you solve a murder that happened so long ago. I mean we're talking nearly thirty years, aren't we?'

The detective agreed, confirming that the most likely date that the event took place was between August and November 1990, when the three-month work visa had been issued.

'It's unlikely we have the resources and capabilities to solve this, but we have filed a case and will await the coroner's determination. Actually, that's the reason for my call. I wanted to request you attend the coronial hearing next month. It will be in Mount Hagen on the second of March.'

'Of course,' Grace agreed, anything she could do to help. 'I'll mark the date now.'

Hanging up, she sat there watching her green tea leaves now calmly settle at the bottom of her glass pot. As she poured a fresh cup, she saw them flutter around furiously and felt that it was symbolic of how she felt at precisely that moment.

# CHAPTER 32: JESS

The city of Munich was a sight to behold. Jess had travelled overseas in the past, but to places in the USA and Asia. Never Europe, let alone Germany.

Munich's historic centre was breathtaking in its architecture, paved pedestrian malls and stylish shopfronts.

Rugged up in her overcoat, beanie, boots and gloves, she strolled down the main thoroughfare, listening to Edward's tour of his precious city as they walked.

They were enjoying a few hours to themselves before this evening's *meet the family* dinner—which Jess was assured was just a welcome home to Edward, who was clearly much missed by his three sisters.

They were staying with Edward's family, and his mother was a warm woman who had instantly made Jess feel welcome when they had arrived the evening before. The long-haul flight from Sydney had taken the best part of twenty-four hours, and Jess was deliriously tired yet happy to be there.

As they meandered through the English garden, they stopped to watch the ducks on the lake and children playing happily on the swings—despite the bitter chill in the air. She took a few photos of the continual waves emanating in a small, narrow section of the Isar River that ran through the park, a truly bizarre sight.

'There's a queue of surfers in the summer, on both sides,' he said, pointing.

'Sure!' she said, laughing off the idea before realising he was being perfectly serious.

'Here, look!' He smirked, handing over his phone, which held a photo of the very same spot with a surfer on one of the waves. He swiped to show her more and more images of the unique surfing spot, and she shook her head in amazement.

They ate white sausage, a delicacy at the traditional Bavarian restaurant Edward had chosen, joining strangers at the long wooden table, enjoying the warmth of the underground cellar. Eventually they headed back to Edward's family home.

Some hours later in the guest room upstairs, Jess could hear the young, hopeful cries of 'Edward? Edward?'

'Come on, Uncle Edward, you're being summoned,' Jess said as she opened the shower screen for Edward to step out so that she could take her turn to jump in.

Pulling her in with him, he kissed her deeply as the warm water and his hands ran down her body.

'Okay, enough of this,' he said, dragging himself away. 'Uncle Edward must get ready!' And he was gone.

Half an hour later, Jess emerged feeling much

sharper than she had earlier—the jetlag rinsed away.

'Here she is,' Edward announced, switching from his fluent German and standing up and motioning to her.

Three golden-haired women—one nursing a small infant—all turned to look at her, and she was relieved when Edward strode across the room and put his protective arm around her.

'This is the beautiful Jessica,' he said proudly. 'Merca is my oldest sister, and these two little tyrants are hers,' he said, playfully grabbing two little boys sprinting past. 'This is Ella, my middle sister, with her baby Ilka. Jessebel is upstairs, but you will meet her soon enough. And here is my baby sister, Harriet, whose children are on their way with Gerhart.'

Edward's sisters all shared his genetically good looks, and their smiles were warm and friendly. Since losing her parents, Jess understood the importance of siblings. It was heartening to see Edward's strong affection for his own.

Dinner was a noisy affair, with Edward clearly the hero among his nieces and nephews, answering lots of questions and receiving cuddles and sloppy kisses as one by one his sisters and their respective husbands and children headed home.

As Jess crawled into bed that night, a sea of tiredness swamped her, and she was asleep in seconds.

A couple of easy sightseeing days ensued before the celebratory party for Edward's grandmother—or Oma as she was affectionately called. A delightful but somewhat formal woman, Oma was forthright and entertaining. She clearly enjoyed being the centre of the family gathering and the cause of the family get-together. Her English was excellent, and she insisted her clan converse in English for Jess's benefit. Speaking in their second language did nothing to slow down the merriment though as Jess fought to keep up with the conversations around her.

A dinner for twenty-four people was hosted at a restaurant by a picturesque lake, and whilst the children were not in attendance, they would be there the following day for the traditional present opening. Tonight it was a sit-down affair for the grown-ups. Jess had brought a sleek blue silk dress to wear, which she accompanied with a stylish black jacket and a chunky silver necklace. She wanted to make a special effort for Edward's grandmother because she knew how important this occasion was for him.

She felt she had struck the right note when they entered the private dining room and she was immediately complimented by Oma on the striking colour of her dress. After wishing her a wonderful birthday, Jess moved to mingle, leaving Edward by his grandmother's side.

Helping herself to a flute of champagne from a passing waiter, she stopped to select a delicious morsel before being embraced by Ella.

'Jessica, you look so beautiful!' Ella said, appraising her outfit.

'Thank you. So do you,' she replied, loving Ella's red Armani pantsuit with sky-high pumps.

'Come, let me introduce you to some more of the family. Our great aunts and uncles.' Jess followed Ella, who steered her around the room to the assembled family.

Edward had been positioned next to Oma at the large dining table, and Jess found herself seated between Edward's youngest sister, Harriet, and

Edward's uncle Klaus. As Klaus was hard of hearing and quite frail, it was Harriet who proved the entertaining dinner companion as she regaled stories of their childhood and the role her big brother had played in keeping his sisters in line.

Jess enjoyed hearing the stories of his youth—as it completed a fuller picture of him and revealed he hadn't always been this suave sophisticate but rather a bossy, older brother and at times a fearsome protector to his sisters.

She knew that she was beginning to fall for Edward, and tonight had confirmed it.

Once they had finished eating, speeches were made by Edward's mother and uncle—who each shared their fondest memories of Oma. Edward proposed a toast to the Great Dame, and they all applauded.

Jess felt so warm and protected as she curled up with Edward in bed that night, believing that she had finally met the man she loved.

# CHAPTER 33: GRACE

John had insisted on accompanying Grace to the coronial hearing in Mount Hagen, and whilst she'd initially told him it wasn't necessary, she was glad he had persisted.

'As the managing director, I should be on hand for any ARC Survey-related business. But also to morally support you and any employees going through something like this.'

Grace was hoping there might be more to it than company policy.

John had been increasingly protective of her these past few months. Her fragility had been on show when the bush grave had been discovered, and he'd witnessed her vulnerability. Something she usually tried to conceal.

She had also noticed his admiring glances when she'd returned from the Cairns weekend away and felt a little buzz that she had elicited such a reaction. The Queensland break had been transformative, restoring her physically and emotionally from the haunted wreck she had been back then to her former self.

Grace and John had flown into Mount Hagen that morning and were now inside the foyer of the District Court with minutes to spare before proceedings got underway. Grace sat twisting her hands nervously, as she sat waiting with Detective Sana and the forensic doctor, who were also scheduled to appear before the magistrate this morning. John had already gone inside to find them seats, and she would join him after her testimony.

Her companions were speaking quietly, seemingly more comfortable and at ease with their surroundings than she was, and so she was relieved to be the first one summoned.

'What prompted you to look in the geographic area where the body was found?' Grace was asked by the counsel for the coroner as she began to give her evidence a short time later.

'Our company, ARC Surveys, headquartered in Port Moresby, is doing a survey for the Department of Main Roads to update the highway between Goroka and Mount Hagen,' she began quietly. 'We had used a drone to survey some of the surrounding area for potential options to position the new roadway. It was when I was looking at the scans on the computer that I saw the vehicle. I then alerted John Mercedes, the managing director of the firm—who is here today,' she said, giving a nervous half smile at John in the gallery.

'What exactly did you see from the images?' asked the lawyer.

'We saw an abandoned vehicle and, at first, thought little of it.' She flicked a sad smile at John. 'But when we noticed it hadn't moved after a few months, we felt compelled to advise the police so that it could be investigated properly on foot.'

After answering a few more questions pertaining to the exact location of the discovery, she was thanked and dismissed, and she went to sit in the pew with John.

As Jess made her way beside him, she discreetly looked around to see if any family representatives had made the trip—but it didn't look like it. There were a few stragglers coming in, possibly media, but no expats to signal that a relative was in attendance.

When Detective Sana took to the stand, Grace leaned in intently to what he had to say.

The detective went through the evidence, outlining the suspicious circumstances surrounding the death, how they had confirmed the identification of the deceased. He then went on to explain something Grace wasn't up to date with.

'We have reason to believe that the deceased was known to the highlands community, as we have recovered photographs on the camera that were taken at various locations in the region. These locations are the Wilhelm National Park and Goroka Festival and a social club in Gumawa, sixty kilometres west of Mount Hagen, one hundred kilometres east of Goroka.'

Detective Sana then went into detail about the extent of time and effort that had gone into identifying and interviewing some of the people in the photos, but that given the photos had been taken nearly three decades earlier, identification had been difficult—let alone locating people to interview.

Whilst no motive had been found, Detective Sana said that the bullet wound confirmed Mr Reynolds had been shot and not simply run off the highway, as the incident had originally appeared.

Next up was the forensic doctor, Dr Gemma Ward, who gave a full account of the autopsy of an otherwise healthy male. Apart, of course, from the single bullet wound in the spinal cord.

'The lumbosacral spine gunshot wound would have resulted in acute bleeding, rendering the patient dead within minutes,' said Dr Ward in her crisp professional tone. 'The gun would have been a low-energy weapon, a pistol or revolver, fired at close range. Because we don't have the bullet, we cannot identify the gun used, but the damage to the surrounding area leads us to believe it may be a 0.22, 0.25, 0.32 or 0.38-calibre handgun.'

A short adjournment was then taken for morning tea, and Grace and John went over to the small table in the corner to pour out coffees.

The inquest invited several more witnesses to take the stand, and one included a frail woman who had met the victim some thirty years earlier.

'He was a lovely young man,' said Bessy Warden, a seventy-eight-year-old Australian woman who fondly recalled meeting the young man on his travels. 'He came into Mount Hagen and asked for some accommodation, and we sorted him out with a room at the hotel. We talked a lot about his travels, as he was a journalist or photographer—one of those—for some nature publication, and he showed me some of his work on his little screen—you know, on the camera.'

'What was the purpose of his visit? Do you recall?' asked counsel.

'He was on an *assignment*,' she said— emphasising the word as if it held the utmost importance. 'I remember him because the Mount Hagen show had just finished, and he arrived like the day or two afterwards, and I said to him that he was too late. That he had missed the big event in our parts. I remember thinking why come now and not last week? He said something about never having been to PNG and was doing an article about the wildlife,' she continued. 'I told him to get to the Goroka Festival in mid-September because that was worth a few photos for his magazine.'

It transpired from her testimony that he had arrived in Mount Hagen by vehicle (she thought it was a Jeep) and had stayed two nights with her before heading east towards Goroka, some 170 kilometres away.

Eventually the hearing the coroner announced he would advise on his ruling after a lunch adjournment.

Despite not feeling hungry, Grace nibbled on a sandwich and drained a strong black coffee, returning to the courthouse an hour later with John. They sat alongside Detective Sana and his team to hear the coroner's decision.

'I have reason to believe that the death of twenty-five-year-old Ryan Reynolds sometime between August and November 1990 was caused by a person or persons unknown, and should the police prosecution secure further evidence, they can take this matter to trial.'

Detective Sana seemed relieved and pleased with the verdict, although he said it would be unlikely it would ever make it to court given the age of the case and the meagre evidence they had been able to unearth.

Arriving at the hotel, Grace joined John at the lobby bar where he organised drinks and an antipasto platter. She was now hungry after not being able to stomach much all day.

'It's surreal to think that he may have gone unnoticed if we hadn't been commissioned to do the survey,' Grace said, still surprised about the chain of events.

'Yes, and he may well have gone unnoticed if you hadn't paid close attention to the scan.' John looked at her intently. 'A toast to you, Grace,' he said, lifting his glass.

Whether Ryan would ever find justice, she didn't know, but his lonely, hidden grave was now gone, and he would be returned to his relations in Australia. It gave her some comfort.

# CHAPTER 34: JESS

As Jess flew down the mountain past Edward, she heard him shout 'Jessica! You're amazing!' She kept her knees bent and in tight. Adrenaline was surging through her.

It had been years since she had skied, and she had forgotten just how exhilarating it was. Especially with the stunning Matterhorn in view and the picturesque village of Zermatt below.

Zermatt had originated as a mountain village in the late 1800s and was initially known for its mountain hiking in summer, thanks to the mighty Matterhorn. It was one of the most spectacular mountains in Switzerland, distinctive in its pyramid shape. Over the past century and a half, it had become one of Switzerland's—and Europe's—most sought-after summer and winter destinations with its unparalleled hiking, mountaineering and of course alpine skiing. The village, which continues to this day to ban motor vehicles, is only accessible by train and uses electric carts to ferry people around.

Edward had booked four nights in Zermatt, and Jess was loving every minute of it.

After two hours of intense skiing, they took a break at the lower section of the mountain and headed to a rustic chalet serving snacks and hot chocolates.

'This is hard work!' Jess laughed as she removed her helmet and goggles and picked up one of the steaming, creamy drinks.

Enjoying the sweet warmth of the hot chocolate, she and Edward quietly watched a succession of skiers navigate their way down the run they had just traversed. The surrounds were truly stunning.

Within twenty minutes they were back outside, skis on, and sliding towards the chairlift to complete another circuit of the mountain.

It was four p.m. before the ski lifts closed, and Jess was relieved to take her weary body back to their gorgeous chalet in the old town.

Unbeknownst to her, Edward had arranged a surprise that afternoon. Within minutes of yanking off her ski boots and padding upstairs, there was a knock downstairs at the door.

'I'll get it,' Edward yelled and was moments later followed up by a man and a woman.

Drinking from a glass at the sink, Jess looked up, puzzled.

'I've organised a massage for us.' Edward beamed and began showing the couple into the living room and instructing them where to set up their portable tables.

The massage was heavenly. Jess could instantly feel her exhausted limbs relaxing—hopefully avoiding the stiffness that would usually result from using muscles that hadn't been utilised for some time. Surrendering to the gentle needling, pummelling and manipulation at the firm hands of her expert masseuse, she felt totally blissed out when the treatment was over.

As Edward escorted the therapists downstairs, Jess drifted into their bathroom and turned on the taps to fill the giant jacuzzi. She dimmed the lights and stepped into the warm, gushing water and closed her eyes.

She had almost dozed off when she felt Edward softly stroke her face. Reluctantly she opened her eyes.

'Hey, sleepyhead. I thought we should have something special to celebrate being here together.' He grinned, holding up a bottle of champagne and leaned in to kiss her.

'Wow, the massage was pretty special,' she said as she watched him pour first hers and then his glass. Handing both flutes of champagne to her, he dropped his towel and slipped into the tub.

Taking his glass from her, he raised his to her.

'Jessica, I love you so much. I would be the happiest man alive if you agreed to be my wife.'

'Edward!' she exclaimed, sitting upright and sending a series of waves across the bath. She had to blink a few times to make sure she was really awake.

'What do you say? Yes?' he pleaded, kissing her languidly. Pulling back, he raised his eyebrows up and down, smiling mischievously, knowing it would prompt a giggle.

'Wow! What a day of surprises. Yes!' Her heart and head were competing for calm. She felt completely overwhelmed.

'Yes!' He pumped the air. 'A toast to you, my

beautiful bride, Jessica McCann.' They clinked glasses and took a sip of the champagne.

Edward placed down his glass before reaching for his towelling robe on the side of the jacuzzi and presented her with a small red velvet box.

Opening it slowly, she saw a stunningly beautiful solitaire engagement ring. The two-carat diamond was as elegant and exquisite as Jess knew Edward's tastes to be, and she felt thoroughly overawed as he slipped it on her finger.

Jess could not remember ever feeling so unbelievably happy. She nestled closely into Edward as he caressed her neck. Drinking their champagne, they talked about the adventures that awaited them.

As the champagne finished, Edward helped Jess out of the jacuzzi and gently and sensuously wiped her down with the towel before placing his lips tenderly all over her body. The feeling became intense, and in moments Jess was reenergised and lost in their lovemaking.

Later dressing in a slinky black jersey dress and boots, Jess looked down again at her sparkling engagement ring. It seemed a shame to hide it now in the warm mitts she put on for their short walk to dinner.

Edward had booked a celebratory dinner at Max's, one of Zermatt's fine dining restaurants, and the soft lighting and moody jazz created the perfect ambience to their romantic occasion. Their table faced a picture window, and outside the snow fell daintily to the ground. Jess knew that Zermatt would forever hold a special place in her heart.

# CHAPTER 35: JESS

'Congratulations!' Emma cried out as Jess let herself in to her sister's Balmain home the following Saturday afternoon.

Jess had revealed the happy news by telephone, but this was the first time the pair had seen each other since Jess's return nearly a week ago.

Whilst Jess had wanted to visit sooner, work had been relentless. She not only had two weeks of emails and correspondence to catch up on, but she had also had to travel out of Sydney for two nights to conduct interviews for a feature she was writing on inspiring women in the lead up to International Women's Day.

It had been an exhausting week, but now she was on her much-valued weekend off and looking forward to catching up properly with Emma and the girls.

The sisters hugged before Emma reached over to switch on the jug. As usual, Jess had picked up a sweet treat, this time a walnut-and-coffee teacake from her local patisserie.

'Where are the girls?' Jess noticed a discernible silence around the house.

'They're with Steve.'

There was enough in that short statement to prompt Jess's curiosity. But it was the flatness of Emma's tone that startled Jess.

Steve had never been a hands-on parent, and besides, today was Saturday—Steve's golf day. A day he didn't give up lightly.

She instinctively knew something wasn't adding up.

'Steve's with all of them?' Jess asked, knowing that Steve rarely took all three girls anywhere on his own, complaining that it was too fraught.

'Yep,' Emma said, refusing to look at Jess, instead focusing intently on making the tea.

'What's going on, Ems?'

'What do you mean?' Her sister's response was defensive.

'Sorry. I just sense that perhaps I've walked into something here.'

'No, you haven't!' Emma shook her head, busying herself with the task of reaching up to the rack to get a large plate for the teacake. But whatever emotions were whirling within her couldn't be contained any longer. Emma stopped reaching and instead collapsed into herself, clutching at the kitchen benchtop to support her shaking body.

Jess watched as her sister visibly crumpled. It was as if the air inside her had been whooshed out by a tight squeeze. Her body slumped, shoulders moving up and down with increasing intensity, and a near silent sob emerging.

Jess was up out of her seat in moments. Holding her from behind, she wrapped her arms around Emma, wanting to inject comfort and strength.

Emma began to eventually settle and then untangle herself from her sister's embrace.

'I'm okay now,' she mumbled. 'Just give me a minute.' She hurriedly walked out of the kitchen.

Jess had never seen her sister cry. She was always the big sister, the mother, the wife. Always in control. Busy, bubbly, the soother to everyone around her.

Jess finished putting the cake on the plate, found serviettes and a knife and brought the cups and teapot to the island bench. Still not sure what was going on or what to do, she patiently sat back on a high stool and waited.

Her sister returned a short time later, and the evidence of her tears was clear. Damp red eyes highlighted a sad, defeated demeanour.

'Hey, Ems. I'm worried about you,' said Jess, reaching out to grab her sister's arm and steer her onto the bar stool.

'Sorry,' Emma said. 'I didn't mean to lose it just there. This is your moment, and I've just ruined it.'

'Of course you haven't, and what do you mean "my moment"? Forget me, let's talk about you. What's going on?'

'It's Steve.' Emma bit her lip nervously. 'He's moved out.'

Jess couldn't believe what she was hearing. How did she not know that her sister's marriage was in trouble? She had enjoyed Christmas with Steve and Emma and had seen Emma just under a month ago before travelling to Europe, and they were perfectly fine. Weren't they?

After a laboured pause, Emma began to slowly talk.

Steve had met an old flame, a woman who had returned to Sydney and begun working at the same bank at Steve. They had decided they *'really loved each other after all,'* Emma said with mock emphasis.

'Steve doesn't want to miss any more years without her, apparently.' Emma rubbed the back of her neck. 'He tried to tell me that he still loves me and the girls, but it's her whom he's in love with,' she said, looking bewildered.

'My God, I just don't believe this!' Jess was astounded, furious, shell-shocked. 'Surely he will come to his senses?'

But Emma reassured her that he would not. She had pleaded with him, suggested counselling, a holiday together... but all to no avail.

'I'm devastated. Not for me so much, because I'll be all right eventually. It's the girls I am most upset for. Their father has chosen an old flame. Instead of growing up in a family home, they will now be bouncing between two houses, not one. I never wanted to do that to my children,' she said with sadness.

Angelina, who would be seven next month, and Clementine who was a year behind, were old enough to realise that their parents had split, and Emma had sat down to explain everything to them as calmly and reassuringly as she could. Baby Annabelle would never know what it was like to have her father living there, as he had already moved out and she was not yet two.

'I should have done something earlier,' Emma said, beginning to blame herself for failing to see the clues.

'I'm angry with myself. Angry at Steve for walking out on us! I'm angry that he gave up on us. He was never here with me and the girls. Always working! Or playing golf or touch footy or sleeping around! God, I'm just so annoyed at myself for not recognising the distance that was growing between us—' She broke down, tears streaming down her face as Jess handed her tissues.

Jess rubbed her back and let Emma cry. She had noticed Steve's absence over the years. Emma often alone with their daughters at home. She'd foolishly thought that Steve was being considerate in giving her and Emma some quality sister time. Now she realised that this was symptomatic of their relationship, with Steve often not home at night and weekends.

'Why didn't you say something?' asked Jess. 'I spend my life coming around here talking about the latest guy I'm dating or what story I'm writing, and yet you never mentioned that you had worries with Steve.'

'I guess I just hoped it would sort itself out as Annabelle got a bit older and Steve felt like he had a bigger role in their lives. You know, like sport or camping... all that stuff that dads apparently love to do with their kids...'

Jess hugged her tightly and then noticed the time on the kitchen clock. Edward had booked an early dinner and movie that evening and she would need to message him to postpone. Over a second pot of tea, this time enjoyed in the comfy lounges in the living room, she sat and listened to Emma as she circled through her competing emotions—from anger to disappointment and hurt. And worst of all to feeling like an utter failure.

Jess just let her talk and listened quietly and sympathetically as her sister's emotions spiralled from fury to regret.

By six thirty, Emma was exhausted and depleted. Jess coaxed her into taking a soothing bath. Insisting, Jess jumped up and headed to the bathroom to find lavender oil and scented candles but instead located frothy blue bubble bath—no doubt for the girls—and turned on the taps. As Emma rested in the bubble bath, Jess fixed them a pasta dish, using the mushrooms, bacon and cream in the fridge. Finding a chilled bottle of Pinot Grigio, she then sat down to wait as a much-restored-looking Emma entered the kitchen. Wearing a kimono-style dressing gown, Jess couldn't help thinking how young her sister looked tonight, young, vulnerable and achingly sad.

Hugging her fiercely, Jess went to pour them wine.

'You and the girls are going to be okay,' Jess said reassuringly. 'I'm here whenever you need me.'

Together they sat back up at the island bench and sipped their wine as the pasta dish was devoured.

Before long, Jess had successfully turned the conversation to the antics of their childhood and had Emma laughing. And once the wine was finished, she insisted Emma head up to bed and get some rest.

She would stay overnight and sleep in the guest room.

Just before eight the next morning, Jess awoke to the sound of cooking noises in the kitchen. Having borrowed a nightie from her sister, Jess sleepily went out to see how she was.

'Good morning,' she said warily as she entered

the sun-filled kitchen.

'Morning,' said Emma brightly, putting the spatula down and turning to Jess. 'Thank you, gorgeous sister, for taking care of me last night.'

'Don't thank me. I just wish I could have made things better.'

'Oh, you did. I slept like a baby last night. Of course, that could have been due to the wine, but seriously I really do feel so much better today. Like I'm back in the driver's seat and not spiralling out of control. For weeks now I've been going around and around in circles, but today I feel steady. I also know that having you back now... the future isn't going to be so bad. I just need to move ahead.'

'I'm so pleased,' Jess responded, smiling and ruffling her sister's hair as she went to make a coffee on the Nespresso machine.

Emma explained that Steve was dropping the girls back in an hour, and she wanted to get some cupcakes baked and iced for morning tea.

'Please stay and see the girls,' she pleaded. 'They've really missed you.'

Agreeing, Jess grabbed an apron and began working side by side with Emma to get the cakes into the oven before the impromptu morning tea began.

# CHAPTER 36: DOM

Dom and Lauren had been dating now casually for two months. Going out to live theatre or a movie or dining at restaurants when their hectic work schedules permitted. They had even enjoyed a few lazy weekends together and were this weekend lounging at his place.

It had become a comfortable routine, and Dom was glad that he had taken the initiative to reignite things with his ex-wife.

Neither had suggested reintroducing their revived relationship to family and friends, not yet. But Dom was aware that this romantic bubble they were in couldn't last forever.

What was holding him back from letting Clancy know that he and Lauren were giving things another go? Why wasn't he inviting Marcus and his wife Chloe around for a dinner with Lauren? Why hadn't he even mentioned the reunion to Marcus?

He felt justifiably cautious. After all, it was a case of second time around, and he guessed that Lauren felt the same way. She too hadn't initiated any social get-together with friends.

He knew that next week would provide him with ample opportunity to speak with Clancy, as Dom had arranged to visit the old man for his seventieth birthday.

Since the heart operation, Clancy had made a strong recovery, and Dom wanted to use his visit to ensure he wasn't overdoing things physically.

Clancy had hit all his milestones in his recovery, and the doctor had given him the six-month all-clear.

Dom watched Lauren now doing the crossword in the back of the Saturday newspaper, her fierce attention to the task. She really was a strikingly beautiful woman, and her concentration was singular. It was as if at this precise moment, the crossword was the only thing that mattered. It was what had made her such a good lawyer. Her complete and utter focus.

Yes, he would enjoy this time with Lauren right now because next week he wouldn't be able to avoid merging reality with this bubble and potentially watching it burst.

****

Dom arrived into Mount Hagen late on Friday afternoon and was now settled on the veranda.

'Here we go,' said Clancy, handing over a cold beer. It was surprisingly easy being back and sharing a drink together. Any residual tension Dom had felt towards Clancy had shifted.

'How's the farm?' he asked, now more keenly interested in the workings of the plantation.

'Good, good,' Clancy boomed.

Things were thriving, and he brought Dom up to speed with the latest news—investors, suppliers, new markets and machinery upgrades. Dom listened intently, occasionally offering his two cents' worth.

Clancy's birthday was the following day, and Mika had organised a small dinner party at her house. But tonight it was just them, and Dom and Clancy were enjoying the quiet serenity of sitting there. Silence always calmed Dom. So often jungles were described as threatening, uneasy environments, stifling with intensity. But Dom had never felt that way. To him, the lush green growth was comforting. It was a living, breathing presence that ensured that he never felt alone, at least not in this part of the world.

The following evening, he and Clancy arrived at Mika's rambling home—a wraparound veranda hanging off the old Queenslander-style property. Whitewashed timber and latticework coloured with vibrant bougainvillea delivered a sense of coolness despite the warmth of the early evening. The interiors were as spacious and white as the exterior, with neutral linen sofas, white shutters and a dash of greenery with large pots of ferns. Mika's art collection was on display, each wall showcasing paintings, carvings and artefacts from local artists.

'Did you hear about that old ute and the poor bastard they found?' Ted Lazenby asked Dom after they'd exchanged hellos on the deck.

Ted had lived in the area almost as long as Clancy, and whilst a good ten years his junior, he had spent his working life running crops on his farm, twenty kilometres north of their plantation. He was a confirmed bachelor and always a good source of gossip in the area. Like Ted, Dom and Clancy were among the first to arrive at Clancy's birthday dinner. Clancy had hung back to chat with Mika whilst she busied herself in the kitchen.

Dom listened intently to the amazing story that Ted shared of a young Australian man found dead in the jungle.

'They say he was a photographer or something in the media and was out here working in these parts in 1990,' said Ted. 'Even came to Gumawa!'

Whilst Dom didn't immediately think of the relevance of these facts, he would later, and it would unravel something he may wish he hadn't.

# CHAPTER 37: JESS

It had been a busy couple of weeks, and as Jess sat across from Edward at the Thai restaurant near her house, she released a deep sigh.

She had shared Emma's marriage woes with Edward over the phone the morning after Emma's revelations, but this had been their first chance to meet up for dinner since. Emma's work demands and Edward's busy travel schedule had conspired to keep them apart. Whilst concerned about Emma's situation, he wasn't as sympathetic as Jess had expected. Instead, he revealed a cool, pragmatic assessment of her sister's situation.

'It is better for this to happen now,' he stated once Jess had updated him on her sister's marriage breakdown over their wine.

'But it's so sad and sudden! The girls are so young,' Jess lamented, disappointed in Edward's matter-of-fact attitude.

'I know,' he said. 'This can't be helped. The alternative is that he will have an affair with this woman, and that would make things more complicated and Emma more unhappy. Yes?'

'Maybe… I guess you're right,' Jess begrudgingly agreed. 'I just wish he would have thought about the bigger picture: his wonderful family and what he is giving up by going back to an old girlfriend. I mean, what if it doesn't work out?'

'It will work,' he said, continuing in his forthright way that she had learned not to take personally. Direct, sometimes brutal, but also not fluffing around with the niceties that were her cultural norm.

Feeling that this exchange wasn't going in the direction she was hoping, Jess changed the subject, instead asking him about work. At least that was safe ground… for now.

# CHAPTER 38: GRACE

The young surveyor had really missed him and wasn't sure how she felt about that. He was, after all, Grace's boss.

John had been away at a survey conference in Australia and had stayed on to visit family in New Zealand over Easter.

It had been a hectic month, initially with the coronial inquest and more recently the constant survey site visits. Every week Grace had flown by light aircraft or helicopter to one of the two key survey projects that were in progress. The first job related to a small island in Milne Bay that wanted to build a jet airstrip and a trio of luxury villas; and the second job was the gas pipeline project that continued on in Kooto, commandeering most of the team at ARC Surveys. She enjoyed the contrast as well as the opportunity to visit different parts of the country.

John was due back that afternoon, and she had been busily ensuring the projects were up to date and ready to present. A briefing had been scheduled for four p.m.

The hours flew by as she revised her reports, returned phone calls and stepped into an impromptu client conference call at late notice. She was needed to reassure the company's newest client—BACI Hotels—that the survey was on track and would be completed within the next two months as per their agreed schedule.

As she walked slowly back to her desk, still digesting the contents of the conference call, John was waiting for her. He was leaning on her desk, scanning his mobile phone, and when he looked up, a broad smile broke out across his face.

She couldn't help smiling back, almost as widely.

'Welcome back,' she said, feeling strangely self-conscious at seeing him again. He looked gorgeous, dressed in smart chinos and a white linen shirt.

'It's good to be back, Grace!' His smile dazzled. 'I just got in and thought I'd come and find you. I heard you were on the BACI call. How'd it go?'

Grace filled him in on the recent phone call, glad to have something concrete to focus on.

'They just needed a bit more reassurance that the survey is progressing on time, on budget. That sort of thing. Am I late?'

As they both looked at the time on John's phone, Grace realised she had kept him waiting and began to bumble her way through an apology. For some reason his presence at her desk was making her feel nervous.

'No worries, we can pick it up in the morning

when Mattius and the guys are in. But I thought perhaps you could share the highlights of the past two weeks over a coldie at the Yachtie?' he asked hopefully.

'That would be great,' she said, relieved to be moving away from the strange tension at her desk. 'Let me just dump this here and log off.'

They left the office together in minutes, John offering to drive them to the club. They'd return for her car.

*Why am I nervous?* Grace wondered, sitting stiffly beside John in his air-conditioned Range Rover. The luxurious SUV had the intoxicating smell of newness—from the plush leather upholstery to the spotless carpets. If only it was a work vehicle, she might feel more relaxed...

'What's got your mind whirring?' he asked, cutting into her thoughts.

'Oh nothing,' she said quickly. 'It's, umm, been a pretty productive couple of weeks. I think you'll be impressed with the team's output while you've been away,' she said to fill the silence but heard the ridiculous formality in her voice. Hoping to shift the focus, she asked about his trip.

John was still sharing the details of the conference with her as they alighted at the Yacht Club, and he humbly admitted that his presentation on the gas pipeline project had been well received.

'I'm sure it was the envy of the room,' she said, knowing how aspirational it was to survey in the wilds of a developing nation such as Papua New Guinea.

'I'm not sure about that.' He laughed as they walked up to the bar. 'Now, what can I get you?'

After giving her order, Grace went out on the deck to find a table.

With the first white wine under her belt, conversation flowed more easily between them. John filled her in on his drive around the South Island of New Zealand with his brother and his family.

'Yep, it's all campers over there. I never thought I'd go for the whole campervan experience—but it was a hell of a lot of fun. I'm not sure if it was because I was doing it with Declan, Mary and their kids, but we had a great four days of travelling slowly and taking in the sights.'

Over the past year or so, Grace had got to know a little bit about John's family. He was close to his twin brother, Declan, and went to see him at least twice a year, and loved being an uncle.

'Jenny's such a cutie—she turned thirteen when we were on the road—but Jake is starting to become that monosyllabic fifteen-year-old, so he took a bit to warm up,' John said proudly, regaling her with stories of winning his nephew over eventually.

Drinks flowed into dinner, and they both opted for the grilled steak, potato wedges, coleslaw salad and a bottle of Merlot.

No work had been discussed, and the few times that Grace had gone to update John, he had waved her off.

'Tomorrow will be early enough to hear about all that,' he said, silencing her on the subject.

It was time to leave, and John dropped her home, promising to call and pick her up for the work in the morning.

'Grace, it's been great catching up,' John said

when the car had pulled to a stop outside her apartment. 'I hope we can do this again—you know, forget the work stuff—just enjoy a night out.'

'That sounds good,' she said casually, unsure if she was interpreting his full meaning or had misread his tone. Irrespective of his intentions, they'd moved into a new, more personal level of their friendship.

He gently squeezed her right arm before turning to unlock her door from his side. A security guard stood waiting to escort her inside.

# CHAPTER 39: DOM

Dom sat on the Qantas flight, looking out the window as they sped down the runway to take off back to Sydney. It had been a good couple of days, and he was glad he had made the effort to return and celebrate Clancy's birthday.

The dinner party at Mika's had been a lot of fun, reminiscing about the old times and Clancy's rogue antics over the past forty-five years of his extraordinary life up here. He had been larger than life in his youth, and whilst he had mellowed in later years, there were still glimpses of Clancy's adventurous spirit.

And there was *that* story—quite an amazing story really—about the discovery of the body of a young man in the jungle, apparently murdered three decades ago. It had been eerily close to where they had all been enjoying Mika's fine food, wine and laughter not less than twenty-four hours earlier.

'Poor bugger. Young bloke, Ryan Reynolds. He apparently passed right through here,' Ted had said as they drank their beers, overlooking Mika's garden. 'I can't say he rings any bells with me, but police reckon he was travelling for some photo piece for *Geographic* magazine or some bloody thing.

'Don't know if he upset some tribe on his travels—probably took a photo without asking,' Ted joked, adding in a more serious tone, 'I mean who else would kill an expat traveller? Anyway, police are investigating, but after more than twenty years, it's not going to be an easy one, probably just get filed away,' finished Ted, as Mika abruptly silenced the morbid conversation to usher them to the dinner table.

'That's enough of that talk, Ted. I'll hear no more about it tonight,' she commanded in an unusually abrasive tone as she led them to their seats.

Dom could see she wasn't happy to have the topic mar what should be an upbeat occasion. Ted exaggeratedly moved his finger over his lips, indicating he'd been suitably chastised, and they'd all moved on to other topics.

For some reason the name stuck with Dom—*Ryan Reynolds*. It must be because of the American actor by the same name. Or is he Canadian? Yeah, that's right he is because he sometimes makes a point of it in his media interviews.

But Dom knew instinctively that there was a stronger association. He just knew there was, but for some reason he couldn't recall what it was.

The drink service had now moved through the aircraft, and Dom sat enjoying his beer and peanuts. His mind drifted back to the vehicle, the country that had spawned him, and the adventures he had had up there as a kid.

It was then, with an abrupt halt, that it came to him. Sitting up very alert in his seat, a strange chill went through Dom, and it had nothing to do with the beer. He knew exactly why the story had rung a bell.

The memory came to him… a normal, everyday weekend at home. He must have been about nine or ten and had run into the house to get something after being out for hours on his bike with Robbo, his good friend at the time.

'Dom, I'd like you to meet a famous photographer,' his mother had said, introducing him to a man sitting beside her on the veranda, sharing wine. He remembered the occasion because his mother had said he was "famous," and he'd never met anyone famous before. It was also unusual for them to have a house guest when Clancy wasn't home as his mother usually kept her own company during his absences. Could that have been the man they'd found in the jungle?

He sat back now in his seat, vainly attempting to recall the features of the man—longish hair? Or was it short? He remembered thinking he looked like a celebrity… or perhaps that was just on hearing he was famous. But he was sure he recalled a big smile and a strong hand shaking his.

Dom had only rushed in to grab his Nintendo and ask if it was okay if he stayed at Robbo's that night as they were going to watch videos. During those days, Dom and Robbo barely spent a night or day away from each other. It had been late afternoon, and he recalled thinking his mum was acting a little like she did sometimes when she had been drinking alcohol at those cocktail parties they went to. Giggly and affectionate. She had hugged him closely before he left, which he also recalled thinking was a little out of character—after all he was only going for one night—

but he had loved her for it all the same.

It had to be the same person that Ted was talking about last night—because he said the guy was a photographer, travelling through the region, and the timing would make sense. He was only about nine or ten. Yes, that's right, definitely ten, because it was the same year his mother had died.

It was then that he had the eeriest sensation. His mother had died in 1990, and Ted said that this person had also died in the same year. Was it the same man who had come to the farm? Did it mean anything?

His mind began to work furiously, returning to his earlier suspicions relating to his mother's death. He had chickened out this weekend in asking Clancy about the baby they'd lost. If he didn't want to talk about it, Dom wasn't going to bring it up. At least not yet.

He felt an impatience to get off the plane and be home. To open his computer and see what he could unearth about the death of this famous Australian photographer.

****

Four interminable hours later and Dom was finally home. Sometimes the flight between Sydney and Port Moresby seemed insufferably long, and today had been one of those times. He recalled feeling the exact same way when he was on the return journey to PNG as a teenage boy, hungry to be back in Gumawa, the land of his birth.

This time though, instead of wishing for the green wilds of home, he had been impatiently counting down the hours to arrive at his Sydney terrace to see what the internet could share about this mysterious stranger that had passed through the highlands and most likely his life. If there was any connection with his mother, he needed to know.

As he fired up his laptop, he filled the coffee machine with fresh filtered water and ripped open one of the packages of coffee he'd brought back. The machine percolated to life, and the rich, familiar smell relaxed him. Taking his strong black coffee over to the kitchen bench where he had set up the laptop, he sat on the bar stool and began clicking through Google, looking at the search results for Ryan Reynolds PNG Highlands.

The first search—the most current—related to the coronial inquest into the death of Ryan Reynolds, and Dom read it eagerly.

He came across a small online story about a body found in PNG jungle and read about the discovery of the skeletal remains of a person in a dense jungle west of Goroka, around halfway to Mount Hagen. The identity had been confirmed as twenty-five-year-old Ryan Reynolds from Cairns.

Making another coffee, Dom took the laptop to the lounge and began to scroll for more information.

# CHAPTER 40: JESS

Jess spoke with Emma daily and sensed her confidence was starting to return. Her sister was attending regular counselling sessions with a psychotherapist, which was helping her to come to terms with her newfound situation. Her loss of identity.

'I've been the girlfriend and wife of one man for twenty years. Since I was a teenager,' Emma lamented. 'No wonder I don't know who I am without him!'

Jess fully supported her decision to meet with a counsellor; it was important for Emma to have a professional guide her through her feelings. And it seemed to be working.

She was thinking of her sister as she looked at the time on her computer, wondering if she could skive off for a half an hour chat instead of addressing the work on her desk. Her latest feature article had just been filed, and because there was only an hour left in the work day, she was half-hearted about starting something new.

Reaching for her features list, she was pondering which one to present at Monday morning's editorial meeting. Should it be the male suicide one, exploring what was now deemed an epidemic in this country? Suicide was becoming the leading cause of death in Australia for men—six males taking their own life every day. A truly shocking number. Or should she go for a lighter story—the one she had been keen to write on the success of Australian filmmakers in Hollywood? The impact of the "Aussie Mafia" (as it was being nicknamed in the US press) and their overwhelming popularity at the box office?

Thankfully she didn't have to make a decision because her mobile rang.

'Jess, it's Dom Jonson,' he said uncertainly.

'Dom, hi. Long time, no speak. How are you?'

'Good, I think,' he responded cryptically. 'Actually, that's the reason for the call. Have you got time to catch up over a coffee?'

'Well, if you make it a drink, I can meet you tonight after work,' Jess said, intrigued by the call.

They agreed to meet an hour later at Leo's wine bar where they had met before Christmas.

Jess arrived punctually and as usual found Dom already there. She smiled when she saw that he had already ordered her a glass of wine—noting her preference for white over his red.

They kissed each other on the cheek, and he pulled out a chair for her to sit down.

After exchanging pleasantries and what they'd done recently, Jess's trip to Europe and Dom's return to PNG, the conversation got to the point.

'Well, actually, PNG is the reason for my call,' he began. 'Did you read about the photographer who was found in the highlands after going missing in 1990? They only just found him. The coronial enquiry was on last month,' he ventured.

Jess recalled hearing something about a discovery of an old vehicle but not much more. 'I've been off the news radar a bit, actually in a bit of a bubble with Munich, my engagement, family stuff. What did the court find?'

'You're engaged?' Dom asked, his face froze.

'Yes! It's all been a bit of a whirlwind actually! Edward asked me when we were overseas,' she gushed.

'Congratulations,' he said, although his stern face didn't convey the sentiment.

'Thank you. Anyway, back to what you were saying. So, tell me what's happened?' she said, keen to move the attention off her and learn more about Dom's story.

He expanded on the discovery of the young man in the highlands and the coroner's finding that he had died of a "suspicious death by persons known or unknown".

'There's not too much online,' he admitted.

'And?' Jess prompted, still curious why this was of interest to him.

'I think there's a link with my mother,' he said, but before Jess could protest, he kept speaking. 'It was *twenty-eight* years ago… 1990. That year is significant. It was the same year Mum died.'

Jess sat back, surprised at the coincidence, but more so at his intense outburst.

'I'm not sure how they are related,' she said, hoping to calm him down but also trying to connect the dots because she was still confused. 'What's your theory on all this?'

'The person they found in the jungle was a photographer or journalist, or both. The thing is, I recall meeting an Australian photographer travelling through the area back then. He visited the plantation. I'm sure he's the same person. He was there at the house, drinking wine with my mother.'

'But, Dom, how could you remember? What age were you?' She was baffled by his strong conviction.

'I was ten. I distinctly remember meeting a famous photographer, and I just know it's the same man.'

'Do you think your mother had something to do with his death?' she asked, unsure what Dom was driving at.

'Of course not!' he exclaimed before continuing more calmly. 'But there is a coincidence. This man ends up dead after being at our place, and my mother dies around the same time. I know it sounds crazy, but I can't let it go. Will you help me unearth more about this man, Ryan Reynolds? I mean, he was apparently a freelancer and worked for *National Geographic*, among other publications.'

Before Jess could reply, he ploughed on. 'As I said, there has just been an inquest, but the information online is scarce. You could access more information, couldn't you?' He looked at her eagerly, finally sitting back in his chair to draw breath, and reached for his red wine.

Jess was intrigued, but surely Dom was trying for a long shot with his suspicions. After all, there might have been plenty of photographers visiting PNG at that time, and Dom was confusing them or even mistakenly thinking he'd met the dead man when it may have been a completely different person.

Then there was the timing of the deaths of Dom's mother and the photojournalist. Surely it didn't spell a connection. He could have died by simply meeting with foul play in the jungles of Papua New Guinea—which wouldn't be unheard of. Or he may have self-harmed, as she had read the statistics on male suicide only that afternoon, and it was alarming.

She voiced her objections, and he began to beg her. 'It's just too much of a coincidence. Please help me. All I want is to learn the facts, and then I'll let it go. I know Dr Willis said that Mum's fall was just that, but after hearing about this—it's just too weird, don't you think? I mean, was my mother having an affair with this man? I clearly remember her being a bit tipsy when a celebrity photographer was over for lunch around that time. Clancy wasn't home, which is why I remember it more. I love my mother; I need to know what she was doing or not doing for that matter. No matter what it reveals.'

Jess eventually found herself agreeing that she would see what her work databases unveiled about the person and the coronial inquest.

As she settled into a taxi for the return trip to her apartment, she thought of what an extraordinary story this was. Even if there was no connection with Dom's mother, the fact that an Australian photographer was murdered in the PNG jungle and not discovered for nearly thirty years was a great feature and one that she couldn't wait to sink her teeth into!

\*\*\*\*

On Monday morning, Jess arrived into the office at six, eventually abandoning the pretence of sleep. So many different thoughts kept going around her head from the manic weekend: Dom's request to look into the PNG story and her fears of what it may uncover; Emma's unhappiness when she saw her over the weekend; and Edward's sudden insistence yesterday that they fast-track their wedding to the end of the year. Things were moving too fast, and her mind had been going around and around in circles all night.

She needed a coffee desperately and had to resort to the Nespresso machine as her regular barista hadn't been open when she'd passed him on her way into the building. Switching on her desktop computer and unpacking her mobile and notebook, she read over the notes she'd scribbled when she got in on Friday night. Dom's conversation was still clear in her head, and she was keen to know more about the mysterious Ryan Reynolds.

> **WRECKAGE FOUND IN PNG JUNGLE**
> Police are investigating the discovery of a vehicle wreckage in the dense jungle between Goroka and Mount Hagen. A human skull and the skeletal remains of a body were found inside the Jeep—and are being scientifically examined at the Port Moresby Forensics Laboratory.
>
> **AUSSIE PHOTOJOURNALIST IDENTIFIED IN THIRTY-YEAR-OLD DISCOVERY**
> Australian freelance photographer and journalist, twenty-five-year-old Ryan

Reynolds, has been confirmed as the victim inside a vehicle discovered in a remote part of the highlands of PNG. Mr Reynolds, originally from Cairns, was a renowned photojournalist working across the world on assignments for publications including *National Geographic* magazine, *Time* magazine and the *Discovery Channel*.

Police have confirmed his death is suspicious due to the nature of the injuries, despite the incident occurring more than two decades ago.

It is believed the victim was on an assignment in Papua New Guinea in 1990, when he met with foul play.

The chronology of the case was riveting, and Jess continued to search for more recent articles on the coronial inquest, which as Dom has said, took place just last month.

### AUSSIE PHOTOGRAPHER MURDERED IN PNG

A Mount Hagen coroner has confirmed that Australian freelance photographer and journalist, twenty-five-year-old Ryan Reynolds, was the victim of foul play when he disappeared in a dense jungle nearly thirty years ago.

The death has been confirmed as suspicious and caused by the hand of a person or persons unknown.

It is believed that Ryan Reynolds

was travelling between Goroka and Mount Hagen between August and November 1990 when he was killed.

It wasn't until January this year that he was found when a surveyor employed by ARC Surveys spotted the wreckage in a series of images produced by a drone that had been surveying the area as part of a highway reconstruction project. Mr Reynolds was discovered inside his vehicle, two kilometres from the roadway, west of Goroka.

Jess sat up. ARC Surveys? She knew people at ARC—her friend Grace Pickering and the managing partner, John Mercedes. Whilst Jess hadn't spoken to Grace since Christmas, months earlier, she now had a very good reason to give her a ring.

Noticing it was just nudging seven thirty a.m. and her barista would now be open, she jumped up, grabbed her phone and went out to find sustenance.

# CHAPTER 41: JESS

After ordering a large almond latte, Jess pounced on an outdoor stool, one of only half a dozen at her small hole-in-the-wall café. They were prized objects, although not necessarily at this hour of the morning when most peak-hour commuters were too busy to sit down for their coffee, instead preferring to snatch a takeaway.

But Jess felt entitled to the small break after her super early start that morning. She'd enjoyed reading some of the old articles Ryan Reynolds had contributed to during his brief lifetime. *National Geographic, Australian Geographic, Bushwalking Annual,* and the *Nature* periodical were just some of the titles he had featured in, as well as international newspapers—the *New York Times, London Gazette* and the *Australian* as well as online and TV editorials with *Discovery* and *World.*

After retrieving her coffee, she looked up Grace's mobile number, inserted her ear pods and dialled. She was getting in early but couldn't wait any longer to speak with her friend and learn more about the discovery.

As the phone rang, Jess pictured Port Moresby on a Monday morning and the slower pace of life there. She missed it.

After the fourth ring, Jess was expecting the voice mail to cut in when Grace breathlessly answered.

'Jess! Is that you?' she said in a rush of air into the phone.

Jess was so glad to hear her voice and felt guilty for not reaching out sooner.

'Don't be silly! We're all busy,' Grace said, dismissing her guilt.

'Well, actually that's why I'm calling,' Jess said, bringing up the grim discovery and ARC Surveys' involvement.

'I know! I nearly called you when it all happened, but then things just kept developing and there was so much to do. Police statements, visiting the site, then visiting the site some more. I'm not sure if you know, but we were working on a new highlands highway, which is how all this came about. And, of course, there was the coronial inquest a few weeks ago, so lots to get ready for that,' Grace explained.

'That's actually the reason for my call. I was hoping you could tell me a bit more about the case because I can't unearth too much online. I'd love to learn anything you know that hasn't yet been shared in the press.'

Grace filled Jess in on their visits to the site and the latest update from Detective Sana—which hadn't been too promising.

'Sadly, it looks like being a cold case. There were some photos that were salvageable from his camera, but given the humidity in the jungle, not to mention the dense rain they get up there, only a few photos survived. At least they provide some clues about his travels—the places he visited. So far, Detective Sana hasn't been able to place any of the faces in the photos, and I'm not sure he's going to try, to be honest. They are a small team and have enough to do with everything else going on up here.'

Ringing off around half an hour later, Jess pocketed her phone and her notebook, which she had been scribbling in furiously in shorthand since dialling Grace.

She knew she had a fascinating story, but whether any of it would help Dom, she couldn't really say. It was impossible to draw any connections from what she had learnt in her call with Grace to the mystery man drinking wine with Dom's mother.

But the photos intrigued her, and she now needed to think about how she could obtain a copy of those. And then she knew. Of course! I'm a journalist, and I'm writing a story about Ryan Reynolds. I'll just plan a visit to interview Detective Sana myself.

With a spring in her step, or perhaps it was the double shot she had just consumed, she knew she had just the story to pitch at this week's editorial meeting.

An hour later, Jess sat back and watched the faces around the table look at her with interest and a hint of admiration.

'So, I just want to get this straight,' said Paul, her news editor. 'You want to do a feature on this historic murder case? Head back to Papua New Guinea to see what you can find out?'

Jess had highlighted that the inquest had not long been on and that the police were still investigating, albeit half-heartedly. But she believed there was a human-interest story in the Australian man at the centre of it all and that their readers would be intrigued to know of this modern-day explorer who had met his fate in the dense jungle of one of the most remote countries on earth.

Okay, she had gone a bit over the top, but so was her desperation to revisit the highlands again and see what she could uncover. She had been careful to avoid any mention of Dom's suspicions regarding his mother's possible connection to the young man.

After some back-and-forth between her and Paul, it was finally agreed that she could head up there in a week's time on the condition that she had obtained the necessary media visa and had also lined up all interviews.

Skipping out of the meeting room, Jess felt exhilarated. There was much to organise, and her first call would be to Grace to get her guest room ready!

\*\*\*\*

She was late! It was Frances's thirty-fifth birthday dinner, and she'd got caught up on phone calls at work.

Thank God she'd brought her party dress to work and hurriedly changed into the slim-fitting black jersey that accentuated her lean frame and adorned it with a chunky art deco pearl necklace and earrings that she had bought at a vintage shop on her trip to Munich. Slipping into her strappy heels, she was off to find a taxi.

Arriving at the Balmain restaurant a short time later, she was shown to a noisy private dining room, which Frances had splurged on for the occasion.

'Happy birthday!' She embraced Frances, whispering, 'I'm so sorry I'm late!'

'We're about to be seated, so your timing is perfect!' Frances was in a jubilant mood. She looked resplendent in a sequinned shift dress in bright purple that shimmered in the light, her dark brown hair loosely piled up on her head, generating a fun yet sophisticated 1960s look.

'But hey, your beloved has been impatiently waiting for you.' She grinned, indicating Edward's presence at the other side of the small room.

Edward looked extremely handsome in his charcoal suit and open-neck shirt, and Jess smiled at him across the table before he excused himself from the couple he was talking to and came over.

'I was getting worried,' he said, kissing her and taking her hands in his.

'Sorry! Work,' she said, rolling her eyes, not wanting to admit how enthralling she'd found it.

'Okay, lovebirds, it's time to be seated,' Frances bossed, as she made her way around the group, helping them to find their seats at the beautifully styled table, brimming with crystal wineglasses, blue water glasses, crimson roses and intricately written name cards.

Edward introduced Jess to the dining companions nearest, work colleagues of his at Bavaria Bank, and in no time the conversation became one of finance, lending markets and returns.

Jess looked over at Frances seated at the top of the table between two smart-suited men whom she didn't know. Perpetually single, yet never short of admirers, the birthday girl looked radiant. Catching her eye, Frances winked, and Jess laughed back.

The wine flowed, the chatter got louder, and they sang a wholehearted 'Happy birthday' to Frances, who flitted around the small candlelit room, excited to have her friends all there to celebrate her milestone.

The Uber drive back to Jess's apartment had been a blur, and before long they were inside and Edward was skimming off Jess's dress and kissing her softly.

'I've missed you,' he said as he gently tugged her dress to the ground. 'Please don't leave me waiting at dinner again. It is unbearable!'

She held his face and pulled it in closely to her, savouring his mouth and the intensity of his kiss and walked out of her dress as they slowly moved towards the lounge.

# CHAPTER 42: JESS

Emma looked terrible. The strain of her marriage breakdown was quite shocking. She wore dark bruises under her eyes and looked fragile in her denim shorts and tangled T-shirt, which Jess noticed hung loosely off her slight frame as she rose to greet her.

But before she could comment, a chorus of 'JESS!' rang out, and she was suddenly encircled by her nieces at the front door. Crouching down for a group hug, she later let them lead her to the giant dollhouse in the centre of the living room, the latest gift from Daddy.

Catching Emma's raised eyebrow, she could see it hadn't been well received.

'Look, Jess!'

'No, I want to show Aunty Jess!'

'Jess!'

'Wow, this is a beauty!' she exclaimed, asking each of her nieces to show her their favourite room in the enormous dollhouse. She listened patiently, although distractedly, as they gleefully talked over each other in their excitement to be heard. Soon they were playing, and she quietly slipped out to find Emma.

'Just when I think I'm making progress, I fall into a heap,' Emma moaned as Jess entered the kitchen.

'Oh, Ems,' she said, hugging her sister closely, hoping to inject some comfort and strength. 'What's happened?' She noticed a marked deterioration since she had last visited. She now felt instantly guilty that she had slackened her visits and phone calls in the past few weeks. But with work, planning the PNG trip and trying to spend some quality time with Edward, her free time had been almost non-existent. Still, she should have made Emma a priority.

Over strong coffee at the island bench, Jess learnt that Emma had Facebooked Steve.

'Oh, Ems!' Jess could now picture what had happened, and sure enough, there for all the social media world to see were images of a gloriously happy Steve with his old—now new—flame, Zandra.

'I know I'm an idiot, but I just wanted to see what she looked like. And now I wish I hadn't. Bloody Steve! Plastered all over her Facebook and all over her!' she blurted, tears streaming down her face.

Jess found a box of tissues on the benchtop and returned, handing some over.

'What am I going to do?' she sobbed as Emma squeezed her hand.

'We will figure this out, okay? Don't worry about Steve. You have your own life to lead now.'

Jess spent a couple of hours at Emma's, workshopping ways that her sister could move forward in her life. It seemed that she'd gone two steps forward, only to regress back three or four in the past month.

With Angelina and Clementine now both at school, that only left two-year-old Annabelle requiring Emma's attention, so Jess encouraged her to consider returning to her nursing.

'I know it's earlier than you were planning, but I think it would be really good for you. It would give you something of your own, get you out of the house.'

Sensing a flash of interest from Emma, Jess proceeded with the topic, debating the merits of working in public versus private health, the hospital system or a role in a medical clinic or nursing home. They agreed that a job that offered school hours, spanned two or three days a week and was close to home would all be crucial factors. A creche was also a must.

Emma committed to calling her former nursing manager and also contacting a recruitment agency that specialised in private nursing positions. Some professional training to update her on the new way of doing things would no doubt be mandatory after a seven-year absence, but it wouldn't be too onerous, Jess blindly reassured, hoping this was true.

'But that can wait until Monday. Right now it's time for you.' Jess clapped her hands excitedly and reached for her mobile.

After a few minutes of quiet persuasion, she ended the call and told Emma to make haste. She'd just booked her in for a four-o'clock appointment with Jess's favourite hairdresser.

'What? No, I can't go today,' Emma said, aghast at the idea of doing something so spontaneous. And probably at the thought of doing something so indulgent for herself.

'Of course you can. Come on, girls!' she called

out, alerting her nieces to their expedition. 'Let's find shoes whilst Mum has a quick shower and gets changed,' Jess instructed as they all busied themselves before leaving the house a short time later.

After depositing Emma in the safe hands of Cheryl, the head stylist at her salon, Jess drove down to Balmoral Beach to spend the last rays of the afternoon on the beach. She played chasey with the girls on the sand, and when that had successfully exhausted them, they sat on the park bench, licking banana paddle pops, watching the waves lightly lap the shore.

It was a blissful end to the day, and an hour later she was picking up her revamped sister.

'My God, she's amazing,' Emma enthused of Cheryl's transformation, proudly showing off her bouncy satin curls that hung flatteringly to her shoulders. It was a marked improvement from her sister's constant limp ponytail that hung halfway down her back.

'Mummy, you look really beautiful,' said Clementine.

'That's the idea,' said Jess with a laugh as she drove them home.

Emma insisted on treating everyone to Thai takeaway, and Jess stayed on for dinner with the hope that her sister had turned the corner.

# CHAPTER 43: DOM

He had been at the bar for the past thirty-five minutes, watching his mobile phone for a message. Eventually he tapped out a quick text to check she was still coming.

As he waited impatiently for her reply to come through, she materialised in front of him.

'Sorry, Dom! I should have texted!'

Jess's face looked so worried he forgave her immediately.

'I was on a call and just couldn't figure out how to text you at the same time on my mobile. Sorry,' she said again, pecking him on the cheek as he stood to greet her.

He couldn't help smiling. She was finally here, with all her vibrant energy. Something he had come to associate with Jess, from the first time she contacted him for an interview nearly a year ago now. She had an electric current running through her—a person perpetually in motion.

After Jess took off her designer denim jacket

and headed to the bathroom, Dom ordered fresh drinks for both of them. He'd abandon the white wine he had bought when he first arrived, because it now looked warm and unappealing in its once frosted glass.

The arrival of their wine timed in with her return to the table, and she now looked more composed. He could see that Jess had applied fresh lipstick, a rich plum shade that highlighted her clear alabaster skin, which was devoid of any noticeable make-up. Her blond-streaked hair had also been tidily combed into some order.

'It's been such a full-on day, but I didn't want to reschedule because I have some exciting news.' Her blue eyes danced, and she took a quick sip of her drink. 'Oooh that's nice,' she said admiringly, looking at the glass of wine before turning her attention back to him. 'So! Guess what?' Pausing for effect only, she announced, 'I'm heading up to PNG next week!'

He sat up even straighter in his seat, his heart beginning to beat a little faster.

'What have you found out?'

'Nothing yet. But either way, I want to do a story for *Leading News* on this,' she said. 'Actually, more than *want*, I *am* doing a story on the mystery around Ryan Reynolds.'

'But we had an understanding,' he began, confused by her turnabout.

'Dom, this story is in the public domain, and I would like to do a feature about it,' she said calmly. 'I give you my word that we can review any mention of anything to do with your family. But let's be honest. That connection is a long shot,' she said kindly.

'Are you doubting what I remember?' Dom was annoyed that she had been industriously planning a feature story and a trip up to PNG without consulting him first.

'Of course not,' she said, trying to placate him. 'Don't you see? If I'm up there interviewing for my feature, it gives me a great opportunity to ask questions, to probe, and then I can still help you to establish what, if anything, links your mother to Ryan Reynolds.'

He was heartened that at least she was still pursuing his suspicions and would canvass any links with his mother.

'I'm coming then!' he found himself saying. 'I want to be there, to see what you find out.' Damned if he was going to be left out any further.

'Dom, that will just arouse suspicion,' she said worriedly. 'Plus, I need to get on and do my job. I promise I'll loop you in.'

'Like you are just getting around to doing now,' he said sarcastically, regretting his tone immediately.

'Dom, I'm sorry. I thought about discussing this with you before now, but I didn't want this situation to arise. I need to be up there independently. The moment you enter the frame, people will start asking why, and they may draw their own conclusions with your family before we do,' she said.

Dom knew what she was saying was possible. But the idea of her flying up there made him feel left out. Powerless and useless. He was determined to find a satisfactory solution for both of them.

Jess filled him in on the details of her trip. She would be departing Sydney the following Monday and overnighting in Port Moresby to catch up with the surveyors who first sighted the wrecked Jeep before flying to Mount Hagen. It would be a four-day trip in total, she would be back on Friday.

'Why don't you extend your trip over the weekend, and I'll meet you at Clancy's?' He looked at her hopefully. He had quickly calculated that he could get away and meet Jess at the end of her work trip to hear what she had unearthed. He would also get to spend time with her, something he was craving more of.

'I guess I could.' She pondered his request, admitting that she would like to catch up with Clancy again. It had been four months since they'd last met up in Sydney at Dom's BBQ, and she would like to see him and Gumawa once more.

'How is he?'

'Oh, you know Clancy!' Dom rolled his eyes. 'I'm sure the doctors have no idea what he and his new heart are doing up there. If he's not tearing around hills with Kila and the boys, he's out at the club, throwing back a few whiskies.'

He enjoyed talking about his father with Jess because she seemed to understand him. He'd seen the attachment, the fondness that had developed between the pair.

Jess said she would see if she could amend her travel plans and hopefully stay on for the weekend as a happy compromise. Dom felt like he'd just had a major win.

# CHAPTER 44: JESS

There was a comfortable familiarity when Jess excitedly walked out into the Arrival Hall at Port Moresby Airport this time. She smiled inwardly at the nervous wreck she'd been last year when she had first flown here, feeling very much a fish out of water.

Today she felt confident as she strode through the sliding doors and towards the beaming faces of both Grace and Ronnie.

Exchanging warm hugs with each of them, Jess relished the feeling of being back, wiser and more experienced. She felt totally at ease in the bustling hall and thrilled to have new friends here to greet her.

'Ronnie insisted on picking you up because you're here *on assignment*,' Grace said mockingly. 'But I couldn't miss an airport reunion, so here I am!' She laughed, giving Jess another hug. 'I've told Ronnie that you're staying with me! No arguments. I have loads of room—I mean I'm in a three-bedroom apartment for crying out loud.'

Jess had also let Ronnie know the deal, relieved

to have had an alternative to sharing the company apartment with her intimidating *Leading News* colleague, the very senior and slightly aloof foreign correspondent, Warwick Hargraves, now back from the US.

After offloading her bags at Grace's spacious apartment overlooking the harbour, they all headed to the Yacht Club for drinks. Her first South Pacific beer never tasted better, and she said so to them.

'Yeah, there's something right about an SP coldie at the Yachtie,' Ronnie agreed, later standing up to say he had to head off. 'But don't get too carried away because they can come back and bite you. See you both at midday at ARC.'

And with that he was gone.

Jess's plan was to interview Grace at the office in the morning before Ronnie arrived, and then Ronnie would arrive for the photos and video. They were going to have Grace and John re-enact looking at the drone images and capture the moment she identified the Jeep, which had sparked the full-blown investigation.

'But we're not doing that now. Tonight I want to hear all your news. You look fantastic!' she exclaimed. It was true. Grace was glowing.

'Well, I do have some news, as a matter of fact,' Grace said shyly. 'John and I have started to see each other outside of work.'

'I knew it!' said Jess. 'And I'm so *not* surprised! You guys looked like a match the first time I met you at this very place.'

'We are keeping things a little quiet. After all, he is my boss, but it feels right and I'm so happy.'

'Well, I'm really thrilled for you…' She paused.

'As it happens, I have a bit of news myself.' Jess held up her left hand and waggled her finger.

'OMG!' squealed Grace, causing a few people to look over at their table.

'It's beautiful,' Grace said, inspecting the diamond.

'We must celebrate your engagement! Come on, I'll grab some champers, and you can tell me all about it!'

As Grace went over to get the drinks, Jess felt content in how far she'd come in just six months with both her career and personal life.

The next morning at the ARC Survey office Jess could see the attraction between the pair as soon as John came out to greet them. The tension in the air was electric, and she quietly smiled to herself, wondering how they thought their colleagues didn't know.

After settling in the meeting room, Jess interviewed Grace on her iPhone recorder whilst taking notes. She corralled John into a couple of quotes and was wrapping up when Ronnie arrived.

Together they set up the re-enactment of Grace and then John scrutinising the imagery on the large computer screen. Ronnie also filmed a short version of the interviews, redone for the purposes of a video news package.

A few short hours later, Jess had left the smitten pair and was in the car with Ronnie on their way to the airport. She couldn't wait to get back to the highlands.

\*\*\*\*

Sitting opposite Detective Sana the following morning at the Mount Hagen Police Station, Jess listened to his overview of the investigation. She'd arranged the interview from Sydney and was glad she had, because the level of approvals to get to this point had been staggering.

The detective was wearing a very smart uniform, which looked like it hadn't been worn... ever. A series of medals were pinned to the front of his blazer, and she wasn't immediately sure what they were in recognition of, but they completed the official look and presented a seemingly accomplished and senior police officer. He was fiddling with a police hat, unsure whether to put it on or not. It also looked new and unworn.

'Why don't you just leave it off for now?' she suggested. 'We'll get some photos of you wearing it later.'

He looked relieved.

The interview had covered much of what Jess had already known.

Ryan Reynolds, twenty-five years of age from Cairns, Australia.

Photojournalist travelling in PNG for a story for *National Geographic* in the USA.

Arrived in PNG on a three-month visa on 12 August 1990 and last sighted in mid-September at a small village just twenty kilometres west of Goroka, on the eve of the town's major show.

Cause of death: a gunshot wound.

Body discovered twenty-eight years later, approximately halfway between Goroka and Mount Hagen in dense jungle off the highway.

Whilst she hadn't learnt anything new, Jess at least had achieved fresh remarks *on the record.*

As she wound up her interview with Detective Sana, he pulled out a manilla folder and opened it. Riffling through, he then produced two plastic sleeves containing a series of six photographs and placed them on his desk.

'This is the only record we have linking Mr Reynolds to his last-known sightings.'

The photos had been the only ones to survive their grassy grave, and each provided a clue to the intrepid traveller's journey.

In one photo, a group of children and adult men stood together. They were highly decorated with brightly painted faces, in purples, yellows, reds and green. They also wore beads and shells around their necks and naked bodies.

'We have spoken to the villagers and believe that this one was taken on the night before the Goroka Show—a big festival here in the highlands. We suspect it was one in a series but haven't been able to recover the other film. It was too badly damaged.'

Whether Ryan had made it to the festival on the 14th of September wasn't known due to a lack of any salvageable imagery.

'Well, there may be,' he said, 'but we can't be sure as not many photos survived. It's a very big event—too many people—lots of expats with cameras. Nobody has come forward to report either way.' He shrugged his shoulders as he sat back in his office chair.

Jess studied the photos one by one. The second and third pictures were close-ups of two spectacular orchids. The intricate flowers looked exotic, delicate and out of place in the wilds around them.

The fourth photo was an artistic shot, overlooking the Goroka district, according to Detective Sana.

The fifth was a close-up of a sign outlining where the photo was taken—Togeric National Park, Goroka—perhaps for his records later on, thought Jess. This was something she had got in the habit of doing herself—taking photos of the place before or after a series of photographs to help remind her where the images had been taken.

Photo six was the only intimate shot in the collection. Taken inside a dimly lit room, it was the only one to include Ryan. The image depicted Ryan with two young women. Despite the poor state of the black-and-white photo, all three were smiling at the camera and holding up their drinks as if asked to chorus "cheers."

'This one looks to have been taken at a social club in the highlands, at Gumawa—about sixty kilometres east of here, heading to Goroka,' he said, piquing Jess's sudden interest. She stared intently at the people in the photo with Ryan, looking for some semblance of familiarity.

'Who are the women in the picture?'

'We don't know.' He shook his head and shrugged. 'We've taken the photo to a few places, including the club in Gumawa, but no one knows who the people are in the image.' He sounded defeated.

*Could one of these women be Dom's mother? Was she actually sitting there having a drink with Ryan?* Her mind was racing, trying to recall Dom's mother's appearance in the few photos she had seen when she visited the family home.

'Can I take a copy of each of these? Just on my

iPhone here?' she asked.

'Why don't I do it, Jess? It'll look better in the story,' Ronnie piped up, reminding Jess of their reason for being there. The newspaper feature she had been commissioned to write.

'Of course!' she said, quickly recovering. 'Can we grab some photocopies as well?'

Detective Sana obliged.

Ronnie and Jess left the police station and checked into the hotel where they'd overnight before making an early start the following day to Goroka—a 170-kilometre drive away.

They were hoping to visit some of the sites in the photos to see what else they could glean. After that they'd circle back to Mount Hagen where Jess would farewell Ronnie and meet up with Dom for the weekend.

Why was that fact eliciting goose bumps? she wondered.

# CHAPTER 45: DOM

Dom had been refreshing his iPhone screen all day, checking he hadn't missed a call or text. But on that front, his phone remained stubbornly silent.

Saying good night to Marcus, he strode out to his car and pressed Jess's number as he started up his car to head home.

'Hey, Jess,' he said, relieved to finally hear her melodic voice on the second ring.

'Dom?' She sounded a little wary at hearing from him. 'Is everything okay?'

'Yeah, fine here. I just wanted to check in and see how things are up there?'

'All good. Yep. All fine here.' Her voice had a strange note to it, and he wished he was with her to read her face for clues.

'Right. So how did today go?' He was dying of curiosity.

'Oh good, good,' she replied vaguely.

'Did you speak with the Mount Hagen police?' Dom tried to hide the eagerness from his voice.

'Yes, it went really well.' Jess sighed, before finally elaborating on some of the information Detective Sana had shared in her interview.

'But nothing new?' he asked hopefully, as everything she had so far shared was what he had already read in the old online news stories.

'Not at this stage,' she said somewhat ambiguously. *Was she hinting there might be something in the future?*

'But there could be?' he asked hopefully.

'Not sure. Hey, give a girl a chance. We've only been up here twenty-four hours,' she said lightly reprimanding, now sounding more like herself.

Finally he let out a chuckle and relaxed his shoulders. 'Yeah, sorry. Just a bit impatient back here, wondering how it's all going up there.'

'Well, it's pretty good to be back,' she exclaimed, sounding genuinely cheery at being in the highlands.

'Looks like PNG has woven its magic,' he said.

Hearing her laughter echo down the line, he wished he was back there too. With her.

# CHAPTER 46: JESS

All in all, the four-day trip had been a mixed bag. Certainly colour, culture and characters were aplenty, but as for information about the mysterious photojournalist, nothing new was forthcoming.

The village people they met with were excited to again see the copy of the photograph featuring their clan before the Goroka Show. Ronnie explained that the photo was very old, and the children in the image would now be grown adults.

After much talk, two male adults were brought forward. They looked about the right age, but Jess failed to see the resemblance given the age difference from then to now.

'Apparently these are two of the young *lik liks*, you know the *children*, posing in the photo,' Ronnie said to Jess.

'That's great.' She felt like they were getting somewhere, only for moments later to have her hopes dashed.

'No, unfortunately they don't remember the

photo being taken. Nor the photojournalist. Apparently, they told the police this,' Ronnie translated.

Feeling a fresh wave of disappointment, she looked over at the two men, who both hung their heads, as if sensing they'd let Jess down.

'You can't blame them, hey? They would have been like two or three? I'm not sure I can remember that much from when I was that age.'

'You're right, Ronnie,' she said, feeling guilty for having had such unrealistic expectations.

'It's okay! No worries,' she said, smiling at the men. 'Ronnie, please thank them for us?'

The only place that really connected Ryan to the region was the club in Gumawa, but as the detective had flagged, the identities of the women in the photo remained a mystery.

She felt a fresh wave of guilt, this time at having evaded Dom's questions on whether she'd unearthed anything new. But the last thing she wanted to do was to build up his hopes, only to have them dashed like hers had been earlier at the village.

The current general manager of the Anzac Club in Gumawa, Miles Davey, was a man in his early forties who had only been in the role for eighteen months. Whilst he couldn't offer any useful information on the members back in 1990, he produced one name for them to try.

'I reckon he'll be able to help,' he had said, handing over the name and phone number of Clancy Jonson.

She felt a tingle taking the slip of paper.

Coincidence or something more?

Irrespective of what Clancy revealed, she

would have enough for a very interesting feature story on Ryan Reynolds at any rate. And perhaps this evening's catch-up with Clancy might provide a clue?

Jess bought a can of Coke at the café at the small airport at Mount Hagen after waving off Ronnie. He and Dom were virtually swapping seats on the thirty-seat Cessna as it completed its daily circuit between Mount Hagen and Port Moresby.

Twenty minutes later, a grinning Dom emerged, wearing his familiar Akubra hat and carrying a small backpack over his shoulder. Casually dressed, he looked carefree and younger somehow. He reminded her of Ryan, and she wondered again about the young man's fate so many years earlier.

Dom grabbed her in a friendly hug, and she held on for a moment, savouring the growing familiarity of this man.

They walked outside the terminal where a Toyota truck was waiting for them. Jess didn't recognise the driver from her previous trip to the plantation, however Dom did and shook the man's hand vigorously. They talked in fluent Motu for much of the trip, and Jess settled in the back seat, relieved that any conversation about Ryan would be postponed for now.

When they pulled up at the front entrance to the homestead, Jess was again stunned by the magnificence of the property.

'Well, hello!' Clancy swaggered over to them with a broad grin as they got out of the truck.

'Clancy, it's great to see you,' Jess said, pecking him on the cheek before Dom clasped his father's hand and went in for a half embrace.

Jess was pleased to see the change that had

come about between the pair since her first meeting with each of them, when Dom seemed resentful and angry with his father. The relationship had indeed softened and developed a closeness that was sorely lacking before.

They settled on the back veranda, Clancy mixing a gin and tonic for Jess and handing two SP beers to Dom to open.

After catching up on general news, Clancy moved the spotlight to Jess.

'So, what brings you up here again?' he asked.

Jess expanded on the feature she was writing for *Leading News* and her attempts to unearth a few more details to ensure the piece had a fresh perspective.

As Dom went to fetch a new round of drinks, Jess opened up her notebook to spell out the village name she and Ronnie had visited just a few days ago. Unfortunately, the photos inside the notebook suddenly spilled to the ground.

The picture of Ryan posing with the two mystery women landed on top of the small pile and was clear to see.

Clancy leant down to pick up the image. 'Where did you get this?' he asked, not taking his eyes off the photo.

'It's one of the photos the police salvaged from the photojournalist's camera. That's him in the middle,' she said, before cautiously adding, 'It was taken here, apparently, at the Anzac Club.'

Clancy continued to stare at the photo in deathly silence.

It was evident that the women's identities were no longer a mystery.

# CHAPTER 47: DOM

Walking back onto the veranda, Dom placed the drinks down.

'Here we go,' he said chirpily before noticing the silent tension at the table. He looked from one to the other and saw the photograph in Clancy's trembling hand.

'What's this? Where did the photo come from?'

No one said anything.

'Is that Mum?' he asked beseechingly of Clancy, who eventually nodded.

'And that's the photojournalist. Ryan Reynolds,' Jess added nervously.

'So, Mum did meet him?' he asked weakly, now feeling oddly deflated at having his own suspicions confirmed.

'Yes,' Clancy replied, dropping the photo as if it were scalding his hands to touch it. He slowly got up from the table and left the veranda.

Picking up the photo, Dom studied it, tracing the image of his mother.

He was still confused and now looked at Jess, raising an eyebrow.

Hurriedly, Jess explained that this was the only photo of its type in the collection of six, showing him the printouts of the others. But they didn't interest him. He couldn't help but come back to this photo of the three smiling faces. One of which was his mother.

'Do you know who the other woman is?' Jess asked cautiously.

'It's Elena,' said Clancy, returning. 'Sarah's cousin. She was visiting from Switzerland.'

Holding a glass of whisky in his hand, Clancy sat down and began to tell a story. His face was still ashen but he seemed to have regained some measure of control.

'They were inseparable,' he began, taking a swig. 'Elena had a real phobia about flying, so she only visited Gumawa the once. She and Sarah wrote all the time. Eventually when phone calls didn't cost the earth, they would call each other and talk.

'I never saw Sarah look so happy as she was when she had her soul sister here.' Clancy paused, as if reflecting on happier times. He looked out at the view, which had now transformed into a pretty sunset of pinks and pastels.

After a time, Jess encouraged Clancy to continue. 'So, this was in 1990, when Ryan was travelling these parts?'

'Must be,' he grumbled. 'Yeah, Elena came at the tail end of harvesting the Majenca coffee crop—which was a big deal at the time. I remember being grateful Elena was here as I was working fourteen-hour days for much of the time and out of town a lot. I had a lot riding on Majenca. It was our first major.'

'Were you there?' Dom asked, looking at the photo.

'No.' Clancy shook his head. 'I don't even recall ever taking Elena to the club.' He looked puzzled. 'But I was away for some of her stay, I remember that.'

After quickly draining his glass, he reached for the beer that Dom had brought back to the table earlier. Stabbing his finger at the photo he said, 'I know exactly who he is. He's exactly what I imagined!'

Dom couldn't believe what he was hearing. His mother knew the missing man. The *murdered* man?

Both he and Jess remained silent; he was too stunned to talk. Clancy clearly had things he wanted to say. Things that Dom had waited a lifetime to hear.

'That's right! Elena met me in Moresby after her stay.' Clancy sounded excited at the recollection.

'Yeah, that's right. I was already in town, and Elena and I flew on to Australia together. She was a nervous flyer, and we thought it would help if I travelled one of the legs with her. I was always flying back and forth to Brisbane back then. I remember getting back to the plantation afterwards and thinking something was up. Nothing major. Just small things. Sarah smiling when she didn't think anyone was looking. Speaking in Swiss German on the phone, being secretive, that sort of thing.'

Clancy looked at Dom, and then his eyes moved to the distant mountain range.

'It's hard to describe, but I also felt that there had been a presence in the home that I didn't like. Yeah, I know it all sounds like superstitious claptrap, but I really sensed someone had been in my home that I didn't know and didn't want to know.'

Sloshing more wine into the glasses, Clancy continued. 'Months went by, and Sarah had withdrawn into herself a bit… a lot. Elena's calls became more frequent—which was unusual as calls to Zurich still cost a bloody fortune.

'And then I saw what was bleedingly obvious—her round stomach. Your mother was pregnant, and I felt like a bloody fool! An idiot!' Clancy thumped the table, worrying Dom, who watched him anxiously.

'I remember being angry that my suspicions were right. No, it was more than that. I was gutted. You see, it wasn't mine. The baby.' He looked at Jess, who calmly stared back at him in understanding.

'I knew,' he said again, stabbing his finger at the blurry face of Ryan. 'He had corrupted her. My Sarah.'

Clancy sat back away from the photo, as if seeking distance from it.

Dom watched his father cautiously now, dreading where this story would go next but powerless to stop it.

'We rowed about it, and I'll never forgive myself for that. Just one night she said it was. But I was so bloody angry. She fell. My God, she just rolled down the stairs like a doll. I ran down after her, but my precious Sarah…'

Clancy began to weep and shake as he put his head into his hands.

Tears slid down Dom's face, too. His memory of that night rushed in. Laying on the grass watching the moon and waking to a noise. He didn't know if it was voices or a crashing thump that had brought him to his feet. His body revolted at the thought of Clancy in full rage and his mother at the top of the stairs, trying to defend herself.

Noticing his son's fearful face, he blurted, 'It was an accident! She just fell. Just stepped back, off the landing.'

Shaking his head now, he pushed his beer away.

'But who am I kidding? I may as well have pushed her, because it was me she was trying to get away from.' He groaned like a wounded animal. His shoulders jerked, and a guttural sound came from within him. It was distressing to watch.

Dom was paralysed with inaction. He had never seen his dad so much as cry, let alone break down like this. He felt powerless to act and could only sit there mutely watching his father's outburst.

Jess shifted uncomfortably in her seat before standing up to pat Dom's shoulder.

'I'm sorry,' she murmured before leaving him alone to sit with a father he didn't recognise.

# CHAPTER 48: JESS

After hiding away for the best part of an hour, Jess walked tentatively down the stairs.

The light was now fading, and Dom and Clancy were still sitting on the veranda, now talking quietly.

She padded into the kitchen to find some sustenance, switching on the kitchen lights and scanning the fridge. There was an abundant range of cheeses, and she pulled out a selection and prepared a plate with olives, tapenade and savoury biscuits. It was an interim measure, but it would do. She doubted anyone would feel like a proper meal tonight.

As she walked out with the platter and an apologetic smile, she could see Clancy reaching for a half-empty bottle of red wine and generously refilling their glasses. He smiled weakly at her and poured her one.

Accepting it, she sat down to join them.

Clancy's anger had dissipated, and a strange mood hung over the table.

She felt the need to say something. 'Sorry about the photo. It's not how I intended to ask you about it. Miles Davey suggested I speak with you, you know, being a long-time member of the club. He thought you may recognise the women, but I honestly didn't know who they were.'

Dom gave her a bemused look, and Clancy nodded.

'I never met the man,' Clancy said, looking at Jess and moving to watch his son. He seemed to want them to believe him. 'Never even sighted him.' Shaking his head, he continued. 'I'd heard what a hit he'd been at the club. And I never knew what that meant. I didn't even know Sarah had been there… It wasn't until months later when I saw Sarah with her stom—' He put his hand on to his stomach but couldn't finish.

Then, his anger returning he said, 'Yeah, he cast his spell all right. The bastard!' Red wine spilled from his glass as he thumped the table. 'I never met him. But I hated him!'

Neither Dom nor Clancy seemed interested in the cheese plate, and one by one they drifted off to their rooms. Dom left first, looking shell-shocked at what he'd learnt, followed by a bedraggled Clancy.

She packed away the food and busied herself in the kitchen, stacking the dishwasher and putting the numerous beer and wine bottles in the recycling before turning out the light.

Back in her room, she thirstily drank two glasses of tap water and made her way to her bed.

Learning of Sarah and Ryan's brief affair was pure gold for her feature, but what did it mean? It provided a good motive for Clancy, but she couldn't see him as a murderer, despite his hatred for this apparent stranger whom he said he'd never seen before. His grief for Sarah was devastating, compelling.

But then again, how do you know what someone is capable of, she pondered? Could any of us have what it takes given the right circumstances? Actually, no! She shook herself with clarity. It takes someone with a different outlook on life and death to do that. Clancy couldn't have hurt either of them.

She was about to turn out the lamp when she remembered she hadn't plugged in her mobile phone and laptop to charge, and so she reluctantly got up to fetch them from the corner chair in her room. That's when she noticed three missed calls from Edward, but as it was nearly midnight, she would call him back in the morning. Without further thought, she switched off the light and fell into a troubled sleep.

Jess awoke to a pounding headache at dawn. Pulling on a pair of denim shorts and floaty floral top, she quietly made her way downstairs with her now powered-up gadgets.

She avoided switching on any lights until she'd made it to the kitchen. Quietly filling the coffee machine, she let it do its work whilst she downed headache tablets with a glass of water.

Taking a mug of coffee to the kitchen table, she then sat down and opened her laptop and began to type.

She was miles away, writing her article, when she heard a ping on her phone and saw a message from Edward.

'Are you awake?'

'Yes xx'

Within moments her phone rang, and she rushed to answer it, hoping it hadn't woken the house.

'Good morning, darling,' said Edward into the phone as Jess stood up to stretch her limbs after sitting still for over an hour or more on her computer.

'Hi,' she murmured quietly.

'I tried you a few times last night. Is everything okay?'

Jess reassured him things were fine, explaining that it had been a late night and the household was all still asleep.

'You can call me anytime, you know that,' he said. 'How is it over there?'

'Oh, where to begin,' she said. 'Let's just say it has been a busy few days and last night was enlightening. I'll fill you in when I get back.'

'Is it difficult to talk?' he asked.

'Yes and no. Everyone is still sleeping here, plus I'm not sure where to begin. Anyway, how are you? Is everything okay at your end?' she asked, keen to change the conversation.

'Actually, that was the reason for my calls last night.' His voice rang with excitement but also a slight reprimand that she hadn't phoned. 'I've been offered a promotion!'

Without missing a beat he continued. 'So, how do you feel about living in Munich?'

Momentarily stunned, Jess clenched the handset as Edward continued to talk.

'My new role is in the global lending leadership team, headquartered out of Munich. They want me back, Jessica. It's so fantastic! It's sooner than I imagined, but it was always a matter of time, so why not now, hey?' He was brimming with excitement, and Jess's feeble head tried to take it in.

She was blindsided by the news and sat down

on the rocking chair in the far corner of the veranda. She hadn't even realised she'd walked out there and was grateful for the fresh morning breeze wafting across the deck.

Eventually she found her voice. 'Edward, I'm really pleased about the promotion, but Munich is a bit of a shock.'

'But you liked Munich when we were there at the start of the year, didn't you?' he asked defensively.

'Yes, it's a beautiful city. But we were just *visiting*. I thought you still had at least a year, maybe more, on your contract in Sydney?' She was confused. 'We didn't discuss where we would live after that.'

'I am German, Jessica,' he stated unnecessarily. 'I could never see myself living anywhere else long-term. Sure, two years here, and maybe in the future other contracts in other countries, but fundamentally Munich is my home. It is where I will always want to live.' He sounded adamant, and it rankled.

Noticing movement and voices inside, Jess was keen to finish the call and collect herself before greeting Clancy and Dom.

'I'll be home on Sunday night, so let's have a good chat about everything then,' she said, trying to sound upbeat, despite feeling completely upended by his news.

'I will come to the airport to pick you up, so just send through your flight details. I love you,' he sang as she ended the call.

Munich? Why did they never discuss the *where* in their future? Was she naive to assume that they would stay in Sydney? But he had never raised the topic of returning home, or had he? Was it always assumed? And why did it have to be so soon!.

# CHAPTER 49: DOM

Dom entered the kitchen to find Clancy cutting up fruit for breakfast. A very normal scene if they hadn't gone through the roller coaster of last night.

'Good morning.' Clancy's voice sounded deeper, hoarser than usual, but otherwise he gave the impression of his regular self, busily chopping up the pineapple. Beside him was a large bowl brimming with pawpaw, banana, watermelon and a myriad of other fruits, revealing he'd been at it for some time.

'Morning,' Dom mumbled, reaching for the coffee like a man dying of thirst. His head felt foggy, and he wasn't sure if it was due to the fraught sleep he'd had, last night's revelations or the concoction of beer, wine and brandy. Possibly all three.

'Hi. How did everyone sleep?' Jess asked, coming in from the veranda.

He'd seen her out there on the phone and wondered if she was already filing her scoop. But when he looked at her properly, he could only see concern etched across her pale face.

'I wish I could say I slept well, Jess, but I'd be lying,' Clancy responded in a weary tone, putting down the knife as if the task no longer interested him. 'Yesterday brought up a lot of memories, seeing that photo of Sarah and Elena after so many years.'

'I'm sure,' Jess soothed. 'Can I get you a coffee?'

'Black. Thank you,' Clancy responded.

'No worries. Let me finish this, and I'll bring it out,' she said kindly as Clancy moved lethargically to the veranda. Dom was touched by her kindness to Clancy and decided to let go of the annoyance he'd felt towards her for harbouring the photo, not forewarning him.

He ferried cereal bowls and spoons to the table, returning to get the muesli, yoghurt and juice.

'I still can't believe there's an old photo of Mum with Ryan Reynolds,' Dom said, now sitting at the table with a second coffee.

'And then for him to turn up after all these years. It doesn't make sense. I mean what happened to him?' he said, more to himself than the others. He thought by understanding how his mother died, he'd have no more questions, but now he had so many.

'I don't know, and I don't really care, if I'm brutally honest,' Clancy said.

'You know how dangerous the highlands can be?' Jess suggested.

'Especially back then,' Clancy added. 'The late eighties and early nineties were the height of problems up here. Post-independence, the place was a basket case. Lots of rascal gangs—and not just in Port Moresby.'

His father reached for the fruit and spooned a

tiny portion into his bowl.

'Clancy, please have more than that,' Jess encouraged. 'Neither of you ate anything last night.'

Clancy shrugged and sat back into his seat, and Dom just toyed with his spoon, not hungry.

'I wouldn't be driving the Mount Hagen highway on my own—not now and certainly not then,' Clancy continued. 'Anyway, that's all a puzzle for the police now, isn't it?'

Dom gave Jess a quick look, curious if she had any more surprises to spring on him. She looked away, instead, burying herself in the task of helping herself to the muesli, yoghurt and fruit. Dom reluctantly joined her, still puzzling over everything.

'I better get off,' Clancy said, picking up his plate and leaving the table. 'I'll be at the roasting shed if you need me.' And with that, he left the kitchen.

'It's a pretty plausible explanation he has. A highway robbery gone wrong maybe?' she murmured. 'It's certainly one of the police theories, and I've read more than a few online articles that paint a vivid picture of the violence and inter-tribal wars in the highlands over the past few decades.'

'Yeah. His death could be a random carjacking. A gang attack. And nothing to do with...' Dom couldn't finish, but he suspected that Jess knew what he was about to say. Or did she? Even he wasn't sure whether it was his mother or Clancy he was now trying to protect.

Suddenly he needed space and stood up abruptly.

'I'll go and help Clancy,' he stammered, just needing to get away.

# CHAPTER 50: JESS

Dom looked spooked, and Jess's heart ached for him, watching him scurry away.

Picking up her mobile phone, she looked up Detective Sana's number and pressed the Call button.

'I have something for you,' she said, biting her lip, still uncertain how to play this. 'I'm actually staying for the weekend here at Gumawa with Clancy Jonson and his son Dom. Do you know them?' She wanted to get this out into the open. Otherwise, what possible reason could she have for showing them the photo?

'Not directly, but I know who Mr Jonson senior is. The large coffee plantation?'

'Yes,' she said, progressing to ramble for a few minutes, emphasising the friendship they'd all developed during her PNG posting last year and Dom's invitation to stay on in the highlands this weekend.

'So, it turns out,' she said, playing for casual but feeling like she was missing the mark by a mile, 'one of the two women in the photo with Ryan Reynolds is, or was, Sarah Jonson. Clancy's wife. She died sometime ago. The second woman is her cousin, who was visiting from Switzerland. She's also deceased.'

What she didn't share was that Sarah and Ryan had had a brief affair. That would be for Clancy to divulge if he chose to.

'You would make a good detective,' he said, impressed. 'I'll speak with Mr Jonson on Monday. I will leave him to enjoy his weekend with you and his son. Perhaps mention this?'

As she ended the call, she noticed a few new emails, including one from a cousin of Ryan's who knew him in Cairns. He'd attached an old photograph of Ryan—who looked to be a teenager in the shot, maybe fifteen or so. He was sitting on a BMX bike and grinning at the camera, his mop of wild blond hair illuminated by the light.

She took her time to study the photo. She was getting to know more about this man, this cheeky teenager, intrepid traveller and solo adventurer who for all intents and purposes lived life to the full.

Jess spent the rest of the day working on her story, with intermittent breaks as Clancy and Dom wandered in and out of the house before jumping in vehicles and driving away.

Lena popped in for a few hours to tidy and fix their lunch, and Jess helped herself to the stack of salad and chicken sandwiches before resuming writing. The men would have theirs later when they returned.

Dinner that night was a casual affair, and Mika came to join them for an outdoor BBQ. As Jess topped up the biscuits on the cheese platter at the outside table, she took the opportunity to watch Dom chatting with Mika. He looked so at ease in this setting, and she wondered why he would choose to leave it behind to return to Sydney if had the choice.

Jess also observed Mika's maternal affection towards Dom and occasional smiles across to Clancy as he cooked the fish on the grill. She wondered, not for the first time, if there was a romance between the pair... or at least the desire for one from a devoted and loyal Mika.

Catching her looking over at them, Dom signalled for her to join them, and she sealed up the biscuit tin and moved over to them.

'I have been telling Dom that we want to see more of him from now on,' Mika said, reaching over to grasp Dom's hand. 'We miss you, don't we, Clancy?' she called over.

Her mothering instincts were on show, and Jess thought how sweet it was that Mika was here for both men.

# CHAPTER 51: DOM

They were sitting hunched over their bitter coffees at the small, crowded café/bar in the Departures lounge in Port Moresby, having landed not long before from Mount Hagen. Jess was absorbed in her phone, reading the download of emails materialising on her screen. Dom couldn't muster the enthusiasm to pull out his device, instead he sat pondering the events of the past few days. Being back at Gumawa. His mother and Ryan Reynolds? Clancy and his look of sadness, possibly regret, when they exchanged goodbyes a few hours earlier. It wasn't normal for Clancy to show his emotions, but this weekend had been anything but normal.

*I could have had a brother or sister,* he thought forlornly at what might have been.

Dom had stayed up late into the night with his father and a bottle of Cointreau. It was the first time the old man had opened up and revealed the depth of his heartache, his despair at having lost his beloved Sarah in the fall. He spoke of his failure, his inability to be a decent father to Dom.

'That's why I sent you away so fast to that boarding school. You just reminded me too much of her,' he had said apologetically.

Clancy had been humiliated by Sarah's actions, her betrayal. He'd been furious, angry and so disappointed that she could do that to him.

'But it was really me I was angry at. I had been a stupid, conceited fool.' He scolded himself for taking Sarah for granted. For not giving her what she most wanted.

Clancy said it had taken a stranger to wake him up and give Sarah what she most wanted—another child. But he stressed that, in time, he would have accepted this child as his own. He knew he would because she—or he—would have been half Sarah.

'It was just a fleeting period in your mother's life, not something that defined her,' he said with strength, looking at Dom intently, as if to say let that be a lesson learnt.

Dom just wished his father had opened up decades before.

'Your mother was a beautiful, precious wife and mother.' He was emphasising this as much to Dom, as to himself.

'Are you okay?' Jess asked, breaking Dom out of his thoughts and returning him back into the bustling café they were sitting in.

Looking over at her worried face, he shrugged. 'Clancy will never forgive himself. He blames himself for, well, for everything. The weird thing is that I forgive him. For so many years I thought he was a crap father, and all along he's been paying the price, suffering guilt and sadness. Their last moments are something that he can never take back.'

He felt Jess's hand reach out and hold his, and he squeezed hers in gratitude. They sat companionably and finished their coffees as the boarding announcement came through.

The flight was uneventful, with Dom closing his eyes and attempting to catch up on missed sleep. The frequent times he opened his eyes, he noticed Jess flicking through the movie options. No doubt she too was distracted and finding it hard to settle.

A few hours later, they were finally off the plane and clearing immigration. As he followed her through into the Arrival Hall at Sydney Airport, a man rushed forward and enveloped Jess, twirling her about before indulging in a passionate kiss.

Dom slowly moved over to the side, feeling awkward during what was clearly an intimate reunion with her fiancé. After a minute or two, they walked over hand in hand, both flushed and smiling.

'Dom, this is Edward. Edward, Dom,' she said, a little flustered.

Edward extended his hand in greeting, and Dom felt compelled to meet him halfway.

'Can I give you a lift, Dom?' he asked politely, although all Dom could see was a smug suit wanting to rub his face in it.

'No, you guys head off. I'm fine to jump in a cab,' he quipped, ushering them off.

As he walked to the cab rank, he felt lonelier than he ever had.


An hour later, back at his apartment, he was restless. He had showered, thrown his clothes into a short wash cycle, finally checked emails and stared at the empty contents of his fridge as if the longer he looked, the sooner something would materialise. He wasn't ready to see Lauren and wasn't sure why. So many emotions going through his head—his mother's affair, his father's admissions and then of course seeing Jess with Edward.

The guy in the suit didn't seem right for her. Too polished and showy. He wasn't what Jess needed. She was soft and fun and relaxed and… He stopped himself from thinking about her. *She's engaged! She's in love, so get over yourself!* he reprimanded.

Grabbing his car keys and flicking a quick text, he headed down to the basement and unlocked his Audi SUV, clambering in and screeching out of the car park. He needed a distraction tonight.

\*\*\*\*

'Dom, you're back?' Lauren looked pleased to see him when he arrived at her front door, having buzzed him in just moments earlier. She lived alone in a high-rise apartment block in Potts Point, and her apartment was stylishly decorated with cream and beige furniture throughout. A statement piece of wall art—swirls of blues, greens and browns— broke up the neutrality.

She had been cooking, and Dom followed her into the kitchen. Opening the fridge, she pulled out a bottle of rosé and suggested he find two glasses.

'I wasn't sure you'd be back so soon. How was it?' she asked as she stirred the risotto on the stovetop.

Not knowing where to start, Dom drained his glass and refilled it.

'Okaaay…' Lauren stopped and watched him carefully.

'Mum had an affair,' he blurted. 'Yeah. It turns out my mother was pregnant when she died. Clancy shared the whole sorry saga,' he said sarcastically, refilling his glass.

'And you believe Clancy is telling the truth?' she asked after hearing the full story. They were now seated together on the lounge. The saucepan of risotto had been put to one side.

'Yeah, I do.' He wished he didn't, but that was the truth.

'I so wanted to blame him for Mum's death, but when he described the events that night, well, it was exactly as I remembered them. Quarrelling, then just silence. He was in shock, the same as me, when we saw Mum on the ground. Just lying there.' He swallowed. 'Clancy's emotions the other night were pure pain. The same as mine. So, yes, I believe him.' *God damnit*, he almost muttered.

Dom found another bottle of rosé and opened it whilst Lauren served up the over-cooked mushroom risotto, and they sat at her oval dining table. The dim lamps and quiet jazz were soothing. So too the wine, which he had been consuming liberally for the past hour.

Lauren cleared their plates to the kitchen, and he heard her rinsing and stacking them in the dishwasher. As she returned to the table, he grabbed her hand and pulled her down on his lap. They locked eyes before he lost himself in kissing her slender neck, her face and eventually her lips.

He felt manic and impatient and didn't want to think about anything but right now.

\*\*\*\*

The next morning, when he woke, he was disorientated until he turned to see Lauren sleeping peacefully beside him. He watched her sleep, her breath quiet and steady, and thought about the feelings he had for this beautiful woman beside him.

She had been his university sweetheart, his wife, his ex-wife, a colleague, a lover and a friend. He knew she would always be a special part of his life, but was it enough? Was he in love with Lauren? He loved her, sure, but was it the same thing? Was he confusing the two? The feelings he had last night at seeing Edward hold Jess had stirred something within him that he couldn't ignore.

As he continued to gaze at Lauren, her eyelids began to flutter and eventually open. She smiled when she saw him staring at her.

Leaning over she kissed him softly on the lips, saying, 'Let's take things slowly this time.'

And they did.

# CHAPTER 52: JESS

Jess had been surprised at Edward's public display of affection at the airport. It was unlike him to be so physically demonstrative, but he'd obviously missed her. He insisted on taking her out to dinner, so they swung by her place first so she could change into a light cotton sweater, jeans and ballet flats. She was already feeling the chill after her brief stint in the tropics. Tying her loose curls into a high ponytail, she added a light moisturiser, mascara and a touch of lip gloss and went to find Edward, who was reclined on the sofa, watching the ABC seven-o'clock news.

'Ready?' he asked, looking up at her adoringly.

'Yes, let's eat! I'll grab a red?' She picked up a bottle from her rack whilst Edward switched off the television.

The local Thai restaurant was just a short walk from her home, and they strolled in hand in hand.

She ordered their dishes whilst Edward poured the wine and raised his glass to her.

'To my darling fiancée. I'm so happy to have

you back,' he said somewhat gushingly.

Jess smiled and clinked her glass to his before savouring a sip. 'So, tell me more about your new role,' she prompted, wanting to release the elephant in the room.

Edward became animated as he filled her in about his new role and the generous salary package that came with it. He then looked a little meek when he said that he would be flying to Munich the following week to meet the global team before the start date in June, six weeks away.

'I can also look for an apartment for us,' he enthused, entwining their fingers. 'Or would you prefer a small cottage, further out of the city?'

The question struck Jess. It was the first time he had asked what she would like, and it rankled.

'What about my job?' she asked lightly, as she began to wrap a prawn in betel leaf before popping the parcel into her mouth to deliciously devour. A deliberate attempt to silence herself from creating waves.

'I'll be making serious money now, so you don't need to worry about that,' he said, looking excessively proud of his newfound status with the bank.

'It's not about money,' she said, attempting to keep the mood calm and conversational. 'You know how much I love working, and let's remember it was me who got a promotion just a few short months ago. Something I'm still pretty excited about.'

Perhaps sensing she wasn't happy with his plan, Edward enthusiastically offered to put some feelers out for a journalist job.

'I don't speak German,' she said tightly. 'And

I'm not sure I want a different job than the one I have now.' She wasn't meaning to be difficult or to sour the mood, but she also didn't like being put into premature retirement this early into her career. A career she felt was finally taking off.

As the entrée was cleared and the main courses served, Edward refilled their glasses and waited for the server to leave.

'What are you saying? Don't you want to move to Munich?' he asked, now looking annoyed that she wasn't embracing his plans.

'I'm not saying anything. I just wish we had talked about this before you accepted the job.' *And before we got engaged,* she thought.

'Darling, we already had this conversation,' he said patiently, as if talking to a child. 'I'm German and I didn't think it would come as a surprise that I would want to live there, at least from time to time.

'The way things work with Bavaria Bank, I could get a contract to work back in Sydney, or Singapore, or New York, or somewhere else in a few years. I thought you loved travel and that you would be excited to have the opportunity to do this together?'

She knew she was being difficult, but she was also feeling decidedly ignored in the whole equation. Was she being unreasonable to expect that Edward would consider her job? Or where she might want to live? She didn't think she was being unfair, but then again, if the tables were turned, would he be so obliging? She knew she was as ambitious as he was, and that had been part of the attraction.

In an effort to lighten the tone and to appear more supportive, she murmured, 'I could probably speak to Paul and find out if *Leading News* has any opportunities or affiliations in Europe.' It wasn't ideal, nor what she wanted, but what else could she do?

The suggestion instantly excited Edward, who eagerly chatted about the media network in Germany and its proximity to the United Kingdom and also the United Nations in Geneva. He began to elaborate on the wealth of communication roles that Germany offered, as if this was the opportunity of a lifetime for her.

Thankfully the dinner had been salvaged, and after eating their way through Penang duck curry, green vegetable stir-fry and rice, they paid the bill and headed back to Jess's apartment.

****

Jess awoke groggily to Edward's five thirty alarm and his warm embrace, before finding herself alone minutes later. Edward had gone home to prepare for the office. Wide awake now, she decided there was no point lying in and got up. Putting on her running gear, she quietly exited the apartment block for a predawn jog. She hadn't run for a while but felt the need to pound the pavement this morning. She still had some residual annoyance to work off.

Jess started off slowly, easing her body back into it, soon finding her natural rhythm. She ran down to Balmoral Beach in time to see a spectacular sunrise over the water before taking a winding route back up the hill to the village of Mosman. After forty minutes, she slowed down to a walk as she entered the shopping village, which was coming alive with the local newsagents and greengrocers now opening, and a queue forming at the small French bakery that sold her favourite pastries and bread. Trucks and vans of all sizes were arriving or departing along the high street, unloading their produce for the new day and the new week ahead. Jess pulled out the five-dollar note she had pocketed in her shorts and picked up a double almond latte to savour on her short walk back to her apartment.

She felt energised by the time she had showered and was waiting for the seven thirty bus to take her into the city. This morning Jess had dressed in her favourite Scanlan and Theodore black slim pants and a floaty silk blouse, adorned with a string of colourful beads and heels. After a week of dressing down in PNG, she enjoyed making an effort for her first day back at work.

As anticipated, the morning editorial meeting was buzzing, with Paul and the editorial team eager to learn of the direction her Ryan Reynolds feature was taking. Whilst she admitted she still had some gaps to fill in—including the backstory on Ryan—she probably had enough to finalise her story for the following weekend's issue.

As she later sat back at her own desk, Jess drummed the table, anxious for an update from Detective Sana about the possible gang murder theory that may solve the puzzle surrounding the death of Ryan Reynolds.

But no phone call was forthcoming, and so Jess left work on the dot of six and headed straight over to her sister Emma's, keen to check in on her.

As she walked up the driveway, the door was thrown open and Angelina and Clementine ran out to meet Jess in their cute pyjamas and dressing gowns.

'Hello, munchkins,' she said, gathering them in for a group cuddle.

Looking up, she saw little Annabelle standing at the door, half hiding behind Emma's legs.

Her sister looked better. So much better. The smile said it all.

They embraced, and in minutes, Jess was handed a bottle of wine to open, and they sat and talked in the kitchen whilst the girls resumed watching *Nick Junior* in the loungeroom.

'Just fifteen more minutes, and then it's time for teeth and bed,' called out Emma.

'So, what's news?' asked Jess.

'I've got a job!' Emma blurted out excitedly.

Jess jumped up and hugged her. 'I knew you would be welcomed back with open arms!'

'You had more faith than me,' she said with a smirk. 'I start next Thursday. It's a nursing job at the private hospital down the road in Gladesville. And the best thing is I can work from nine thirty to two thirty, so I can still do drop-offs and pickups with the girls. I've also found childcare for Annabelle for three days, and Steve's parents will take her for one day, so things are starting to fall into place,' she said, her face beaming.

'You've been busy!' Jess was impressed with the progress her sister had made and wondered if they were like a see-saw, she and Emma. Whenever one of their lives was coasting along, the other's seemed up in the air. She had a feeling it was going to be her turn to take the upheaval route next.

She had mulled over the idea of Munich and done a list of pros and cons, which just left her more confused than ever.

She knew she loved Edward, but she wasn't yet ready to give up on her own life here in Sydney—leave

Emma and her nieces, her friends and her job. It had been less than six months since she had got the promotion to Features editor, and she doubted she would land anything quite this good in a publishing company where she was an unknown.

Her sister sensed something was on Jess's mind, and soon Jess found herself pouring everything out.

'Germany!' she exclaimed. 'I don't know whether to be excited for you or sad for me. It's so far away! What about your job?'

'Exactly! I'm so torn because I just love my role here. I'm finally past the stage of being sent out at the whim of an overzealous news editor and now able to dictate the types of stories I cover. I love my work, not to mention the autonomy I have.'

'Can you convince Edward to stay on here?' she probed.

'I gather this promotion is a big deal to him, like mine was to me, so I understand why he wants to do it.'

'But if you had another year or two to really sink your teeth into the Features role, you might then be ready to try something different in Europe,' said Emma.

'If only Edward would see it that way. No, I'm afraid he thinks if he turns this one down, then it's a black mark against his name.'

'Could you do the long-distance thing?' asked Emma tentatively.

Jess had also suggested that and wondered why Edward was so against the idea. After all, it was so easy to connect these days with Skype, Zoom, Facetime. But he had argued that they were engaged and he wanted them to be married and not live separately.

'That's the other thing,' said Jess. 'Edward is really keen for the wedding to take place in Germany so that his grandmother can attend. He thinks we should get married between Christmas and New Year so that you and our Sydney friends can make a bit of a holiday around it and enjoy a white Christmas.'

Emma was ecstatic at the prospect of an overseas wedding and voiced as much to Jess. The conversation then flowed around wedding dresses and how the three little girls could be the flower girls and what they would wear.

Sometime later back at home, as Jess prepared for bed, she thought of what Emma had said about commuting and felt that it would be a reasonable short-term solution. That way they would both get to enjoy their elevated roles, and she could postpone moving to Germany until the end of the year. Notching up a solid year as Features editor in Sydney would then put her in good stead when looking for a similarly high-level media role in Europe.

It was over an early breakfast two mornings later that she broached the idea to Edward.

They were sitting at an outside bench table at the *Boathouse*, a chic café located on the water at Balmoral, sharing a plate of scrambled eggs and sourdough toast.

It was a typical Sydney morning—the sun already warming up the sand, as locals and visitors arrived to walk along the esplanade, sipping coffees or exercising their dogs. All forming part of the never-ending trail of walking, cycling and running groups keen to get their morning off to an energetic start.

From their table on the timber deck, which was elevated over the water, they had a bird's-eye view of the swimmers, kayakers and other sea craft moving around them. It was Sydney at its finest and provided a calm backdrop for Jess to broach the topic.

'I'd like to propose a compromise,' she began nervously. 'Yes, I agree that we move to Germany when we get married. And, yes, let's get married in Munich in late December, like you suggested. Emma just loves the idea! But I want to keep working here until then.'

Edward's face went from a broad smile to serious contemplation.

'Darling, if this is what will make you happy, then this is what we will do,' he said conciliatorily, leaning in to kiss her lightly. 'The Splendour Hotel at Titisee will be perfect. We could get married at the historic church, and everyone could stay at the hotel, which overlooks the lake,' he said, expanding on the region and segueing to his thoughts on which areas of Munich they should look for a home.

Jess felt a lightness at having reached a solution with Edward on their future plans. Everything would be okay… wouldn't it?

# CHAPTER 53: JESS

A week later Edward had departed for Munich. What was meant to be a short reconnaissance had now evolved into him moving permanently for the new role.

'It just makes sense. Otherwise, I will come back for perhaps a month at the most? It's better just to get on with it,' he said with determination.

A packing company would oversee his relocation, and Jess wished there was another service that could just as easily have dealt with the highs and lows of her emotions.

His eagerness to be gone so fast felt a little callous, but she knew this was a career move for him, and it wouldn't be fair to voice her hurt at the fast pace this was taking.

And so, in less than a week she found herself back at Sydney Airport, kissing Edward goodbye. Suddenly he was gone, swallowed by the sea of fellow travellers all filing into the immigration hall.

As Jess slowly walked back to her car, her phone pinged and she looked down. It was a missed call from Dom.

She was halfway home when her phone rang, reminding her of the earlier missed call from Dom. She answered on speakerphone.

'Jess, it's Dom. I've been trying to reach you.' He sounded urgent.

'Sorry, I saw the missed call and was going to buzz you back later,' she said.

'Mika has been arrested,' he blurted. 'Clancy called last night. Mika was taken into custody yesterday for murder! The murder of Ryan Reynolds.'

'What? My God.' The news was too astounding, and Jess tried to comprehend what she was hearing whilst steering her vehicle through the traffic. 'I'm driving and trying to process what you just said. Where are you? Can we talk?'

Arriving just twenty minutes later at Dom's Kirribilli address, Jess took almost as long to find a parking spot. The harbourside suburb was heaving with Saturday-morning markets, and its cafés were overflowing. Boasting stunning terraces, architecturally designed homes and an increasing number of apartment blocks, the suburb had one of the best views of Sydney. It overlooked sparkling Sydney Harbour and its two biggest assets—the Opera House and the Sydney Harbour Bridge.

Dom had clinched one of the million-dollar views along the harbourfront, and she buzzed before making her way inside.

A sombre-looking Dom led her through to the terrace and fixed her a sparkling water.

'The police spoke to Clancy and a couple of others from the Anzac Club. One conversation led to another, and they arrested Mika.'

'What? I don't believe it.' Jess couldn't work any of this out.

'Clancy doesn't know what hard evidence they have, but apparently there was enough to make an arrest.'

'I didn't even know Mika lived in the highlands back then,' said Jess, recollecting a conversation she had had with Mika when they first met at Clancy's last year.

'Oh, Mika's always lived in the highlands… ever since I can remember, and I'm nearly forty,' said Dom. 'Her husband, Ren, left many years ago, and she might have gone away for short periods, but she always came back. She might have bought her house in Gumawa twenty years ago, but she's definitely been in the highlands for much longer.'

'Clancy must be devastated.' She sighed. 'I mean, they're a couple, aren't they?'

'No, no. Just friends,' said Dom dismissively. 'I think she may have liked him more at one time, but Clancy never took it beyond friendship. I know he loves her in his own way, and she's probably his closest mate, but there's nothing romantic in it. I'm sure of it.'

Again, Jess was puzzled. She recalled a distinct feeling that Mika was in a relationship with Clancy. Was it something she had said or the way she had behaved? Jess just wasn't sure which.

# CHAPTER 54: GRACE

The arrest had been sudden and caught Grace unaware. The first she'd learnt about it was reading an online news site on Monday morning at work.

### WOMAN CHARGED WITH PNG MURDER

HIGHLANDS resident, Mika Julen aged sixty-eight, has been charged with the murder of an Australian man in 1990. The historic murder case only came to light in February this year, following the discovery of his skeletal remains inside an abandoned vehicle in the highlands of Papua New Guinea.

Mika Julen has not entered a plea and has been remanded in custody until a further court appearance on 20 May in the Mount Hagen District Court.

She immediately dialled Jess's mobile.

'Jess, have you seen the news? They've arrested someone for Ryan's murder!'

'Yes, isn't it shocking!' Jess said, explaining that she'd learned of it through Dom on the weekend. 'Dom doesn't believe there is any evidence, as such, but there must be something concrete to make an arrest.' She sounded perplexed. 'I'm going to telephone Detective Sana shortly, hear what they have.'

'I'll do it,' Grace found herself offering. 'I've got his mobile, and he'll probably open up to me a bit more given our history on this case.'

Hanging up shortly afterwards, Grace dialled Detective Sana's number and was surprised to get him on the first ring.

'You've seen the news,' he said without preamble.

'Hi, Detective Sana. Yes, have I ever! What's happened?'

'I can't say too much at the moment, Grace,' he replied calmly.

'What evidence was there? What did you find?' Grace asked. 'I thought you said it was going to be near impossible to solve, given the time lag on this and the degradation of the crime scene.'

'Yes, I thought so too. Look, don't spread this around yet, although it'll be in tomorrow's newspaper anyway,' he said, resigned to the runaway story emerging. 'We located a weapon, a handgun, that was registered to Mr Ren Julen, the former husband of Mrs Julen. This weapon is the one we believe that killed Mr Reynolds.'

'But that doesn't make it the wife!'

'Mr Julen had left the highlands some years previously,' he said patiently. 'We also have uncorroborated and conflicting stories as to the whereabouts of Mrs Julen at the time of the murder.'

He explained that the procedure would now take its course, and the case against Mika would not be in court for some months as each side prepared their evidence.

'What was her motive?' asked Grace, still dumbfounded over the fast arrest.

'I'm afraid I can't say any more, Grace. Please understand.'

# CHAPTER 55: JESS

Jess dialled Detective Sana immediately after Grace's call. Something wasn't adding up, and she had a niggling feeling why.

Studying an enlarged image of the photograph of Sarah, Elena and Ryan, clarity was now emerging.

The detective had been guarded in his responses to her questions, but he had provided a few snippets that had given her confidence in her theory. And a new angle to pursue.

She hung up the phone and walked into the conference room and impatiently awaited Paul's arrival for the morning news conference. Moments later, he and his ever-present assistant strolled in, closing the door and taking their seats.

After an agonising half an hour, it was finally Jess's turn, and she began her pitch. It was definitely a pitch because she desperately needed Paul to support her on this—both professionally and financially—as it would require yet more of the company's lean travel budget.

'I'd like to do a follow-up piece on the murder mystery in the PNG Highlands,' she said in a confident *I can clinch this* tone. 'There was an arrest on the weekend of an expat woman.' She handed over the printout for Paul's perusal. 'Whilst I know it appears to be a straight crime story, and you'll probably want Warwick to handle it, I really want to write it.' She tried to sound as commanding as she could with a dozen senior editors listening in. 'It's a new angle to include in what can be a larger feature than the one I already have, or even a two-part feature?' She knew Paul liked story instalments to keep readers engaged. 'Plus I have all the contacts now,' she said, another tick when it came to how Paul judged assignments. 'This feature would be the story of an Aussie backpacker killed by a woman avenging the man she loves.'

She now had the full table's attention, and even Paul was listening intently.

She continued. 'I've spoken with the local PNG detective this morning, and whilst he didn't confirm it, the woman they've arrested has a motive related to unrequited love. The case has been set for the first week of June, and I'd like to attend and cover it and use it in the original feature.'

'You want to travel back up there?' Paul asked, comprehending what she was now asking.

'Yes. That way I can report on the subtleties of the court case, speak with those people who are close to the woman who's been arrested, Mika Julen, and ideally interview her. I have met her a few times, so that should help gain me access,' she said, hoping the personal connection would win her further points as Paul weighed up her request.

She knew Paul was all for contacts in this game.

He was forever sounding off about the journalist's 'little black book' and how crucial it was to seizing the big stories first.

And so, with that little pearl delivered at the end, Paul agreed to delay Jess's original feature, earmarked to appear in that weekend's paper. She could attend the court case next month and finalise the feature then.

But Jess's trip didn't eventuate, or at least not in the way she had planned.

Early the following morning, as she was buried in research at her desk, Dom rang.

'Jess, it's Mika. She's dead!'

'What?'

His voice sounded strangled as he said, 'She hanged herself last night.'

Jess was shocked at the news but quickly became concerned for Dom, who sounded at breaking point. 'Where are you?'

She marched across the city to Dom's office and met him at a nearby café. Placing two coffee orders at the entrance, she then rushed over to hug him. She could feel his body tremble, as if weeping or attempting not to. Her heart squeezed.

He recovered his composure after a few minutes, stepping back and wiping his face with his hand. 'God, if I'm like this, I can't imagine what Clancy's like.' He ushered her to sit.

'How is he?'

'Oh, you know Clancy. He's not saying much, but he's completely gutted. First her arrest, and now this.'

Dom announced that he was flying up in the

morning to support Clancy and also help with funeral arrangements for their dear friend.

Jess felt sadness at the chain of events that had come about. She leant over and held Dom's hand as he talked about his many memories of Mika.

'She's always been there. Always.' He wept quietly.

# CHAPTER 56: DOM

*My beloved Clancy,*
*I have done something that I don't regret because I did it for you,*
*my dearest man. I will always be loyal to you and love you. Please*
*know that I only wanted to protect you from heartache.*
*All my love everlasting, Mika*

Dom sat quietly after reading the letter for a third time. Clancy had handed it to him when he'd arrived that evening, explaining that it was in an addressed envelope that had been passed on to the prison guard.

'I never knew,' Clancy said solemnly.

'You mean that she was responsible for murder? Or that she felt that way about you?' asked Dom gently.

'Both,' he replied, looking baffled. 'Mika was my mate. I thought I knew her... I can't believe she's gone.'

He looked frail and alone.

'What did the police say?'

'Not much,' Clancy grunted, getting up to pace the veranda. 'Mika seemed fine when I visited her on Monday morning. She didn't want to talk about the arrest, and I thought there'd be time later on.

'She was calm and sort of resigned to her fate, but definitely not suicidal,' he said adamantly. 'No way. Nor did the police think she was.'

Despite this, Mika had hanged herself in her cell.

Clancy wiped a hand over his dripping face, dropping back into a chair.

'Oh, Dad, it's bloody awful,' said Dom, instantly leaning forward to grasp his arm.

Clancy shook him gently off and took a deep breath. 'Anyway. The police say Mika's confession and the gun pretty much closes the case now.'

'But how? Why?' Dom then thought, perhaps the *why* had now been explained. Mika had been in love with Clancy and had gone to extreme measures to protect him—but protect him from what? Why kill a young backpacker who was just passing through? She couldn't have known about his affair with Sarah, surely?

The following day, Dom determined he would drive into Mount Hagen and learn more about the circumstances surrounding Mika's suicide and indeed the murder she had been charged with.

\*\*\*\*

'Hello, Mr Jonson,' Detective Sana said as he showed Dom into his office.

'Dom, please,' he replied, taking one of the two seats facing the desk.

'I'm sorry for the loss of your friend, Mrs Julen,' the detective said kindly.

'Thank you. As I said on the phone, I just want to know more about Mika's arrest. How you came to the conclusion that she was involved in any of this.'

'Of course,' he said and poured them each a glass of water.

'An evidence trail led us to match the bullet which we managed to find at the scene to a gun that was in the possession of Mrs Julen. It was located in her home in Gumawa.'

'But what does that prove? It was probably her ex-husband's,' Dom blustered.

'Yes, it was registered to her former husband, you are right,' he said patiently. 'Mr Ren Dietrich is the registered owner of the handgun, and we have so far been unable to locate him—he disappeared many, many years ago, you understand. Because of their different surnames, we did not immediately establish any connection between Mr Dietrich and Mrs Julen. However, eventually this came to light in the data search, and we then executed a search warrant on Mrs Julen's home.'

'But why would Mika kill someone? It could have been Ren? Jealous of his wife?'

'Mr Dietrich and Mrs Julen had separated in 1988, two years prior to Mr Reynolds being shot,' the detective said, looking at him sympathetically. 'I am sorry, but Mrs Julen had confessed.'

# CHAPTER 57: JESS

Jess saw an airmail envelope on her desk when she arrived at work and assumed it was from Edward. Once or twice he'd slipped things into the post, and so she opened it whilst logging on to her computer.

As she pulled out the letter, she paused, seeing handwriting that she didn't recognise.

She studied the envelope more closely and now noticed the PNG stamp. Quickly flicking to the second page, she saw the name Mika Julen.

A shiver went up Jess's spine as she sat still and read.

*Dear Jessica,*

*Time is running out, and it is time to tell my story, if only to protect Clancy from any false accusations by your article or from misinformation by others. Clancy is blameless in all of this. What I did, I did alone.*

*The police visited me today and have taken away my handgun. They know it was me, and I expect that by this time tomorrow I will be arrested.*

*Yes, it is true. I am responsible for the death of Ryan Reynolds. You can report that.*

*But first let me tell you why.*

*Ryan Reynolds was careless and dangerous, with no regard for the consequences of his behaviour. He was going to destroy our loyal community, what I hold most dear, and I couldn't let it happen. I had married a philanderer who was never stopped in his ways, and I wasn't going to sit by and watch it happen again. I saw Ryan's animal instincts that night, so long ago, when Sarah became his prey. So innocent and so vulnerable without Clancy by her side. Our great protector.*

*Ryan barely remembered me when we bumped into each other at the Goroka Festival soon after. But I knew exactly who he was and what he had done. Imagine my anger when he spoke so nonchalantly about returning to Gumawa and staying on.*

*He was threatening the harmony of our small community. Clancy was never going to be cuckolded by this man. I wouldn't let it happen.*

*I followed him that night. His tyre burst, as I knew it would because I had worked at it doing just that. And I pulled the trigger, silencing him and his bravado from wreaking havoc on the life of my dearest friend.*

*I don't regret shooting him, and never shall.*

*Regards*

*Mika Julen*

# CHAPTER 58: DOM

Dom sat beside his father's slumped figure at Mika's funeral. It was a large turnout, with no one appearing to hold it against Mika that she had been arrested for murder. Instead, the locals celebrated a fine woman and friend, whom they had known and loved for the best part of forty years. A patron of indigenous art, a lady of grace, and an intellectual among their small tight-knit town.

As Dom listened to Clancy's glowing eulogy, he realised the inadequacy of his feelings for Lauren. They were insufficient to sustain the lifetime of memories his father now shared for his dear friend.

Dom suddenly wanted more for himself in this life. He needed someone who made his heart beat faster, got his pulse racing, and who could share his life unequivocally.

It was now or never. He'd had enough of being Mr Nice Guy. It was time to act.

# CHAPTER 59: JESS

She had been curled up watching *The Proposal*, featuring her favourite actress Sandra Bullock... and of course that name now forever etched in her memory—Ryan Reynolds. She had seen the film many times before, and it never disappointed. The romance of it and the humour as hard-nosed boss (Sandra) and conscientious employee (Ryan) switch things around and battle it out in the gorgeous setting of Alaska.

She had paused the film to top up her camomile tea when the front door buzzer sounded.

Noticing it was after nine, she was tempted to ignore it, but fearing a neighbour may be locked out, she jumped up. It wouldn't be Edward; they weren't scheduled to see each other for a few weeks in Malaysia.

After identifying Dom on the small video screen, she nervously let him in. She didn't realise he had returned and hadn't yet worked out what to do about the letter.

'I just flew back in,' he explained, misreading

her worried face. 'Sorry to call unannounced. I had to see you.'

'Come in,' she ushered. 'Can I get you a tea or something stronger?' She was almost about to reach for the wine in the fridge when he stopped her.

'No, no, I just needed to say something.' He shifted awkwardly in her small living room.

'Is everything okay? How's Clancy? Did it go okay?' She barraged him with questions, his anxiety firing hers.

Stopping, he reached out to grab her hands in his.

'Are you okay?' She was worried because he looked like a caged animal. *Did he know about the letter?*

'Jess, it's been a gruelling couple of days, but the one good thing to come out of all of this is clarity.'

Jess could see the shining brightness in his eyes and waited uncertainly.

'I want you in my life,' he said, catching her by complete surprise. This was not what she was expecting.

'I've loved you since the moment you browbeat me into an interview for Clancy's coffee story,' he said with a lopsided smile. 'I've wanted you even more since the whole Ryan discovery, and I want you so much right now.'

Stepping closer, he moved his hands to cup her face and leant forward.

Momentarily caught off guard, she lost herself for a few moments in the sensation of his soft lips before quickly stepping back.

'Dom. Stop!' she spluttered, feeling both flustered and confused.

'I know you're engaged. But Edward's not right

for you,' he said earnestly.

'Dom! Don't!' She moved further away, angry at his remark.

'Listen to me, Jess. I've been muddling my whole life with the wrong women—well more like one wrong woman. Does he make your heart race? Does he get you like I do?'

'Oh, Dom, you can't ask me that.' She sighed, not wanting any more seeds of doubt to creep in about her and Edward. Not now.

'I love you, Jess. I know that you feel something for me. If you don't, then I've really lost my mind here, but I can feel it. Can't you?'

Jess sat down on the sofa, feeling defeated and totally blindsided.

Yes, she did harbour feelings for Dom, and didn't realise how strongly until he kissed her. But she needed to regain control of the situation and extricate herself immediately.

Plus she had something she needed to share.

She leapt up to retrieve the letter from her handbag and handed it to him.

He looked confused at the folded piece of paper.

'Take it home. Read it. I'm sorry, but it came whilst you were with Clancy. I have to use it,' she said, knowing that Dom's first impression of her would now be vindicated. An exploitative journalist. But what could she do?

Dom looked perplexed and went to open it.

'No. Please take it home. Read it when you're at home,' she urged. Reluctantly he left.

Her movie now abandoned, she reached for her journal and wrote and wrote and wrote, channelling her conflicting emotions on paper.

She loved Edward! He was everything she wanted in a man—charming, loving, caring, successful... but her mind kept wandering to Dom. It was as if a movie reel of every moment they'd shared began to play in her head. Their first sighting at the airport in his Akubra hat, his less-than-friendly welcoming at Gumawa, to the sensitive soul asking for her help in learning about his mother. So many memories flooded her head, and her heart ached.

And now this. What would he think when he read the letter? Should she have been there with him when he saw Mika's confession? And would he hate her for using those words to expose things so publicly?

# CHAPTER 60: JESS

Edward had chosen a beautiful resort in Langkawi, an island off the mainland of Malaysia, for their holiday. It had been four weeks since he'd departed for Germany, and whilst they spoke regularly, it was their first time together in all that time. She felt the slight awkwardness of two people, once intimate, now relearning the familiarity they'd once shared.

Their villa overlooked a stunning series of six pools at the beachfront resort and was spacious and bright. She was disappointed to see the room empty when she swiped her magnetic room key.

There was evidence all around her of Edward's arrival—his laptop open on the low timber coffee table and his suitcase on the bed, not yet unpacked but certainly rummaged through.

Tossing between going out to find him and hitting the shower to wash away the travel stench, she opted for the latter and was glad she did as it helped to revive her mood. Slipping into a fluffy white robe, she massaged moisturiser into her face and combed her wet hair, leaving it to dry naturally.

She then heard the click of the door, and Edward strode in.

Jess's heart gave a leap at the sight of him, his features even more handsome than she remembered.

'Sorry I wasn't here when you arrived,' he said, walking over and kissing her tenderly.

His warm embrace was enveloping and reassuring, and Jess quickly dismissed her initial annoyance at not being met.

'I think I could just fall asleep in this position,' she said, leaning into his body and closing her eyes.

'My poor baby, do you want to lie down?' Edward led her into the bedroom and pulled back the bedclothes for her to get in.

'Don't tempt me,' she said, sitting on the bed but not ready for sleep.

Whilst it was inviting, Jess didn't want to play havoc with jetlag and resisted the urge to clamber in. She had also been hoping for a more romantic reunion than sleeping off her weariness alone.

'What about a walk?'

A short time later, Jess and Edward were strolling along the beach, a long sandy strip with hotels and holiday apartments on one side and a gentle lapping ocean at their feet. It was late in the day, and the temperature was mild and the surf flat.

'You have to drive out to a point on the other side of the island to catch the waves,' Edward remarked, nodding in the near distance. 'It's fantastic! I was there all afternoon.'

Trying not to be offended that he had chosen a surf over greeting her—for the first time in a month—she swallowed her disappointment and enquired about his new job.

That evening they dined on the beachfront at one of their neighbouring restaurants. The crayfish was delicious, and she ate it ravenously as she sipped crisp white wine. Candles and fire torches created a beautiful ambience, and she finally felt herself relaxing into her stay.

Edward reached out and held her hand, as if reading the shift in her mood.

Jess filled Edward in on the unfolding story she'd been working on.

Whilst Edward had met Dom, he had a habit of feigning a lapse in memory when she brought him up.

'Dom? Have I met him? Which one is Dom?' These types of comments frustrated her, especially tonight when she was overtired. 'How do you know Dom again?'

'PNG, Edward. Remember? I met him for the coffee story. He's the son of Clancy? The coffee baron,' she replied tightly, removing her hand and letting out a sigh.

Edward didn't sense her annoyance and let her continue.

'They just had the funeral for Mika—the woman accused of murdering the young Australian backpacker. Anyway, Dom went to the funeral with Clancy up in the highlands, and when I saw him in Sydney, he just seemed so distraught about the whole thing. And then I had to hand him her confessional. I felt awful.'

'This is understandable,' Edward reassured her. 'Hopefully you have now finished this article?'

'Yes, it's been filed for this weekend's paper,'

she said, relieved but uneasy about finalising the feature which would appear as a four-page exclusive.

'Well, that deserves to be celebrated!' Edward raised his glass 'Well done, darling. Here's to the conclusion of your PNG adventure,' he announced.

Jess automatically raised her glass to the toast, but the wine felt nasty and acidic as it slipped down her throat.

The next morning, she woke early, her body clock still on Sydney time. Edward was peacefully sleeping beside her, and so she crept out of bed and sat on the balcony to watch the sunrise. It was a beautiful time of day, and the fishermen were wading out with their nets, and it was oh so peaceful.

Jess felt calmer today, less anxious and uptight. The joys of long-distance relationships, she lamented. She had been in knots about seeing Edward again and was glad they would now get into a rhythm for their long weekend together.

But her mind still returned to Dom and that astonishing kiss that still sent tingles through her two weeks later. She hadn't expected the outpouring of emotion from Dom and felt conflicted and torn. She cared for Dom, deeply, which is surely why she was still thinking about him, worried about him. And wondering what he would make of Mika's letter.

But she was here now with Edward and needed to concentrate on that. Marriage and a life in Europe were her future.

'Hey, what are you thinking?' asked a gravelly voice, switching her thoughts immediately back to the present.

Edward leaned down to kiss her gently on the

lips and lifted her water glass to refill it, returning to sit with her and watch the final rays of colour from the spectacular sunrise.

The days went quickly, as Jess swam in the sea each morning and Edward headed off to the other side of the island for a surf, before returning to spend the rest of the day together. They agreed to hire a vehicle and explore the island one day and take a boat trip on another. Jess also coaxed Edward to do a gentle hike one morning, skipping his beloved surf so they could avoid the heat of the day.

Before she was ready, their break was over, and she was sitting in the resort reception awaiting their lift to the airport. Edward was still in the room on another conference call, ensuring he was on top of things for his return.

The tropical atmosphere of the resort transported her back to the highlands of PNG. She felt so relaxed sitting and listening to the sounds of crickets, frogs and birds, and savouring the smell of light rain falling outside.

It hadn't been a sublimely romantic nor an easy reunion, but surely that was normal and to be expected, given their recent absence. Once they were back living in the same city, things would be different, of that she was convinced.

Edward arrived in the lobby at the same time as their car pulled up to take them to the airport where they would go on their separate journeys, once more.

# CHAPTER 61: DOM

Dom sat back as he finished reading Jess's feature. He knew it would be appearing in today's edition of the *Weekend Leading News* and had been uneasily anticipating it.

It had been a well-written, balanced and sympathetic article, painting a picture of life in the remote highlands of Papua New Guinea in the 1990s and the parallel stories of a young intrepid photographer, Ryan Reynolds, and his fateful meeting with Mika Julen. The story shared details about Mika's life that Dom didn't clearly recall, including her husband's neglect and philandering ways, before eventually abandoning her in the highlands. It shared how the local community had rallied, becoming her second family, and one that she would protect to the end.

Clancy and Sarah were also referenced in the article, but Jess had been efficient and tactful in her choice of words. She shared a story of lives complicated by a series of events—rejection by Mika's husband, her loneliness and unnatural attachment to Sarah and Clancy, and her fierce protectiveness in killing a young man she believed would ruin the life of her most beloved friends and destroy the harmony of their tight-knit community.

Excerpts of Mika's letter were included, as he knew they would be.

What most surprised him was the enlarged image of the black-and-white photo of his mother, Elena, and Ryan. He hadn't seen it before in the smaller print he'd seen, but there in the corner of the enlarged image was Mika staring at the trio, a disapproving look etched on her face.

Dom thought of life and all its intricacies… and of unrequited love.

# CHAPTER 62: JESS

Jess had returned to work early, keen to go through her inbox, which had been ignored during her holiday with Edward. She always made it a rule to tune off work emails when she took leave, and whilst it was a pleasure to do so, there was the small matter of catching up on hundreds of emails when she returned.

Many were internal emails imparting company updates, media alerts from around the globe that she subscribed to, Publicists pitching story ideas, and there were also a few messages from readers sharing feedback to her features. Today she opened those first, keen to see what readers wrote about her PNG feature.

One of the emails was from Dom.

Her heart stopped for a brief moment, and she pressed open.

*Jess, thank you for the sensitivity of your article. I enjoyed reading it, and whilst it was painful in parts, it was beautifully written and respectfully shared. Dom.'*

Before overthinking it, she fired back a quick reply, thanking him for his message. Short and sweet.

*'Hi, Dom, and thanks for the note. I'm glad that you enjoyed the article. Jess.'*

She then got into her day, and before she knew it, six o'clock had come, and she packed up to head home.

She hadn't heard back from Dom, and whilst she told herself that this was good, she was a bit deflated.

For the rest of the week, Jess vowed to get her life back on track by running each morning before work or taking her goggles to the pool afterwards. And she immersed herself in her writing, working like a demon on her next two features.

But when the week ended, she had too much time on her hands. Edward was away at a conference in France and hard to reach, and Emma and her girls were on school holidays, staying at a friend's farm.

She tried Frances, who she knew would have a multitude of options to choose from—shopping mornings, spa treatments and drinks parties—but she too was busy on a date.

Jess resolved to make the most of her solitary weekend, stocking up on fresh food and finally tackling the task of decluttering her apartment. She put to one side the items that would need to go into storage for her move to Munich: ornaments, books and knick-knacks. Her relocation was still months away but she felt compelled to start the process.

Whilst she had managed to fill both days, her nights were lonely, and by Sunday night, she was feeling flat from the solitude. As she sat in front of the television, eating an early dinner of home-made chicken soup, her phone pinged with a text.

It was from Edward.

*'Darling, missing you xx Speak tomorrow x'*
Jubilant, she pressed Call but it went directly to voice mail. *What the hell?* she thought, annoyed, as she tossed her phone on the sofa.

# CHAPTER 63: DOM

Dom had seen her email flash up on the screen last week, and after three failed attempts to compose a light-hearted, casual response, he left it unanswered. But now as he settled into Sunday evening, it irked him, and he felt guilty that he hadn't replied.

In all honesty, he had been hoping for something more from Jess's text, considering it was their first contact since his declaration of love in her apartment nearly three weeks ago.

Dom also felt a bit foolish about it now, but dammit, at least he'd put it out there and she would know how he felt.

He had been sure there was a connection between them… more fool him.

At least it had propelled him to pull the Band-Aid off and terminate his relationship with Lauren. She hadn't been surprised when he had gone over to explain things. She, too, had sensed that the relationship was cooling and an all-too-familiar distance creeping back into their relationship.

So, he spent the weekend attempting to distract himself by finalising documents for a court appearance on Tuesday, glad that the pressure of the case was giving him something else to focus on.

# CHAPTER 64: JESS

Jess hadn't seen Edward for a month, since their holiday in Malaysia, and she was counting down the days to Friday when he'd be returning. She desperately needed to feel reassured about *them*, after silly bouts of insecurity and uncertainty. He'd amended his business in Hong Kong and Japan to include a weekend dash across the Pacific at her request.

However, when she logged on at work that morning, her joy turned to rage. He wasn't coming. Whilst he would be in Asia, he couldn't spare the additional days away, blah, blah, blah. He was flying back to Munich and then London for business commitments.

She sat looking at the email and felt disappointment and then rising frustration that work had yet again been his first priority.

Instead of composing a response, she stood up and walked to the tearoom. But after filling the jug and opening the tea box, she thought, *Stuff it, I'm getting a proper coffee*. Grabbing her purse, she made her way back to her friendly barista.

As she waited for her latte, she messaged Frances to suggest a glass of wine after work and received an immediate 'Yes!' Glad to have plans, she walked back into the office minutes later, feeling much happier.

Early that evening, as she and Frances sat sipping an Aperol Spritz in the moody bar across from Frances's office, they caught up on their busy lives. Frances's role at the bank continued to expand, and soon she would commence regular trips to Munich to work in the head office. The news pleased Jess because it meant that she would at least have a friend when the time came for her to relocate. Perhaps detecting Jess needed a few laughs, Frances cheered her up with exaggerated tales of her more recent dating disasters.

'No wonder I'm still single,' she wailed, but Jess felt she was more than content with the steady stream of eligible men in her jet-set lifestyle.

They laughed a lot together, and Jess was glad she hadn't gone home to mope.

Eventually the conversation moved to Edward.

'He's an ambitious man, that one,' Frances remarked as she returned to the table with a second round of drinks—this time chilled glasses of sauvignon blancs. The white wine was calming, and Jess was enjoying its soothing effects.

'He's taken on a big role and determined not to say no to anything—including representing Bavaria Bank at the zillions of conferences on the financial industry schedule,' Frances said admiringly. 'Don't get me wrong,' she continued. 'Edward's a very impressive speaker, but he's also juggling this enormous new role and attempting a personal life. Long distance! I don't know how he does it!'

'Yes, I'm feeling a little lost,' admitted Jess.

'I don't blame you, honey,' said Frances. 'I should have warned you at the beginning that young Edward is a man on the move. He's certainly got ambitions for his future.' She winked.

When the girlfriends parted, Jess opted to walk to the bus station rather than jump into a taxi. It was still relatively early, and she wasn't in any rush to get home. She pondered what Frances had said, especially her point about Edward's ambitions and determination to succeed. She had admired his career focus, but now she was wondering what it would cost them.

As she passed Leo's, the small bar below Dom's office where they'd met a few times, Jess was suddenly hopeful that she might see him sitting inside. The bar was reasonably busy for a Tuesday night, and she scoured the dimly lit room for a sign of him, but he wasn't there. Disappointed, she went to leave but decided to see if he was upstairs at work instead.

Ordering a glass of pinot, more for Dutch courage than anything else, she sat at a quiet corner table and sent a text.

*Dom, I'm downstairs at Leo's. Please let me know if you're close by? Jess.*

As she sat back to observe the crowd around her, she felt the atmosphere momentarily shift. Looking towards the door, she saw him. An electric current passed through her, and she couldn't repress the relief she felt at seeing him after so long. Her beaming smile couldn't be contained.

'Jess,' he said, kissing her on the cheek as she sat stupidly staring up at him. 'I didn't expect your message.' He looked both happy to see her but also curious.

'Thanks for coming,' she managed to say.

'Actually, it was good timing. I was just wrapping up things in the office when your text came through. Thanks for the invitation,' he said, smiling shyly.

Seeing that Jess had a full glass of wine, he went to the bar and returned with a beer.

There was none of the awkwardness that she had been dreading, instead they chatted easily about work and the court case that had kept Dom working late. The conversation moved to Jess's work, and she expanded on the different stories she was exploring before addressing what she most wanted to know.

'Were you okay about the PNG piece? I had to include the connection between Ryan and Sarah in the story. And Mika, naturally,' she said.

'Yeah, of course. I emailed you,' he replied, and she nodded, acknowledging that he had.

'How's Clancy?' she asked now, realising he wasn't going to say anything more.

'Much better. He's a resilient bugger, that's for sure. I think the initial shock of what Mika did has passed, and he's getting on with things. I'm thinking of returning up there to see him in a couple of months. I've not been up since...' And then he paused. 'Well, since the funeral.' Looking embarrassed, he added, 'I'm sorry for my outpouring at your apartment that night, Jess.'

'It's okay,' she said, hoping to dismiss the topic.

'No, it was really immature of me. You're engaged, and I acted like a lovesick teenager. It's just that I had this crazy notion that if I didn't tell you how

I felt, it would be a disaster. The disaster is that I did.' He grimaced. 'It never pans out that way when the hero does it in the movies.'

His vulnerability was on full display, and Jess's heart gave a tight tug. The feeling was intense, and she felt so torn.

Placing her drink on the table, she leaned over, indicating for Dom to lean in as well. And then she kissed his lips so softly, prolonging their touch for as long as possible.

It was a gentle, long kiss, and it conveyed so much of what she was feeling. Connection, hope, reassurance. He kissed her back just the same way, and then they pulled apart, their eyes not moving from each other's.

'I'm sorry. I just had to do that,' she said, watching his eyes, his face, his mouth.

'I'm glad you did.' He smiled hopefully.

Feeling suddenly unsure, self-conscious and confused she asked, 'Do you mind if we call it a night?'

They collected their coats and bags and quietly left the bar.

As they walked out, Jess tried to find a way of smoothing things over. 'Dom, sorry, I don't know what came over me just there.'

Dom grabbed her hand and squeezed it gently. 'Shhh, it's okay. We're even now.'

And they shared a small smile.

A taxi moved slowly past them in anticipation of a fare, and she was disappointed as Dom quickly hailed it. She had been half hoping he may convince her to prolong their evening and see where things led. Together they clambered in, Dom making a point of taking the front seat and directing the driver.

During the short cab ride, Jess found herself unable to stop talking, as she rambled on and on to a patiently listening Dom and no doubt an enthralled taxi driver.

'Sorry about earlier, Dom. It's just been such a weird time, you know with work and things… I blame that extra glass of wine. I shouldn't have had it. I just feel a bit emotional, you know? And tired, soooo tired,' she continued to rave from the back seat, hoping Dom would think she was drunk, overemotional and weary.

Alighting at his home, Dom leaned in at her car window and reassured her that everything was fine. Touching her face kindly, he smiled and stood back to let her continue her ride home.

But that night as she lay in bed, all Jess could think about was the beautiful lingering, soft kiss and the look in Dom's eyes afterwards. It was hope mixed with affection and love—genuine, wholehearted love.

She knew she should be feeling guilty about Edward, but she didn't. He had chosen work over her.

# CHAPTER 65: JESS

The next morning Jess woke to the sound of her phone. Edward's name flashed on the screen. No doubt calling because he hadn't received a reply to yesterday's email cancelling his visit. She had been childish not to respond, and the price would be a clipped lecture. Reluctantly, she answered.

'Sorry to call so early, darling, but I have good news,' he excitedly began, catching Jess by surprise. 'I've rearranged things so I will be in Sydney on Friday night!'

Jess sat upright in excitement. 'Really? That's so great! How?'

Edward began explaining that he had pulled a few strings and they would now have their weekend together.

Brushing away memories of last night and what was clearly a momentary lapse in judgement, she headed to the shower and dressed for the day ahead. She had a spring in her step when she left her apartment and walked to the bus stop. After replying to a sweet text from Dom enquiring if she was okay, he was promptly forgotten as she excitedly prepared for Edward's return in two days' time.

But the weekend got off to a bad start and never seemed to fully recover. Edward's flight was four hours late, and so Jess cancelled their Friday dinner plans at Felix, a French bistro in town. She made a pasta dish and bought a rich chocolate mousse for their supper, but Edward faded before dessert. He revived on Saturday morning, waking her with gentle kisses down her back before things turned more passionate, and later they walked down to the beach for brunch.

The bacon and egg rolls were delicious as they sat out on the deck with the outdoor heating system getting rid of any residual morning chill. Whilst Sydneysiders couldn't complain about chilly winters, the weather was brisk, and they sat under café blankets in the warm sunshine.

It was just as she was savouring the moment that Edward mentioned they would need to make a move.

'I've got to head into the office for a few hours,' he said.

'But it's Saturday,' Jess moaned.

'Yes, but it was part of the deal in me being here,' he said, slightly patronisingly, she felt. Or was she just feeling oversensitive? 'I agreed to join a few of the Sydney team today for a debrief, and it will only be for a few hours. It's how I wrangled coming to Sydney to see my darling,' he said, giving her a kiss on her forehead.

After Edward left, Jess potted around at home and visited Emma and her nieces for a few hours.

'I am too tired to go out for dinner,' Edward

said wearily when he came in the door several hours later.

'We can't cancel. This place is near impossible to get into. I also think they'll sting my credit card for a late cancellation fee if we don't go,' she said, half joking and half serious.

'I'll cover the cost,' he said dismissively.

The comment annoyed her, but she didn't rise to it and instead tried a different approach. 'I've been really looking forward to going to Yak Sek, especially with my gorgeous fiancée,' she purred, moving into his arms.

The Japanese bistro had generated rave reviews by both the restaurant writers and food bloggers, and she really wanted to go, plus it would be a romantic evening out for them.

'Why don't you have a lie down and I'll wake you?'

'All right,' he relented, kissing her lightly.

Jess woke a groggy Edward a few hours later, and after a shower and a shave he looked like his old self.

She had dressed in a new blue velvet jacket she had splurged on, and together with slim black pants and sky-high boots she felt sexy and sophisticated. She had made a conscious effort to wow Edward this evening, to remind him that work wasn't the only dazzling thing he had in his life. And she was chuffed when he complimented her halfway through their aperitifs.

'A toast to you. You look simply stunning this evening, darling,' he said.

Dinner was lovely, but she couldn't help noticing that their conversation always seemed to get back to work. She attempted to find mutually interesting topics, but the sad realisation hit her that they didn't have many. They had only been dating a short time when Edward was posted back in Germany, and their mutual friends consisted of Frances and colleagues at the bank.

To move the conversation away from work, Jess enquired about his parents, as well as his sisters and nieces, and listened to his effusive updates on his family.

Disappointingly, Edward didn't reciprocate with questions about her family, but she decided to bring him up to date anyway.

'Emma and the girls are doing great these days!'

'Oh, that's good,' he murmured.

'Yes, I'm so proud of Emma. She's now working four days a week. She and Steve are sharing custody of the kids, so she has every second week to herself, which she's using with her study and rebuilding a social life. Did I tell you she's doing post grad studies in nursing as she wants to move into administration?'

Edward didn't know this, and so she decided to continue to talk until she had felt her side of the family had had their equal share of the conversation. Immature, she knew, but she wanted Edward to be engaged in her life, and if that meant updating him on the full story of Emma's life, then that was what she would do.

\*\*\*\*

After dropping Edward at the airport at midday on Sunday for his afternoon flight, Jess began driving home, and realised that they hadn't confirmed when they would next see each other nor had they talked about their wedding plans, which was actually a relief. There had been enough tension already without arguing over arrangements for their big day or where they'd live or what she'd do in Munich for work.

Jess decided not to head directly home but instead drive down to the water's edge at Kirribilli. She got out of the car and strolled over to the grass and sat down in the warm sun, watching the boats, yachts and ferries manoeuvre across Sydney Harbour.

It had been an unsatisfactory weekend, if she was being brutally honest with herself. She and Edward didn't have a lot to talk about. But surely that would grow in time?

Looking out at the splendour of the harbour, Jess wondered if she truly wanted to give up all this and move to the other side of the world. For Edward, a man she clearly didn't really know.

The sudden ringing of her phone, knocked Jess out of her idle thoughts.

'It's Clancy. He's had a heart attack,' said Dom, breathlessly.

'My God, which hospital?'

'He didn't make it.'

Everything going on in Jess's life suddenly seemed irrelevant.

A life extinguished in those few simple words.

'Oh, Dom, I'm so sorry,' she said, feeling her heart break for this beautiful man and the relationship he had only just started to rebuild with his father.

'I can't believe it. He was fine when I spoke to him two days ago. He was just regular Clancy.' He sounded guttered.

'I'm actually right here in Kirribilli. Shall I

come over?' she offered.

'No. I'm not home. I'm in the city and need to tie up a few things before I fly up tomorrow,' he said, diminishing Jess's hopes of comforting him. 'I just thought you should know.' His voice cracked. 'He always had a soft spot for you, Jess, and I think it was reciprocated.'

Confirming that it was indeed reciprocated, Jess hung up, feeling even more alone and sad than she had earlier that morning when she had farewelled her fiancé.

# CHAPTER 66: JESS

As winter began in earnest, Jess felt a clarity that she hadn't experienced in some time.

She had been regularly emailing Dom over the past two weeks, checking in on him and his plans for the plantation now that Clancy was gone.

To her astonishment, he said that he might take time out and work on the farm for the next six months and see out the contracts before either selling it or putting in a new manager. He admitted that good managers were hard to find for such remote locations.

'It will also give me a chance to see how it fits being back for a while. If it sucks, then selling is the only option. Otherwise, I'll just delay the decision-making. I might as well get on with it,' he said.

And Jess knew what he meant but in an entirely different context. She too had been stalling when her gut had been telling her what to do for months.

And so she began to type.

*Dear Edward,*

*Our time together was so special but I fear too short to build a happy marriage on.*

*I was so besotted when you asked me to be your wife—the greatest privilege a woman could ask for. But so much has changed since our fun-filled, carefree days in Sydney and holiday in Zermatt when you proposed. Trying to snatch a week or even weekend together has been so difficult this year, and I know that your career is on the rise, and you should take every opportunity you can.*

*But I have come to realise that I need to live my life, and not yours.*

*We are truly different people with different lives ahead of us. Your love is to be in Munich, and mine is to be closer to home. Our beautiful families deserve to have us each near, and I fear that moving to Munich isn't right for me or for my beloved sister, nieces and friends whom I cherish.*

*Nor would living in Sydney be fair to your mother, treasured sisters and extended family—especially Oma!*

*I don't think marriage is our future. I will always have fond memories of our Sydney days.*

*Love*

*Jess*

*x*

She didn't hesitate before pressing Send, and for the next couple of days a lightness came over her. It was as if she had unloaded a burden she hadn't even known was there.

Edward called her three days later. He was calm and crisply professional. 'I didn't know what to think, how to respond, anything. Why Jessica?' he implored.

'I'm sorry. I know it would have been best to speak, but things are so distant with us—work, time zones... there's never a good time to just talk. I needed to communicate this properly, not in a hurried conversation.'

Edward's disappointment filtered through the phone, but as Jess talked more to Edward about the exciting life he had ahead of him, and their different goals, his tone eventually began to shift.

'On our last visit I felt we didn't have the foundations, the common ground, the structure.'

'But that comes,' Edward had protested.

'Does it? Or should it be there from the start? Edward, you are an amazing man. But we are from different countries, with different lives to lead. I will always love you, but I now realise that I want more and deserve more. As do you. Please understand.'

Edward did—at least he said he did—and Jess was relieved when he clearly conceded that perhaps she was right.

She hung up and wiped the tears from her face before preparing for bed. Despite the raw emotions of the phone conversation, she slept peacefully. She knew in her heart of hearts that she was doing the right thing.

# CHAPTER 67: DOM

Dom was back in Sydney for a few days to tidy up his affairs before moving to the coffee plantation for at least six months. He was looking forward to road-testing managing the farm before making a decision on whether to sell it.

He could have skipped this trip back to Sydney but in all honesty, he wanted to see Jess. She had emailed him the week before with the news of her broken engagement, and he had contacted her straightaway.

As he listened hopefully on why she wasn't going to marry Edward, he quietly prayed that he had in some small part played a role in her reaching that decision.

He tried to reassure her she had done the right thing. 'I'm speaking from experience, Jess.'

Dom loved Jess, but he knew that right now was not the time to pursue her with any more heartfelt declarations. She was fragile and still coming to terms with her decision. That's why, when Jess offered to pick him up at the airport, he declined, preferring to meet up for a drink that evening instead. There were things he needed to get at the office beforehand.

# CHAPTER 68: JESS

Jess sat nervously at the same corner table at Leo's, nursing a fast-disappearing gin and tonic. The drink reminded her of Papua New Guinea, from her first nervous sip en route to Port Moresby to the happy times at the Yacht Club or sitting on Clancy's veranda.

So much had happened in one year, and she sat back to contemplate how different her life would be today if she had never volunteered for the PNG role.

She wouldn't have met Clancy, or Dom, and that made her feel downhearted. They had been such a big part of her life.

She began to feel butterflies at Dom's imminent arrival. And then there he was. Suntanned and beaming. Hair a little longer than she had seen it, and a battered Akubra being tightly gripped as he made his way towards her.

Jess stood up when he approached, and they looked into each other's eyes so keenly—each trying to read the other's thoughts. They had bonded so closely over the past month in their phone calls and emails, and the intensity of this reunion felt enormous.

He pulled her into an enormous hug, and she fiercely held him close, savouring his physical presence.

Jess had told him about her broken engagement, and whilst she hadn't signalled what this could mean for them, her body language said it all. He drew back and looked into her now watery eyes and kissed her.

The kiss was magical. It was the kiss of life for Jess, and her whole body reacted. She put her arms around his neck and kissed him passionately back.

'I love you,' he said, standing back to look at her.

'I know. I'm only just admitting it to myself, but I love you too. More than I ever knew,' she said, and they kissed again.

# EPILOGUE

The rain lashed at the windows as Jess worked in the kitchen with Lena, Clancy's devoted housekeeper who had stayed on after the funeral.

It was Christmas Eve and Jess wanted to have most of the arrangements done ahead of time for tomorrow's lunch. Lena was an enormous help to Jess as she worked on the meal preparations, determined to have everything just perfect for her Christmas feast. They were mixing the seasoning for the large turkey they were going to roast the next morning and had already made up the tangy sauce for tomorrow's seafood cocktails.

Emma and the girls had arrived two days earlier, and she could now hear their squeals in the bath. Grace and John were on their way, and Jess was so happy to have them all there for their first Gumawa Christmas.

Jess had moved to the plantation a month after Dom's return, desperate not to be away from him ever again.

They had agreed to give PNG life one year and were so far loving their time up there together.

Jess had taken a leave of absence and offered her freelance services to *Leading News* and was hoping to fill in for Warwick from time to time. In the interim, she would try immersing herself in fiction writing.

Meanwhile, Dom was working alongside Clancy's loyal team and endeavouring to put his own stamp on the business. Jess felt that Clancy and Sarah would have been overjoyed to see Dom finally settled back at home.

A senior lawyer had been employed to hold the fort, providing Dom with all the time he needed to determine whether his future would be in Papua New Guinea as a coffee plantation man or back in Australia.

Since arriving nearly three months ago, Jess had never felt happier or more at peace. She knew instantly that this was the life that was meant for her. This exotic tropical paradise had got under her skin right from the start. She could never have imagined that a three-month work stint would shake up her life the way it had, and smiled at the thought.

Dom walked into the kitchen with a bottle of champagne and two flutes.

'I've come to steal you away so we can quietly toast this moment before John and Grace get here and those three little cherubs get out of the bath,' he said.

Jess untied her apron and followed Dom onto the veranda.

He uncorked the bottle, and the fizz was magical as it poured into the glass.

Raising his glass, he went to make a toast, but she put her fingers on his lips.

'To our PNG adventure.'

# ACKNOWLEDGEMENTS

I would like to thank my husband for his enormous support and encouragement, and for inspiring me to bring my fiction to fruition.

I am so grateful to my sister, author C.A. Larmer for so generously and patiently sharing the wealth of her writing and self-publishing experience. Without her support this book wouldn't be released.

And I would like to thank friends and family who have assisted in reading early drafts and providing comments and encouragement. Simone, Sandy and Andrea, I value your input.

And finally, thank you for reading *The Plantation*. It means so much to me.

## ABOUT THE AUTHOR

Michelle Larmer was born and raised in Port Moresby, Papua New Guinea and now lives in Sydney, Australia with her husband. She is a former regional television journalist and today splits her time between working in public relations and fiction writing. *The Plantation* is Michelle's first novel.

www.ingramcontent.com/pod-product-compliance
Lightning Source LLC
Chambersburg PA
CBHW050014120726
47903CB00006B/1764